"EXPLOSION ABOARD!"

Even from the lower deck they heard the pilot's shout as the shuttle shuddered and then began to break apart.

"Emergency separation!"

There was a bang and then the breath was driven out of their lungs as something shoved with enormous force against the rear bulkhead. Looking like a larger version of an ancient Apollo capsule, the separated nose section immediately flipped over to reentry attitude, and for a moment they saw the crumpled shuttle falling away behind them. Haloed with a flickering blue light, the stub-winged craft was falling in on itself.

It's imploding!

"Is everyone okay down there?" the pilot shouted. "Brace yourselves. We're going to hit!"

J. BRIAN CLARKE

THE EXPEDITER

DAW BOOKS, INC.

DONALD A. WOLLHEIM, PUBLISHER

1633 Broadway, New York, NY 10019

Cover art by Vincent DiFate.

DAW Book Collectors No. 811.

First Printing, March 1990

1 2 3 4 5 6 7 8 9

PRINTED IN THE U.S.A.

PROLOGUE

I am all.
  We are one.
  We are therefore "I."

The universe was young. On a planet which had cooled; which had produced oceans, continents, and an atmosphere while the rest of the cosmos was still largely in its primeval state, the miracle which is life first appeared. It spread through the oceans, crawled up on the dry land, branched into a million species—of which one finally knew itself and became "we." We filled our world. We built ships of space and spread to the planets and moons of our solar system. We tinkered with spacetime and reached the stars. The galaxy opened before us.

In an even greater adventure, we explored inward into ourselves. We probed into, experimented with, and finally determined our own evolution. Time and space became mere footsteps to anywhere and anywhen, and ultimately "we" became "I."

With my new mass awareness, I looked at the universe as "we" had never seen it. And discovered, to my infinite sadness, that there were no others.

I was alone.

So I launched new explorations. I looked for life and found it on many worlds. But everywhere it was primitive; its behavior based on instinct, its survival dependent on the vagaries of nature. Nevertheless, patiently, I watched and waited. Sometimes, I even encouraged. Two such life-bearing spheres received special attention. On neither were the developing forms more promising than those I had investigated elsewhere. Together, however, they were unique. Nowhere else in the galaxy had life manifestated in two locations as extraordinarily coincident in time as well as space. The possibilities were clear. In the same sense I needed contact with "another" to stimulate my own development to new heights of awareness, the potential of these two species was a sum much greater than their separate parts. It was to that end, I designed and then built the greatest engineering work of my eons of history. Again, I waited.

Knowing, of course, that before there could be a beginning there had to be a meeting—

ONE

THE TESTAMENT OF GEOFFREY

This testament was written for humans by one who was not human. Nevertheless it shines with what the sentients of the planet called Earth identify as "humanity." Perhaps it contains a lesson for all beings who consider themselves intelligent; be they humanoid or any other organization of matter which knows itself as "I."

So to those who fear.

Or hide.

Or above all, who hate . . .

Read this and learn.

I am Phuili.

My name is Gefapronikitafrekazanzis, or Geoffrey to the humans who knew me. Now I am old, with not much time remaining before I must leave this sequence and enter the next. However I still have modest notoriety as the one who made first contact with members of your species. Much has happened since that moment of my youth; the gates have been opened to the universe, and together we are exploring the mighty system of suns known so unappropriately by humans as the Milky Way.

I know however that a great curiosity still exists about that pivotal meeting so long ago. So to please my human friends, I now record what this Phuili did and saw when the long strangers first came to The Shouter.

The Phuili had been on that small world for many

turns when the humans came. The Shouter is a desert planet with a thin atmosphere which is frequently obscured by windblown dust. Much like your Mars, I am told. Normally our explorers would have passed it by like hundreds of other worlds we had seen of its kind, if it was not for the artifacts which cover its surface in many thousands. Now, of course, we know the purpose of those artifacts. But until the humans came, the mighty structures had remained one of the universe's more spectacular mysteries.

They called them alien artifacts, or AA's. And because the structures loudly signaled their existence to the universe, the planet on which they were located was known appropriately as The Shouter. Beyond that simple acknowledgment that the artifacts did exist, neither Phuili nor humans were aware that they were in fact the means to bring the planets of nearly twenty thousand suns to within a step of distance and a moment of time. It was knowledge that neither Phuili nor humans would, or could ever know.

Unless, as a unity of two—

The arrival of the strange spacecraft into orbit above The Shouter would become an event with catastrophic implications for the Phuili. The beliefs and traditions of ten thousand generations had taught us that under the Maker we are the only beings in the universe who are self-aware; who have the ability to think and create. It is an ancient concept of ourselves which made us extremely vulnerable against something we *knew* could not and did not exist.

I remember very clearly the messenger who told me about the strange ship. "What do you mean?" I asked. "How can there be such a thing?"

"No one knows. But it is there, and it has been seen."

"What is it like?"

"Smaller than a Far-Explorer, with some kind of primitive ion propulsion system. It was detected when it phase-shifted into normal space outside the orbit of Planet Seven, but was not reported until it penetrated the ComNet."

That was understandable. Although ships from the home world arrived and departed according to rigid schedule, Far-Explorers could not, of course, be bound by such restraints. Which explained why at first detection it had been assumed that the stranger was, in fact, a returning Far-Explorer whose crew could have no knowledge of schedules which had been in place for less than a generation. The strange nature of the ship would consequently not have become evident until it activated one of the robots which, at twenty diameters, form The Shouter's communications and detection network.

Not that immediate realization came to us. Even as I was being informed, it had already been presumed that by some combination of errors which in any other circumstance would have been deemed close to a statistical zero, the entire net had somehow misidentified a returning Far-Explorer.

To state that I was surprised when I was called into the First's presence and told to investigate a reported sub-craft landing is, I suppose, an exaggeration. I was, after all, the most junior as well as the youngest at the station, so was therefore the most expendable. Naturally, that was not mentioned as the First pointed at the map.

"It landed here, at Artifact nine thousand and three. You may take a wingship, but I suggest you do not overfly the site. Instead, land beyond that ridge so that they will not suspect your presence."

"You wish me to approach on foot?"

"I believe it would be prudent. If, as seems most logical, the crew of a lost Far-Explorer have returned in a ship they have had to build from the wreckage of the old, it explains the strangeness of the ship. It is also why I advise caution. We do not know how such a long separation from the home world will have affected those lost children."

"Rationalization" has no equivalent in the Phuili language. The human concept of Occam's Razor similarly has no place in our philosophy. Which is why I did not doubt that the First's unwieldly explanation—which did at least avoid the statistical improbability of a ComNet error—was the true one. Because the lost ones had probably forgotten much of the ancient wisdom, it was only fitting that I take great care.

How do I explain what happened to me when I first saw the long strangers? Frankly, it is difficult. How would a human react if he saw a crab write a mathematical equation in the sand? Perhaps that will help you to partially understand, but it is far from enough. A human would be shocked, he would deny, but ultimately he yields to even the most unpalatable truth. That is your flexibility.

That is not, unfortunately, the way of the Phuili. Before we yield, we break.

I had dutifully landed the wingship far enough away that the strangers could have no advance warning of my presence. With pride that I had been selected for this delicate mission, and rehearsing in my thoughts how I would address these lost ones if circumstance made it proper for me to approach them, I ascended the back of the dune which overlooked the place of landing and eased myself into a clear viewing position at the top.

Impossibly huge, a symbol of ancient mystery, the artifact towered over me. The great horizontal bowl blocked half the sky, its supporting pylon so slender it seemed no more than a heavy line joining the base of the bowl to the ground. The artifact's shadow resembled a black lake in the desert, and on the lake's nearer shore stood a four-legged craft of strange design. At first glance the craft seemed totally primitive, clearly designed for no other purpose than to transport a bare minimum of payload with what was probably an equally primitive system of propulsion. But if the thought crossed my mind that the crew of a wrecked Far-Explorer could only have survived if they had the use of functioning sub-craft which were incomparably more advanced than the frail construct on the desert, then I promptly dismissed that thought as a flight of fancy inappropriate to the solemnity of the moment.

I felt tempted to move down, but caution held me back as I looked for those I had come to find. Because it is difficult for unaided vision to adjust to the brilliant contrasts of light and shade which are normal on The Shouter, I did not at first see those who were still within the artifact's shadow. But when they suddenly emerged into the light, casting long shadows which rippled over the uneven ground like writhing fingers pointed in my direction, I think it was then I began to break.

For a few moments I was in mental stasis; not understanding, not even caring about this thing which could not be. And then as control returned, so did an almost irresistible urge to go back to the wingship and return home. It would bring great shame, of course, perhaps to the extent I might have to consider an early termination of myself from this sequence. But even as I considered this terrible denial of proper function, I found I could not move because stronger than my fear was my sense of duty; the knowledge that if the powers beyond the end and the beginning had intended that I should not be here, then I would not be so. Forcing my unwilling hand into action, I unclipped the far-viewer from my equipment belt and attached it to the visor of my helmet. Looking back on that moment, knowing what I thought I had just seen with my unaided eyes, I now marvel at the extreme of madness which made me expose myself to the incomprehensibility of a close-up of those beings. If it was duty, then that stern aspect of my being was guiding my muscles without recourse to my frightened brain.

Focusing was automatic, so I had no control over the rapidity with which the image snapped into crystal clarity. At first, I tried to close my eyes. Then I tried to turn away. I even wished I had the ability to turn off my mind like a lamp. Instead, like an innocent staring unwinking into the sun's burning eye, I looked.

And I shattered.

I suppose a human physician would say I experienced a mental overload and withdrew from reality. Perhaps that is possible, even for a Phuili, although such a condition is unrecorded in our Archives of Medical Science. I do know, however, that when I finally recovered my senses the sun had moved halfway down the sky, a measure of at least two hours. It is also certain that something had changed within me during that time, as if my horror had triggered the formation of a psychic shield. It was with no hesitation at all that I again activated the far-viewer and looked down at the strange sub-craft.

The three beings were no longer visible, so I presumed they had returned inside their vehicle. The ground about was heavily scuffed with their foot marks, and I saw several pieces of equipment linked by cable to a small solar collector.

Humans have said that what I did next was an unparalleled act of courage. It is not true, of course, because I am Phuili and not human. I did what was necessary, and even that was only possible because of the protection my previously vulnerable mind had put about itself.

It was almost as if I had split into two halves, as part of me stood apart and watched with interest as I went down the slope to where the ungainly machine stood on a flat area of rocky ground. At first I walked around, stooping low under the twin windows which looked like the eyes of an enormously magnified insect. To my amazement, the energy of propulsion was entirely chemical. The two big reaction nozzles at the base and the smaller steering thrusters in the upper hull, were of designs we had discarded in a past so distant it was almost forgotten. But there was a clear contradiction—to fly and land such an unstable configuration was far beyond the capabilities of even the most experienced pilot. Which implied a sophistication of automatic control quite remarkable by any standard.

It seemed my briefly acquired impartiality was being sundered by a gamut of unfamiliar emotions; fear, contempt, wonder, and puzzlement being only a few. What was I to do? Report what I had found and be judged insane by my friends and colleagues? Or continue what I had started, to an end I could not see and dared not think about?

Logically, for me there was no choice. These strangers, whoever or *what*ever they were, were on The Shouter and could not be ignored. Somehow my colleagues would have to be convinced of their existence, which would seem to involve—for every one of the one hundred and thirty who currently staffed the base—a traumatic shock similar to what I had already experienced. Whether or not any or all of them had the necessary flexibility to accept and then to adapt to this new shape of the universe was something I did not know. It had become terribly clear that I was burdened with a responsibility even the greatest of the Elites would hesitate to accept.

Again that impartial side of me watched as I walked in front of the machine and stood in a position from where I could be seen through its windows. The reaction from those inside was almost immediate. First, I saw a vague movement within the darkness behind the transparent panels, followed by a sputtering in my helmet phones which evolved into a series of harsh syllables as my receiver found and locked in on the transmitting frequency. Not being sure how I should respond, I simply said "I do not understand," and lifted my arms in the accepted gesture of welcome.

In terms of what they consider strange, humans are flexible. The "we are not alone" syndrome has been a factor in their social and intellectual development since their shaggy ancestors first peopled the sky with gods. For the humans called Schendist, Alcorn, and Devany, the appearance of the small alien before their lander was an inevitability which was bound to happen sooner or later. It was merely their good fortune it had happened to them. So what they did next had already been rehearsed countless times in countless imagined circumstances. This was an event which humanity, by nature, was prepared for.

But not the Phuili—

When a door opened and one of the creatures descended a metal ladder, I stood my ground like an expendable remote which was being controlled from a safe distance. My second self was still observing dispassionately as the Phuili organism waited for whatever was about to happen.

After it reached the ground, the being did not immediately move from the base of the ladder. Instead, it faced me with its upper limbs lifted. The being's pressure suit was a clumsy affair which to a large extent concealed its true appearance. Nevertheless, it was clearly of what we now know as the "humanoid" form, although it was at least half a height taller than I was, and with a narrower body. It was difficult to see what was behind the front transparency of the helmet, but I gained the impression of flattened features and a slit of a mouth. It pointed at itself and made a single sound.

" 'Uman'?" I said.

The strange head bobbed vigorously. *"Human,"* it repeated, again pointing at itself.

I considered. Either its name was "Human," or it was of a race called "human." I decided the latter and pointed at myself. "Phuili."

"Fooli?" It took one step in my direction.

"Phuili," I said again, and took a countering step forward.

"Human, Barry." The being looked at me expectantly.

I was nonplussed. Although my altered mental state had enabled me to accept the existence of this "human," I was not willing to acknowledge any initiative other than my own. That it had seemed to be initiating communication with me was, I decided, an illusion born of my own confusion. Nevertheless, if communication were possible at all, I had to find out just how far this strange exchange could take us.

It had added the sound "Barry" to "human." So in turn, I said. "Phuili. Gefapronikitafrekazanzis."

Not all human myths are benign. There exists a pantheon of malevolence in the collective psyche, a darkness of the id against which individuals of that volatile race are always on guard. To human ears, the Phuili language of undiluted consonants is harsh; on the instinctive level it is a sound of menace. The threat imagined by the simple sounding of a Phuili name; causing the humans to retreat to their machine and prepare for hurried ingress—such was the misunderstanding which had the dubious distinction of being the first of many.

Of course, I did not know the true reason for the human's nervous behavior, but I did not think I needed to. Obviously, my appearance had created an unexpected flaw in its concept of the universe, as the fact of its own existence created a flaw in mine. However, the overwhelming question still remained. How to explain this new reality to the one who had sent me here? The more I considered the problem, the more I began to realize that in this matter, at least, communication with humans would entail considerably less difficulty than communication with my own kind.

I activated the First's frequency. "I am at the place of landing," I reported. "The creatures aboard this craft are not Phuili." There was no immediate response. Either the message had been recorded for later playback, or the First had heard and was deliberating the state of my sanity.

The Barry human reluctantly moved away from the ladder as another human emerged and came down. The third human remained inside their machine. The Barry human spoke at length to the newcomer. I found the harsh syllabic speech irritating, so I turned down the gain. Finally the new human turned and pointed at itself. "Katherine." Its voice was lighter and less unpleasant.

"Gefapronikitafrekazanzis," I repeated.

This time, I think they understood. They both walked half the distance to me and stopped. "Gefaproni . . ." the Katherine human began and stopped. It seemed to be having difficulty with consonantal speech. Then, triumphantly, "I know. I will call you Geoffrey!"

I wanted to be angry. To be addressed by any shortname is an insult worthy of trial and consequent compensation. But because these humans could hardly be faulted for the limitations of their speech organs, it seemed they were more to be pitied than condemned.

Limitations . . .

It was then I had the germ of an idea.

The notion of humans being "intelligent animals" was conceived by Geoffrey as much to protect his own people as it was an excuse to bring two of the strange creatures to the Phuili base. It was undoubtedly an unfortunate beginning for the humans, although it was a correct one for Geoffrey. He knew that the tradition of Phuili uniqueness had existed for too long; it was not so much learned as inherited as part of the Phuili psyche. Consider the convoluted rationalizing which allows for an animal that can build spacecraft, and the power of that tradition can be better perceived. Only later generations were not afraid to acknowledge humans as friends. Geoffrey's insanity had, in fact, made him a Phuili who was ahead of his time.

Three days later, with the Kurt human remaining aboard the lander, the Barry and Katherine humans accompanied me in the wingship back to the base. An empty ground car was waiting for us as arranged, and I immediately drove my guests to the building which had been set aside for us. The humans expressed surprise at the base's extent and obvious permanence, and wondered why they had not seen it from orbit. I pointed at the flickering haze which hemisphered the base. "Shield diverts dust around and over," I explained in their language. "From top, softens outlines. Not see."

"You mean the concealment is only a byproduct? Not intended?"

"Of course," I replied. "Why we want to conceal?"

My facility with the human language should not be surprising. The language is simple and completely without subtlety, and with the aid of a radio link to the Computer Core I had become conversant with meanings in less than two days. Unfortunately, I doubt any human will master Phuili talk. Not only is the human jaw ill-constructed for its use and the human ear equally deficient, but because at birth the human mind is virtually empty and needs to be fed everything it must know, it can never benefit from the reservoir of instinctive knowledge which our Phuili young already possess when they enter this sequence.

The First joined us after the supplies had been unpacked. The humans (their sleep cycle was only slightly longer than our own) had placed their mattresses in a small alcove, their food containers close by. Although it was reasonably certain our sustenance needs were mutually compatible, it had been decided we would wait for a full analysis before the humans would be allowed to sample any Phuili foodstuff. It had also been agreed that the First would determine if full quarantine would be maintained, or if the humans would be allowed access to the base and its personnel. To a large extent, that depended on the First's powers of persuasion. Although he himself had accepted my description of the humans as tool-using animals, there remained some doubt that everyone would accept this lesser yet still mind-twisting concept and remain fully sane.

When Averponekatupenavizis finally entered, I knew he had already been observing the humans for some time. Nevertheless, the signs of strain were evident as he stayed at the far side of the room and fixed his gaze on me rather than the vistors. He was aware of the limitations of the human tongue, so did not object when he heard himself called Avery. He had also tapped into what I had fed into the Computer Core, so was able to communicate with the humans without my assistance. But as he exchanged verbal data with them, his eyes remained steadfast in my direction.

"I am called the First because I am the first of equals," he replied to the initial question. "It is my function to point the way."

Although the Phuili have a hereditary ruling class known as the Elites, in the human context there is nothing equivalent to the formal selection of a single leader. Instead, there is an "instinct" which in any group situation allows the will of many to be expressed through one. It is merely one aspect of an exceedingly strong empathetic sense—a sense which on occasion can even reach out to humans.

It was difficult for us all, although I think less difficult for the humans. They had always accepted the possibility of other intelligences in the universe, so had been stimulated rather than demoralized by my unexpected appearance. For us Phuili, however, the mere existence of the humans threatened a crisis of first magnitude. And that was an unaccustomed burden for Averponekatupenaviziz, who was forced to bear this responsibility totally alone, without the support which is normally a First's right. As I watched and listened, I tried to aid him with my own humble singularity, with sadly little effect. I supposed fatigue and the unprecedented excitements of the last few days had temporarily reduced my ability to empath. But in desire if not ability, I remained with Averponekatupenaviziz as he continued,

"What is your planet?"

"It is called Earth."

"Humans are the premier species?"

"Yes."

"How long have humans been traveling space?"

The Barry human named a number which I translated to Phuili units. "About three hundred years."

"But that is only—" Averponekatupenaviziz turned to me. "Gefapronikitafrekazanzis, three centuries ago is but yesterday. Can a seed become a forest in only a day?"

"Ask them when they built their first starship," I suggested. I was being cruel, but I knew it was necessary.

"Fifty years ago," was the Katherine human's reply to that question.

Averponekatupenaviziz agitatedly ushered me into the next chamber. His distress showed on his features, his shaking hands. "I cannot believe such a thing. Yet they are telling the truth. I know it!"

"You can tell?"

He looked at me with surprise. "Of course. The sense was very strong."

"But they are aliens!" I protested. "Their emotions, their ideas—" Then words faltered, as I understood the terrible price I had paid for becoming adjusted to the humans.

"What is it? Do you have a problem, my friend?" Averponekatupenaviziz was concerned. The signs were in his words and physical reactions; the flexing of his jaw, the lift of his hands. But the important signals, those of mind to mind, were missing. The confirmation of my worst fear came as he added, "Gefapronikitafrekazanzis, you are blank. In my mind you are not there. What has happened to you?"

I lied. For the first time in my life I told a deliberate untruth, and it cost me dearly. But he already had problems no First should ever be called upon to bear, and I doubted he could carry more. In any case, I was suddenly in the unique position of being the only Phuili who could conceal an untruth, which perhaps had potential as a useful talent as well as being a curse. "Nothing is wrong," I replied. "I believe we are both fatigued."

Again I was in that peculiar mode in which I stood apart from myself as I rationalized the possibilities. I had prepared "Avery" in advance, and he had not broken. Neither, I now believed, would any Phuili if he or she was similarly prepared. But I was not so sure how the humans would react to an official proclamation of their inferiority. In my clumsy fashion I had explained, and I think they had understood, the "intelligent animal" aspect of their introduction to the First. But would they accept a permanent relationship based on an acknowledgment of Phuili superiority? I did not know. I only sensed we were all poised on an uneasy fulcrum, that at this moment the choice between two very dissimilar futures was more in human hands than Phuili.

So I felt a great lightening of spirit as Averponeka-tupenaviziz, anticipating a large part of the problem, said flatly, "The others must be informed. But it will have to be done gently, in the same manner you led me to the knowledge." He touched my arm. "I am grateful for your caution, Gefapronikitafrekazanzis."

I inclined my head. "It is a difficult knowledge."

"Very difficult. So I am puzzled. How did you manage to come through this experience so unchanged? After all, there was no one to prepare you for what you found out there."

"I do not know," I replied, amazed at the ease with which I was learning to deceive. I added, "Perhaps it was meant to be, for whoever was the one to contact the humans."

I knew Averponekatupenaviziz was of a somewhat mystical nature, so it did not surprise me as he nodded thoughtfully. "I will assemble our colleagues and prepare them. Some may already have seen our guests from a distance, so it is better they know the truth before their imaginations conjure something worse. You and the humans will remain concealed until I tell you otherwise."

I acknowledged silently, then returned to the humans. I did not know enough of their language to be subtle, so instead I decided to use an analogy. "You breathe our air," I said. "It is difficult?"

The Barry human replied. "It sustains us. But it does have an unpleasant odor."

That was logical. The odds against their native atmosphere being precisely the same as ours, were astronomical. So what was "different" to their organs of smell could be, I supposed, unpleasant. I pointed at the cylinders they had brought with their other supplies. "Why do you have those?"

"They are for emergency use. Otherwise, in time we expect we will get used to—" His face wrinkled. "—your gases."

"Because it is necessary?"

He nodded. I was learning not to be surprised at the similarity of body gestures; for instance the nodding for acquiescence, the sideways shaking of the head for a negative. Even the lifting of both corners of the slit like mouth was clearly a smile, although the barking humans refer to as "laughter" would probably be accepted by my colleagues as proof of their animalistic nature.

I said, "If you or any of your species wish to continue your presence on this world, it will be necessary that you accept other unpleasant but necessary things."

"What things?"

"Most important, that you continue to recognize that the Phuili are a superior species. But also that you accept limitations of your numbers and activities on this world, as well as permanent status as subjects for Phuili scientific study."

They stared at me. I knew my use of their language was still inadequate, that I had difficulty with many of the sounds. But I also knew they understood the content if not the details of my message, and that the rising pink flush on their exposed areas of flesh was probably resentment.

"Why?" the Barry human asked at last. "What gives you the right—" The female stopped him with a sharp word.

I tried to explain. Much of what I said was relative to what I had learned about the human species, which made it new even to me—and consequently difficult.

"The Phuili are an ancient people. Much of what we are is therefore ours from the moment of birth, and is not learned as you know learning. Therefore, we have certain beliefs about ourselves which cannot be changed without risk of insanity. You humans may be what you think you are, but to the Phuili that can never be."

The Katherine human said shrewdly, "Forgive me if I am wrong, but I have the feeling *you* believe we are more than inferiors. Geoffrey, doesn't that conflict with what you have just told us?"

She had made a painful point, one I knew I had to answer. "There is no conflict. You see, this Phuili is insane."

They looked at each other. Then, "I don't understand," the Barry human said puzzledly. "You seem rational to me."

I tried to explain. Using what I knew of their language was like trying to describe sight to one without eyes. "We have a sense. It is like—" I struggled, continued. "Imagine being able to perceive between hot and cold without having to know the degree of hot or cold. Or recognizing the optical band from the radio band, but not individual frequencies." I tried to think of other similes, but was forestalled as the human female said with a smile,

"I am guessing, of course, but I think you are talking about empathy. The ability to sense mood as distinct from individual thoughts. Am I right?"

I marveled at this one's powers of discernment. "Yes, you are right. Do humans have it?"

"Not to the extent it can be trusted. Not without some physical signs, at any rate. As far as the mind-to-mind part of it is concerned—" The small, strange eyes opened wide. "Is that what you have? Like telepathy?"

The word was unfamiliar, but I thought I understood. "The method of transmission is not important.

It is the content. For the Phuili, words are the embedded fruit in a cake. It is the cake's whole taste which is the message, not merely the sum of the fruit it contains."

"I think—" The female came closer to me. There was sympathy on the strange face, in the moistened eyes. "You have lost the taste, haven't you?"

I sighed. "Yes. At first I thought it was fatigue. But I knew otherwise when Averponekatupenaviziz told me he had no problem reading your sincerity. I had sensed nothing."

That seemed to disturb the Barry human. "Are you telling us he—?" His oddly articulated fingers clenched and unclenched. "Dammit, Kath, we won't be able to keep anything from these people!"

The Katherine human nodded. "It certainly seems that way. And if the Phuili know when we lie, then there is obviously no point continuing the charade of inferiority. Not when any one of them can sense it is only an act."

"Ah, but in that case what is sensed is not important." After a moment of hesitation, I added solemnly, "Does it matter, if in its ignorance the leaf thinks it is equal to the flower?"

It is ironic that as the Phuili increasingly acknowledge that perhaps the leaf IS equal to the flower, they must necessarily also come to terms with the phenomenon of human hypocrisy. Because on the psychic level humans are insulated from each other, they practice deceits which the empathetic Phuili cannot ignore—yet at the same time find impossible to accept. So which will come first? That Phuili will accept what humans say? That humans will mean what they say? Or that crabs will write equations in the sand?

Perhaps, before anything else changes, there will be reports of mathematical crustaceans.

It would have taken ninety-three minutes, as humans measure time, to fly to the location of the human lander at Artifact 9003. But at sixty minutes, I had to crash-land the wingship.

It was a bad place for such an emergency, in a depression crisscrossed with gullies and littered with boulders. But somehow the four of us survived, although we were all injured. Pakegoknerfronakipilasis was the worst, with a crushed leg. Least injured was the Barry human, with cracked ribs. Fortunately, we had enough sealant to restore the integrity of our pressure garments, although much of our air supply was gone before the last rent was sealed. We were alive, but our situation was not good. The wingship was damaged beyond repair, the communications module had been torn out at first impact, and we were considerably off course because I had diverted to avoid a dust storm.

"It is unheard of," the one the humans called "Packer" said peevishly. "There has never been a failure like this." His look, as he glared at the humans, was accusing.

The Barry human moved uncomfortably. "What did he say?"

"He believes you humans are to blame."

The Barry human shrugged. "So he doesn't like us. It's why he came, isn't it?"

There was no need to reply. When Averponeka-tupenaviziz had failed to gain acceptance for the humans, it was inevitable that the successful spokesman for the opposition accompany us to make sure the humans left the planet. I was wary of Pakegoknerfro-nakipilasis. Whatever emotion had been powerful enough to overcome his loathing of these beings to the extent he would tolerate their close proximity made him unpredictable. He knew of my insanity, so he was aware I could not read his intentions. Neither, of course, could he read mine. Not that either advantage counted for much, especially considering the unexpected nature of the terrain and our injuries.

The Katherine human made a noise of pain as she lifted her upper body to an upright position against a boulder. Although the injuries to her lower limbs were not as severe as the damage to Pakegoknerfronakipilasis, she was equally as immobile. "We must take stock," she announced.

My own damage was that of a dislocated upper limb which was also fractured. Although the pain was severe, I disciplined it to a lesser status as I asked interestedly, "What is stock?"

"A list of everything that affects our situation. What we can use to improve it."

I translated for Pakegoknerfronakipilasis. "An illogical hope," he said. "It is merely further proof of what we already know; that the humans are primitive beings who are not intelligent enough to know they will soon die."

Despite her pain, the human female made a laughing noise. "If hope makes us primitive, then, by golly, we are primitive!" She looked at the other human. "How is our air supply?"

"Not good." He gestured at the single cylinder he had pulled from the wreckage. "With that and what we have on our backs, four or perhaps five hours at the most."

"Much less for us," I said sadly. "Phuili do not allow for what we believe will not happen."

"How long can you keep going with what you have?"

"By your time, three hours. No more."

The Katherine human changed the subject. "Communications?"

"We're communicating, aren't we?" the male retorted. I was learning a little more about that strange type of speech humans call sarcasm.

"Yes, dear, but unfortunately only with each other." The Katherine human turned to me. "Geoffrey, how powerful is your suit radio?"

"The equipment we carry is very limited," I informed her. "Always, we relay through the long-range sets in our vehicles."

"My god, talk about bare bones! Don't you people have emergencies?"

"It is not efficient to design for anything more than an intended use," I told the Barry human. I pointed at the slender rod which extended above his shoulders. "Can you talk further?"

"It depends—" he began, then stopped. He carefully got to his feet and turned toward a high promontory which extended into the depression southwest of us. "How far are we from the lander?"

I told him.

"Hmm. About two hundred klicks."

The Katherine human was also staring at the promontory. "Do you think it is possible? That is a tough climb."

"With no guarantee there will be line-of-sight when I get there." The Barry human shrugged. "But it's all we've got."

Now I understood. "It will take much energy. You will need more oxygen than you have."

We looked at the spare cylinder.

"What are the beasts planning?" Pakegoknerfronakipilasis asked me. "Be careful, or they will take what little of life remains to us."

I felt an illogical annoyance at my Phuili colleague, although I knew his warning was proper and should be heeded. But my insanity was making me consider both sides; a broadened vision as remarkable in its own way as the perception I had lost. "That one," I said, pointing at the human male, "will climb to that high point, and from there will attempt to communicate with the human who waits in the lander at Artifact nine thousand and three. It is the only way help can be brought to us in time."

"In time for what, Gefapronikitafrekazanzis? If the beast takes the extra air container, I agree he may survive long enough to make his signal. But for the rest of us, including the female, it answers nothing."

His argument, although hostile, was logical. I translated for the humans.

The Katherine human said, "There is still a way."

*   *   *

Beasts are programmed for self-survival. If possible, they avoid danger. No beast will place itself in jeopardy merely to save individuals of other species who happen to share the same danger.

Geoffrey knew that humans are more than beasts. Even more than so-called "intelligent animals," although he was willing to accept a lesser status if only to gain for humans some kind of official Phuili acceptance. But unless the individual known as Pakegoknerfronakipilasis could be persuaded otherwise, Geoffrey's sponsorship would inevitably fail in its purpose.

Were Geoffrey's thoughts running along those lines as he piloted the wingship which also carried Pakegok-nerfronakipilasis and the two humans? Perhaps there is a clue in his comment about the unexpected nature of the terrain.

Consider.

If, before the humans were gone from The Shouter forever, they could be presented with an opportunity to demonstrate unbeastlike compassion and inventiveness, even the most dogmatic of skeptics might be persuaded to change his opinion. An emergency landing, at a place where in any case they would be "found" after a reasonable interval of time, could perhaps stimulate such a demonstration. Of course, even the most contrived scenario can be overtaken by events.

Such as, for instance, a dust storm and an unplanned course correction.

The First summoned me as soon as I was sufficiently recovered. "You are well," he said without preliminary. "Pakegoknerfronakipilasis is not. Do you know why that is so?"

I inclined my head. "He is ill for the same reason I am insane."

"The humans?"

"It has to do with them."

"I see." He considered a moment. "I am not insane. Neither am I ill. Yet I also had contact with those beings."

"You were prepared. Also, you are the First."

He looked a question.

"The unexpected is difficult. Yet the unexpected does happen. You hold your office because of all of us, you are the most—" I struggled to find a word. "—flexible."

"An interesting concept. You learned it from the humans?"

"I believe it is what makes them successful as a species. However, there is a strange side to their character which seems to counter that advantage."

"Explain."

"Logically, by eliminating the two Phuili, the humans could have gained enough extra air to guarantee their own survival. It would have been, after all, a clear case of an invokation of the law of necessity."

"An ancient and honorable law," Averponekatupenaviziz agreed. "So why wasn't it invoked? Compared with you and Pakegoknerfronakipilasis, the Barry human was relatively undamaged. So surely he could have done what was necessary."

"This is true. And if the choice had been an absolute one—such as, for instance, matching the certain death of four against the probable survival of two—then I do not doubt the Barry human would have properly invoked the law. But because he and the female perceived a statistical possibility that all four of us could survive, they selected a course of action which not only reduced their own chances, but which also placed the human female into a greater jeopardy than before."

I will go to sleep, the Katherine human had said after the male departed with his own tanks replenished from the spare. She then did something with the control unit on the front of her pressure garment, and promptly lapsed into an unconscious state.

Pakegoknerfronakipilasis and I were completely mystified. Finally, his contempt suggested an answer. "She has turned off her mind because she fears the pain of death. For her kind, there is clearly no next sequence. Their end is a terrible finality."

There was a logic in his pronouncement which chilled me. But if he was correct, then why were we still alive while the Barry human was a distant speck plodding toward a doubtful destiny?

I went to the Katherine human and touched the chest area. Her breathing was slow. "There is possibly another explanation."

"Be brief. Talk uses air."

"It has to do with the air." Using my sound arm, I dragged the spare cylinder to Pakegoknerfronakipilasis's side. Then I produced what remained of the pressure-sealant. "With your two good arms, I think it may be possible to adapt this alien fitting to replenish our own containers."

Although his prejudice was extreme, "Packer" was too intelligent not to realize this life-extending opportunity. He accepted the sealant without comment and worked painstakingly until at last the extra gas was feeding into our helmets. Then, as he returned his attention to our situation, his attitude seemed to change. "Because the female is unconscious," he announced, "she therefore breathes less."

It was, of course, a statement of fact. It was also an uncharacteristic concession which hinted that perhaps my gentle prodding had turned him in a direction his rigid inflexibility of nature would not otherwise allow. Fearing to disturb this new chain of reasoning, I remained silent as he continued,

"The male took some of the air, because without it he will certainly exhaust his own supply before he reaches his destination on that height. Although he could have taken the entire container and left us nothing, he chose not to."

I was greatly tempted to lead him further toward consideration of the unthinkable. However, I restrained the impulse and instead said simply, "That is true."

"That the female turned herself off, or that the male did not take or exhaust the container—each by itself can be considered a fortunate coincidence from which you and I have benefited. Taken, however, together . . ."

Pakegoknerfronakipilasis was suffering. His speech had become irregular, his vocal chords hoarse as if from too much use. I had been through a similar experience, so was aware of the schizophrenic turmoil of his thoughts—caused, in his case, by the extremes of his innate conservatism versus his machinelike ability to gather and analyze facts. Because humans were irrefutably inferior, it was equally certain that they were incapable of behavior beyond that dedicated to simple self-preservation—although there was a slight statistical probability that the behavior of a single human might be misinterpreted as compassion for others not of its kind. Unfortunately, the impossible juxtaposition of *two* of the creatures simultaneously displaying such altruism, represented an insane conflict of absolutes that Pakegoknerfronakipilasis' own implacable logic was forcing him to confront without hope of justification or compromise.

In a similar situation, I had shattered. But his was a different, more deliberate personality. He withdrew like a threatened flex-snake shrinking itself into insignificance.

Pakegoknerfronakipilasis crumpled.

After I had finished describing the events in the desert, the First lapsed into a deeply contemplative silence. Sharing the silence but not the contemplation, I waited. Although I was learning to accept the gulf which for the rest of my life would isolate me behind the lesser senses of touch and sight and hearing, moments like this would always be a painful reminder of my handicap—and there would necessarily be many such moments, as long as I continued to serve the cause I had precipitated. Which I knew I must.

Finally, Averponekatupenaviziz sighed and looked up. I think he grieved for me, even as we both knew my loss was as nothing compared with the future waiting to be born within this austere room deep in bedrock. "Pakegoknerfronakipilasis endlessly repeats the argument which destroyed him," he mused, half to himself.

I nodded. "It is a sad thing."

"He is apparently not aware of what is happening. So he does not suffer as you do, my friend."

I bowed my head. "I have a consolation. I still function."

"Gefapronikitafrekazanzis, what you have is more than that. You are unique among Phuili in that you are restricted to sensing the external world as humans sense it. That may be of great value."

It was like a ray of light through storm clouds. "We are to continue a relationship with humans?"

"We must. Unfortunately, they share our universe."

"It will be difficult to change what is already decided. Pakegoknerfronakipilasis has many supporters."

"Exactly."

If I had been normal, I would have immediately recognized the First's meaning. But already I was using deductive reasoning to an extent I would have thought impossible before the humans came, and after only a slight hesitation I asked, "Are you sure exposure to his words will not push others over the edge?"

"They will be prepared. They will be reminded of their mentor's rigidity, of the fact that proof of anything contrary to his beliefs would in any case have sufficed to destroy the foundations which supported his concept of reality."

Despite the tragedy we were discussing, it was difficult not to be heartened by its positive implications. "Instinct being proved as intelligence," I said, "must have been as shattering as black being proved white."

"You remain perceptive, Gefapronikitafrekazanzis, despite your sickness. Of course, you and I know the truth is somewhere between, and I am certain our colleagues will accept that truth when they realize humans represent a new classification of being. For most of them, I suspect the scientific challenge will be irresistible."

"The humans are proud. I am still not sure they will accept a lesser role."

"You have already told me they are an adaptable people. They are also realists, as we must be. In other words, it will be your function to prepare the humans for that lesser role—as I must prepare our own people for what is, I believe, a new universe."

So the testament ends. It is a matter of record that the human known as Barry Devany did finally contact his colleague aboard the lander, although when he was picked up he was nearly dead from oxygen deprivation and took months to recover. On the other hand, Katherine Alcorn's fast recovery so impressed the Phuili that they adopted the use of stasis drugs—implying a remarkable admission that even their own advanced technology was not always immune from error.

Geoffrey was assigned to the Permanent Earth Research Unit which was later established on The Shouter, and it was only due to his ceaseless activities as a mediator; on Phuili itself as well as on The Shouter; that PERU survived the first critical years.

Perhaps Geoffrey himself should have the final word. This is what he wrote to a human colleague shortly before he returned to his home world for the last time—

We will not meet again. But that is as it should be because change is, after all, a vital component of the living universe. Nevertheless, the problems will remain. Our successors will have to resolve those problems as they arise, or all that you and I have worked for, for so long, will be as nothing.

We are so few, those of us of both races who seek to unify our thrust into the universe. But I sincerely believe there are forces which have already predetermined that unity of purpose. Surely it is no coincidence that The Shouter, our gateway to the galaxy, is located almost precisely equidistant between your home world and mine. And although we are so different, what are those differences except images on both sides of the same coin? Together, humanity and Phuili are greater than their separate parts. Apart, we are less than that sum.

Much less.

My friend, I need hardly remind you of the continuing threat to your species from uncontrolled misuse of its profligate technology. And I know you have studied the Phuili enough to suspect, as I do, that our fate is the ultimate stagnation of an inflexible heritage. That two such self-destructive extremes can be melded into a vital new force, may seem impossible. But it is necessary, if only for survival's sake. Although I am sure there is more to a unified future than mere survival.

To paraphrase what a wise human once said, this Phuili has "walked a mile in human moccasins." Perceiving the universe as humans perceive it, I discovered to my astonishment that I had gained more than I had lost.

So should it be for all of us. Because only then will every Phuili and human at last realize that in all things essential, we are the same.

Your friend,
Geoffrey.

TWO

THE EXPEDITER

One world was called Earth by its inhabitants who, in turn, were of the race of man, or "humans." The other world was Phuili. Its inhabitants, of the same name as their planet, developed in a gentler and more equitable environment than Earth's, without the stimulus of competing carnivores which forced humankind to evolve rapidly or perish. It is true, therefore, that although man and Phuili share many similarities, they are also remarkably different. It is also true that humans (who were still using stone tools when the Phuili were already experimenting with powered flight) have an instinctive competitiveness which the conservative Phuili could neither understand nor tolerate. If there was to be a melding of the widely divergent talents of these two races, it would have to be done gently.

With great subtlety.

If it was not for the Pleiades Star Cluster, we would have found The Shouter a couple of centuries ago.

So until the *Far Seeker* and its crew of visionaries cruised out of the Pleiades shadow and detected a screaming source of radiation a couple of hundred lights beyond that nebula-hazed cluster, Earth's expansion into space had proceeded at the plodding pace decreed by the xenophobic World Union Council when the phase-shift drive was first developed. It is still not clear what bureaucratic blunder enabled a crew of star-gazing rebels to commandeer a phase ship and take off on their own, but it is certain *Far Seeker*'s triumphant return eight years later was the final straw which brought down that small-minded and nit-picking administration like the house of cards it really was.

But that, of course, is another story.

As is the one in which man made the first contact with another intelligent race, the Phuili, who had been drawn to The Shouter from their empire of worlds four hundred lights farther on toward the Hub. When *Far Seeker II* arrived off The Shouter during August of 2416 AD, the Phuili had already been on that remarkable world for so long they considered it their private reserve. But intelligence is apparently such a rare phenomenon in the galaxy, they permitted the establishment of a permanent Earth research unit (PERU) so they, in turn, could research humans—which they did with aggravating persistence.

Still, that seemed a small price for the privilege of being stationed for a while on this galactic mystery. So I was like a small boy being introduced to his first two-wheeled bicycle as I emerged from the shuttle and confronted the awesome structure towering from the plain a few kilometers away.

"Iss large, iss not?"

Imagine a dog given vocal chords and a flexible jaw; such is the speech of a Phuili. The being was in the driver's seat of a small runabout parked next to the ramp, his wide-eyed canine head regarding me solemnly through the elongated bubble which was his helmet. I had not immediately noticed him because even one's first alien becomes upstaged against the incomprehensibility on the plain. Awed and embarrassed at the same time I started to stammer an apology, but was halted by the sight of a fanged grin. "When I come," the voice rasped in my helmet phones, "I too could only see zat." A stubby arm gestured. "But now I take you to your kind. Pleese to sit on here."

"On here" presuming the seat next to him, I gingerly climbed aboard and hung on as the vehicle accelerated with a jerk. My small driver swung the steering bar hard over and we turned like a top, bouncing through our own dust cloud and then down the graveled road at a speed which would have made me nervous on a paved highway.

The Shouter has a thin atmosphere of mostly nitrogen with barely detectable traces of oxygen and a few of the noble gases. So the sky was a magnificent velvet blue, paling off at the horizon where the other component of the atmosphere—dust—was lofted by vagrant winds over the bone-dry landscape. I suppose some part of me appreciated the austere beauty of the planet, but my mind was still on the colossus behind us. I would like to have looked some more at it, but it was behind me and in any case my helmet was not as swivelable as my head. So instead I watched The Shouter's only metropolis race toward us.

My driver pointed at a rectangular structure set apart from the Phuili domes and pyramids. "Humans zere," he announced as the runabout shuddered over a series of ruts and I tasted blood where I bit my tongue. I wished I knew the polite way to get the Phuili to stop so I could save myself a few bruises and walk the rest of the way. But not desiring to offend unknown sensibilities, I held my peace and continued to hold on for dear life.

We whizzed by a graceful pyramid. "Phuili on here five ten hands of years," my driver said. "We always stay."

I had been warned to expect this bit of propaganda, so despite my aches and pains I was aware enough not to be surprised. With two fingers and two opposed thumbs, the Phuili numerical system is based on eight. "Five ten hands" is therefore four hundred which, even considering their shorter year, is a pretty long time. In other words, The Shouter is Phuili's by longstanding right of possession, and every Phuili had apparently been instructed to make sure humans were frequently reminded of the fact. The "we always stay" bit was optional but used often, so I suspect our innocent human intentions with regard to The Shouter were not entirely accepted by this likable but sometimes irascible species.

We stopped with a teeth-rattling jerk inside the main air lock of the rectangular building which, on closer approach, had become a modest four-story structure. The outer doors closed and air whistled in with a rush, blowing dust from the frame of the runabout. The whistling stopped, and as the dust began to settle a tall human entered the lock from the interior of the building. He was trim and white haired. "Mr. Digonness?"

I flipped my helmet back on my shoulders and climbed stiffly from the runabout. " 'Digger,' please," I replied as I accepted his handshake. He was even taller than I thought, a good half head more than my own not inconsiderable one hundred and eighty-seven centimeters.

His mouth twitched into a smile. "All right, Digger, you may call me Clarence. Short for Clarence Van Standmeer, Assistant Research Administrator on this noisy sphere."

I swallowed. Familiarity with the boss is not normally my style. "Yes, sir . . . er . . . Clarence."

The smile expanded into a laugh. "We're strictly informal here, believe me." Seriously, "Though we do expect you to perform, of course." He turned to my Phuili driver. "Bertram, how are you? Haven't seen you around lately."

The Phuili had removed his own helmet, proving the similarity between his native atmosphere and ours. His head, though canine, was pink and hairless. The eyes were remarkable: large, dark, and intelligent. "I am well, Clawence my fwiend. I had temporwawy function in administwation until awival of new human. Now I assigned zis one."

The A.R.A. nodded. "I am pleased. I know by experience he could not have a better guide and companion."

"Zat is twue," the Phuili agreed modestly. Before

he replaced his helmet, he turned to me. "I and you meet soon."

I hoped my embarrassment did not show. Not only had I been mouthy with the boss, it seemed I had been aloofly uncommunicative with my future partner. "I am looking forward to it," I said, hoping my shyness toward this small alien had not been interpreted as prejudice.

Clarence touched my arm. "Let's go." I hurried after him into the building. The door closed behind us and I heard the thrumming of compressors as they evacuated the lock. "First, your quarters," my guide said, leading me up a narrow stairway to the second floor. The room he showed me was small but comfortable, with a folding bunk, a couple of chairs, and a standard screen-terminal recessed next to a compact food prep unit. "Your things won't be delivered for a while," he told me as I discarded my gear and wriggled out of the P-suit. "So I suggest we trot up to the lounge and see who is there. Old faces always like to meet new ones."

"And vice versa," I said as we walked along the narrow door-lined corridor. "About Bertram . . ."

Clarence stopped and looked at me. One elegant eyebrow was raised, giving him a saturnine expression. "What about Bertram?"

"How does a Phuili get a name like that?"

He frowned. "Their own names are a mess of clicks and consonants, absolutely unpronounceable by humans. So those we know have accepted the nearest human equivalent. They don't seem to mind; in fact, I suspect they are quite flattered. Weren't you briefed about that?"

I shook my head. "No."

"I see." Clarence seemed irritated. "You *were* briefed, I suppose?"

"Of course." I added lamely, "It's just that I did not expect to meet my Phuili partner so soon."

The irritation faded, was replaced with a thoughtfulness. "I would have met you myself, except I was informed someone else had volunteered. If I had known it was Bertram . . ."

"Something unusual about that?"

"Digger, you are the first human arrival to be met at the pad by a Phuili. Frankly, I am not sure if you should be flattered. Or apprehensive."

I felt a sinking feeling. "What do I do?"

He looked at me soberly. "Just be careful. And when I know more, I'll advise more."

I sensed the source of his concern. If I, for some unknown reason, was special to the Phuili, then it followed I had become equally special to The Shouter's human community. It was as if a new and untried staff member of an overseas embassy had immediately been promoted—by choice of the host country—to something approaching the rank of ambassador. The diplomatic hazards were obvious. It would also be extremely unnerving to the junior, being way beyond the scope of his expected responsibilities. Which was exactly how I felt as I followed the A.R.A. to a spiral stairway which wound up the central well of the building. As we climbed, I tried hard to convince myself I was overreacting.

To a certain extent I succeeded, so that when I was ushered into the Observation Lounge and again saw the monster on the plain, my burden—imagined or otherwise—seemed not so important. There were people in the room, but at that moment they did not seem so important either. Instead, I walked over to the huge window and stared, fascinated. For a while I was permitted my reverie. They had been there and understood. Finally, one of them came and stood at my side. "Gets to you, doesn't it?" The voice was low, husky, and pleasantly female.

That's an understatement, I thought, momentarily oblivious to the charm of those dulcet tones. Imagine a shallow, two-kilometer-wide saucer balanced horizontally atop a slender pylon three kilometers high. Add a flickering sphere of pale flame a further kilometer above that incredible assembly, and there you have it. A reasonable description of a reality which in essence is undescribable. Alien Artifact Number One.

More time passed. To me it was not long, but to the others it must have seemed I was stuck in a time warp. A slender hand moved up and down in front of my eyes. "You must come down now," the pleasant voice said, "before you grow moss."

I shook myself back to reality. "Sorry," I apologized, turning to the owner of the hand. She was small and nicely formed, with dark hair and intense green eyes. I am shy with women and somehow this one squared the trait. So I stammered like a fool. "H . . . how long?"

She grinned. "Two minutes. Three minutes. Does it matter? Nothing wrong with being a romantic, Mr. Digonness."

"My first name is Peter," I said, surprising myself.

"It is?" Though her lips curved into a frown, somehow her eyes continued smiling. "Clarence just told us you prefer Digger."

"To you, Peter," I persisted, wondering why. Only my mother called me Peter, and this vivacious beauty was certainly not my mother.

"Okay, you may call me Jenny. Short for Genevieve Hagan. And these are Helda, Jock, Dewinton (who will be insulted if you don't call him Dewy), Allan, and Rhiddian. Clarence, our dear lord and master, you have met. Anyway, everyone will later tell you their last names and what they do here—if they can remember either. But now you are the new boy and are allowed three questions. Number one?"

Instant immersion. I knew then she was the base psychologist—not in the formal sense perhaps—but the one who by inclination and personality usually assumes the role. It seems to happen wherever there is an isolated group of humans, though in this case I was already biased enough to be certain Jenny was better than most. I felt a twinge of disappointment in the realization her interest in me was kind rather than romantic. Nevertheless, I accepted her invitation.

"How many of them are there?" I asked, gesturing at the object on the plain.

"The AAs? Nineteen thousand, six hundred and fifty-four. But you know that, surely?"

I shrugged. "I thought I did. But after seeing that *one* . . ." I gestured helplessly.

The girl pointed toward a range of low hills humped on the horizon. Something flickered between two of them.

"Another?" I asked.

She nodded. "About sixty klicks from here. Actually, that and AA One are the only two within five hundred klicks. Planetary distribution is quite random."

"I know where there are three so close together you can visit 'em all on foot within hours," the one called Jock said. He was stocky with red hair and freckles, so typical a type I immediately tagged him as an ethnic Scot with haggis in his veins. But my theory fell apart when he stuck out his hand and introduced himself. "Jean DeLaforte, geologist and com tech. Otherwise known as Jock, which is terribly degrading for one with my sensitive Gallic temperament."

"It's no worse than Digger," I sympathized as I accepted his limp handshake. "You're from Garson's Planet, aren't you?"

He withdrew his hand like one who had been stung. "Who told you that?"

I grinned. "An angel."

His face cleared. "Well, I'm damned. So you know about Garson's angels, huh?"

"They're raising a colony on Luna. Something to do with 'social interactions between species.' A bit more intelligent than chimps, a lot more affectionate than puppies, and about as frail as one-meter butterflies." I pointed at his hand. "I don't wonder you have to watch your strength. Where you come from, it must be damned difficult to avoid hurting the natives."

Jock nodded. "Unfortunately, we don't always succeed," he said sadly.

"Well, no one around here need worry about hurting the Phuili," Helda said, brusquely halting the conversation's downturn. A big woman, she had a tough but good-natured face. "Not only are the little buggers made out of concrete, they don't like to hug or shake hands." She chuckled. "Which is probably good for *our* state of health. Right?"

"As far as I am concerned, the only thing about the Phuili is that they are a frigging nuisance," the small man called Dewy grumbled. "They're always there, like an itch you can't scratch. One of these days I might just sneak out on my own and . . ."

"I do not advise it," Clarence interrupted coldly. His voice knife-edged, he continued, "You know the conditions of our agreement with the Phuili, and as your A.R.A. I expect you to abide by it. You are members of PERU, and as such you are each assigned a Phuili partner to facilitate your work here. In return, you accept the fact you are *his* project, and learn to put up with his frequent presence and always nagging questions. As you investigate The Shouter, your partner investigates you. It's that simple." The A.R.A. paused, somehow catching my eye. "None of us like it, but we learn to live with it. Because we damn well have to!"

Though he was not addressing me directly, I sensed he was reminding me of the peculiar circumstances of my arrival. But already I was beginning to doubt its significance. There is a first time for everything, and in that light I failed to find anything remarkable in the fact I had been met at the pad by a Phuili rather than by one of my own kind. If the aliens desired human company—for whatever reason—it seemed logical they would want to commence the acquaintanceship as soon as possible. Even at shuttle disembarkation.

Jenny said, "Clarence, while we are on the subject of Phuili partners, what about Dig . . . er, Peter's? Has one been assigned?"

"Oh, indeed," the A.R.A. replied dryly.

"I have already met him," I told her.

"You have?"

"He was waiting for me at the pad. His name is Bertram."

"Bertram? *He* met you?"

"Quite a precedent," Helda said thoughtfully.

Clarence smiled a thin smile. "Quite."

I was embarrassed. Everyone was looking at me as if I had shed my skin and become something else. "I don't know why you're making such a fuss," I said uncomfortably. "So I was met by a Phuili . . ."

"*The* Phuili," Jenny interrupted firmly. "Dear man, don't you know? Bertram is Clarence's opposite number here. The Phuili boss."

My first trip was obvious. I knew where I wanted to go and it was expected. Not only by my fellow humans but also by Bertram when I contacted him after breakfast the next morning. His image on the screen nodded politely when I made the request. "Ah, Mister Digonness who I to call Digger. You wish to go AA One. I be at your lock in fwaction of hour."

When a Phuili makes a promise, he keeps it. (For that matter, so did everyone of PERU. Being a minority had made Earth's representatives on The Shouter somewhat sensitive about the less laudable aspects of human nature, so for Phuili consumption we did our best to act like saints. Though Moses could not have imagined a less likely setting for adherence to the Commandments, by and large, I think he would have approved.) Anyway, it was only twenty minutes later when my Phuili partner rocked his runabout to a halt outside the lock and I climbed aboard.

"No," Bertram said, stepping down from the vehicle. With a sudden and completely startling demonstration of the power contained within his compact body, he leaped clean over the runabout and landed lightly on my side. Though the leap had lofted him at least three times his own height, he was not breathing any differently than normal as he told me, "You dwive. Iss pwoper you learn."

"Er . . . yes." Wondering what other surprises this

small being had in store for me, I obediently slid over and wedged myself behind the controls. Somehow I found the lever which moved the seat back, so at least my knees were not at the level of my shoulders. Then I found the speed control, which worked by pushing the steering bar forward. There was no reverse, I soon discovered. If there was not enough room for the vehicle to switch ends in its normal toplike fashion, the procedure was to push it back by hand until there was. It seemed primitive, but the runabout was so light I think I could have lifted the whole thing with only one hand. Bertram could probably have swung it over his head. Traction for this ultralight machine involved intensification of attraction between chassis and ground, a wondrously useful item of Phuili technology which made me marvel. But which at the same time added another load to my already sagging ego.

I had, in other words, become somewhat depressed. Physical plus technical superiority equals mental superiority, a simplistic equation which at that confused moment seemed entirely logical. If Bertram had been a three-meter humanoid with piercing eyes and a noble brow, and not a half-human sized caricature of a bull terrier in a silver suit, I suspect I would not have been bothered by my newly discovered inferiority. But I do know I would have been in a much worse state if I had not been otherwise occupied driving the runabout and answering my partner's endless questions.

It was tough at first. As AA One rose before us, irritation increasingly supplanted depression as my attention wandered between driving, the enigma ahead, and Bertram's inquisitiveness. He wanted to know about my home in New Mexico, my education, my politics, even about my sex life—though he soon lost interest in the latter when he learned I was middle-of-the-road-normal. But it was when he asked me about my scientific specialty, that the conversation suddenly began to get interesting.

"I do not have one," I told him.

A heavy paw pressed down on my arm. "Pleese make stop."

We jolted to a standstill amid a swirling cloud of brown dust. Ahead, AA One was unbelievable, a surrealistic fantasy. Above its enormous dish the flickering sphere of light was an ethereal sun, at this distance close enough to cast faint but blurry shadows.

My alien guide turned to me, his snouted head enigmatic behind the reflected highlights of his helmet. "Zen what iss expediter?"

There was no blinding flash of realization. But at that moment I got the first hint of the reason behind Bertram's interest in me. I chose my answer carefully. "Do you know what a catalyst is?"

The head shook slightly. "The word iss . . . not familiar."

"A catalyst is a substance which increases the rate of a chemical or nuclear reaction, but which itself remains unchanged."

There was a silence. Then an explosive, complex cluster of sounds which neither my tongue nor voice writer could ever hope to reproduce. Bertram continued, ". . . iss happen in stars wiz carbon. What you call 'Phoenix.' "

"That's it!" I said, surprised. "Hydrogen into helium plus energy, with carbon as the catalyst. Hence the analog. My job here is to act as a human catalyst; in effect 'expediting' reactions between those of the various scientific disciplines. Do you understand?"

The silence this time was a long one, enough for me to rationalize some of my own thoughts. I knew applications for PERU were routinely submitted to the Phuili for final clearance, which explained Bertram's knowledge that I was an expediter. But whether or not my explanation bore any similarity to what he had already been told, I had no way of knowing. What was clear was that I was the first of my kind on The Shouter. It also further explained Bertram's interest, and with that realization my spirits began to recover from their previous low. In this matter, at least, it seemed I had the advantage, and I felt myself warm toward the little alien. Within the alchemy of my reasoning, Bertram was becoming more "human."

"How do human become . . . expediter?"

"In my case, via my former profession of science writer," I replied. Sensing his puzzlement, I continued, "It was my job to use the media to explain scientific matters to nonscientists, to simplify . . ."

"No," Bertram said.

Cut off in mid sentence, I could only stare at him. "No?"

"Entities who not scientists not wequired to know science. Zerefore you not speak twue. Also you say you not have specialty. Zen perhaps you not scientist like ozers. So why you on Shouter?"

It seemed I had committed a *faux pas*. Nonplussed, I stared at my companion, wondering how to restore what I had hoped was a developing relationship. "Not scientist" had been grated with the kind of contempt which could only come from one who considered himself a member of an aristocratic elite; an elite which by practice and custom held itself aloof from plebeian involvement. If I was right, it was a devastating revelation. But at that moment, my only concern was to seek the right words to get me out of trouble. One thing was certain; I would not apologize. Aside from my pride, I had the gut feeling that eating humble pie would only make matters worse. So I decided to concentrate on science and scientists. My own connection.

I took a deep breath of canned air. "I know a lot of science. But instead of being concentrated on one discipline, the knowledge I have is spread over many. That is what makes me useful, because I am equipped to explain biology to a physicist, chemistry to an astronomer, and so on. After all, we are here to study a planet, and planetology is a composite of *all* the sciences. So with my help, each member of our team can better understand what his colleagues in the other disciplines are doing. Overall, it increases our efficiency."

I felt pretty smug as I mentioned efficiency. I was

sure it was one argument which would appeal to the notoriously logical mind of a Phuili. But I was disappointed. Instead of pursuing the subject, Bertram pointed toward AA One. "We continue now."

So we rolled again, approaching up to and under the towering artifact. Bertram was uncharacteristically silent, allowing my senses to soar up the sunlit side of the AA's pylon, to the half illuminated bowl suspended between ground and the stars. I vaguely remember stopping near the pylon and stepping out of the runabout, all the time gawking like a star-struck tourist. Sixty-eight meters across its base, it rose up out of the rocky ground, tapering up . . . and up . . .

It was an awesome experience. Above me, the bowl was a mass which seemed to block out half the sky; its whole enormous weight held aloft by a column so incredibly frail that for a moment I felt an insane urge to run for my life—before the whole assembly gave way, crushing me like an ant below a falling mountain.

Swallowing my nervousness, I uneasily approached the base of the pylon. It was farther than I thought, requiring me to walk several dozen paces to get within touching distance. To the eye it was a smooth and lustrous gray, while to the touch there was almost a tacky feel—a definite resistance as I trailed my gloved fingertips across the surface. Then I noticed faint marks irregularly distributed around the pylon's base. Above about the three-meter level, the great shaft rose unblemished.

"Done by Phuili," Bertram said. He had followed me to the pylon and was watching with interest. He pointed at the marks. "Phuili tools made zose. Not useful." He moved farther along and indicated a patch of discoloration. "Laser. Still not useful."

I marveled as I examined the discoloration. A material which could resist a laser's solar intensity was something worth knowing about. "Were you able to analyze the material?"

"Iron," Bertram replied. "Carbon. Ozer elements we not identify."

"But that's a steel alloy! How . . . ?"

"Not know. Not molecular bond we know. Matewial feel funny. Act funny. Perhaps PERU find answer."

So a Phuili could be sarcastic, a sour reminder that we humans could hardly be expected to acomplish what the Phuili had failed to do after centuries of effort. I decided to ignore the thinly disguised goad. "I am sure my people are trying," I said carefully.

Again an offering of Phuili propaganda. "Beacons here much before Phuili come. Beacons here when Phuili go, zough Phuili not leave for long time. We permit humans to study beacons because Phuili want know more about humans. At end, we know more about humans zan humans know about beacons."

An angry response trembled on my lips but remained unvoiced. Despite my companion's needling and assumption of Phuili superiority, I still found myself liking him. So I restrained myself as much for personal reasons as diplomatic. I also decided not much could be gained by staying at AA One this trip, though if I had surrendered to my druthers I could have remained for hours. But I wanted to return to PERU and find Clarence. A wild idea had surfaced in my mind and I needed the A.R.A.'s reaction.

"Interesting," he said.

We were within his office on the main floor. It was comfortably furnished with soft pastel wall hangings and furniture of subtle shades and shapes. The room reeked restraint, betraying a facet of the A.R.A.'s character which made me uneasy.

I said defensively, "You have to admit it fits the facts better than the beacon idea."

"I admit nothing. Yet."

"Look at the word 'beacon.' It implies some kind of cosmic lighthouse, a concept which is absolute nonsense if you consider the billions of stellar beacons nature has already provided. Neither can I accept that The Shouter is a planetsized billboard, a sort of galactic exercise in P.R. Because if so, what is it advertising? And where are the salesmen?"

"Good point," Clarence said with an irritating half smile which further increased my nervousness. My thoughts churned as I looked for the flaw the A.R.A. had presumably spotted in my argument. Then:

"You are good, you know." The half smile broadened into a grin. "Especially for one so new here."

I felt like a child, expecting a spanking, who is instead given a candy. While I was sorting out my response, the door opened and there was an agreeable whiff of perfume. "Sorry," Jenny said. "Didn't know you were busy." She turned to leave.

"Just a moment." Clarence pointed to a vacant chair. "Digger has a theory. I want you to hear it."

She came in. "Oh?"

"According to this young man, The Shouter is not a beacon. Moreover, he claims he knows the true purpose of the AAs."

"Well." The girl sat down and crossed her trim legs. "My curiosity is piqued."

Both of them looked at me expectantly, causing me to flush with mixed embarrassment and apprehension. But I was neatly backed into a corner, so I decided to come out fighting. "The people who built the AAs are still here. On The Shouter."

Hazel eyes widened. "Here? Peter, you cannot be serious! Except for the Phuili and us humans, there is nothing on this planet which walks, crawls, flies, or whatever. The Phuili declared The Shouter sterile long ago, and they should know. They have been here long enough!"

Clarence coughed. "I think, dear, you did not cover all the possible means of living locomotion."

I carefully studied my hands. Though I did not think the A.R.A. would deliberately ridicule my theory before the girl, I still wished I could turn back the clock—at least so I could shut my own mouth before I unleashed the malevolent genie which was now haunting me.

". . . burrowing?" Jenny was asking. "Like moles?"

"Or like humans," Clarence said. "Take the Luna complex of Lansberg, for instance. It's a complete underground city."

She looked doubtful. "Yes, but . . ."

I thought I had better reassert myself before Clarence took complete control. So far he seemed on my side, though I still had my suspicions. "Jenny, have you ever been to Lansberg?"

"Often. Why?"

"There is a big structure on the east wall of the crater. Do you know the one I mean?"

She frowned. "I think so. It's a condenser, isn't it?"

"Exactly. A device to reject heat by radiating it into space. It's needed because heat is the ultimate end product of every kind of activity, from the wriggling of a bacterium to the motion of the universe. So if . . ."

"Entropy," Jenny said. "Time's arrow."

Fortunately, there was no note of condescension in her voice. Otherwise I would have shut up like a clam and stayed that way. It was perhaps the most difficult part of my job; to avoid being too basic when dealing with a bunch of scientific prima donnas. So I was grateful for Jenny's gentle curb on my runaway tongue. Not for that girl, bless her, the look of withering scorn or the sarcastic put down. So I continued:

"Consider an advanced underground society like Lansberg's, but on a scale so vast its tunnels and galleries house an entire planetary population. Perhaps several populations, if the planet is old enough not to have a fluid core. Now consider the energy that society would require, for manufacturing and life support, for creating new living space . . ."

"They'd need condensers. My god, Peter, would they need condensers!" Jenny's eyes were round with excitement. "The Shouter could be like one of those ivory puzzle balls, a whole series of concentric shells layer upon layer . . ." She paused, breathless.

I loved the way she called me Peter. "Of course, the AAs are not condensers in the accepted sense," I went on, hoping I was not blushing. "No pipes, for instance, no radiators to condense a vapor back into its liquid state, no circulating system of any kind which is apparent. But there must be others ways to reject surplus energy, using devices our science—even Phuili science—can barely imagine. That is why I am convinced that sphere of light above AA One must be investigated in detail, especially if we can determine how much energy it is putting out. Using that as a base, we can then . . ."

"Just a moment, Digger." The A.R.A. turned to Jenny. "Well? What do you think?"

"I love it!" Eyes sparkling, she jumped to her feet, came over and firmly tucked my arm within hers. "Clarence, give this man a raise. He deserves it!"

He smiled. "Perhaps."

It seemed I had every reason to feel euphoric. The A.R.A.'s unexpected support and Jenny's bubbling enthusiasm should have been enough to melt the heart of even the most ardent pessimist. But something jarred.

Clarence said, "Digger, though Jenny has been with us for only a few months, she has managed to become one of the most respected members of PERU's team. Aside from her obvious charms, she is a talented astrophysicist who has added considerably to what we know about this star system. So don't take her endorsement lightly. Okay?"

"Okay," I agreed, which was academic anyway. I would have welcomed Jenny's endorsement if she had only been the cook and not one of PERU's resident geniuses. Still, Clarence's flattering remarks about her seemed out of context and I wondered what was behind it.

So, apparently, did Jenny. "Clarence, I am not going to thank you for those kind words because I know you too well for that. You have an ulterior motive tucked in there somewhere." She smiled sweetly. "Don't you?"

His answer was as blunt as her challenge. And to me, devastating. "Digger's theory is not new. The Phuili thought of it two centuries ago, and were so convinced of its merit they squandered most of their resources on the subsequent investigation. All they found was rock and magma. No tunnels. No subsurface civilization."

"Damn," I muttered.

"Jenny, you chose exactly the right moment to come through that door. Telling a man he is wrong is one thing, making him feel foolish is another. Because of your reaction, Digger does not have to feel foolish."

"Balls," Jenny said succinctly. Having relieved herself of that unladylike observation, she dismissed our white-haired boss and turned to me. Hands on hips, she was both provocative and formidable. "Peter, there is a bottle of rather good wine in my quarters. For a while, anyway, I think you and I should concentrate on better things. Will you come?"

My heart thumped as I drowned in her unwavering green gaze. Somewhere in the background Clarence had faded to unimportance, a frowning vagueness on the edge of my awareness. Lovely images floated through my mind; erotic images with immediate promise of reality. Finally my tongue unraveled, and with an effort I replied weakly,

"I would love that drink."

The planetary system was old and—quite literally— scorched. Once its family of eleven planets had followed the usual pattern, ranging from an assortment of smaller solid bodies near the sun, through five gas giants, to an ill-defined cometary halo marking the boundary between planetary and interstellar space. The fourth planet once bore oceans, continents, and ice caps. There had been life-forms, one of which developed intelligence and ultimately attained the stars.

When its home sun showed signs of instability, the race made certain preparations. Many worlds felt their presence during this brief interregnum. But when the preparations were complete, they returned to their own world. From there they departed this space-time continuum and went . . . elsewhere.

Slowly the sun swelled until it was a red giant whose tenuous surface encompassed the two innermost planets. Then, equally as slowly, the sun shrank—until it was a white dwarf with a miserly energy output which could outlast the universe. Early during this dull near-eternity, a fragment of matter fell inward from what was left of the cometary halo. For centuries it journeyed along a groove dictated by celestial mechanics, until it fell through the sky of the now barren fourth planet—

"It came down near AA Eight-o-three," Clarence told me over the intercom. "A briefing has been arranged for us in the Phuili Head Sphere, so please get dressed and meet us in the dock A.S.A.P."

He broke contact before I could comment. Rubbing the sleep from my eyes I groped my way to the bathroom a few doors down from my quarters, then hurried back and clambered into my clothes. I was going to miss breakfast, but I didn't mind. I had had joyous reasons for sleeping late, and in any case the cold shower had shivered me to life. So within minutes I was aboard PERU's pressurized minibus as we rolled sedately out of the lock and turned toward the Phuili complex. Jenny was two seats ahead of me in the bus, but other than a slight smile as I edged by her, she did not acknowledge our new relationship. Jean DeLaforte leaned across and said something which made Jenny laugh and me a little jealous. So I turned and stared through the window at the approaching cluster of buildings.

Finally, we stopped under a large spherical structure, out of which a broad tube descended and locked firmly to the pressure hull of the minibus. From his seat at the front, Clarence went to the door and tripped the opening mechanism. Pressures had been equalized, so the door swung easily inward, revealing a flight of small steps rising through the tube. Treading cautiously on the narrow treads, the A.R.A. led us into the Phuili Head Sphere.

We emerged into a low room filled with rows of

padded benches. The air was damp, with an odd smell which made me think of burned toast and horses. The eleven of us sat gingerly on the small benches and waited. Jenny had plumped herself beside me, and into my ear she whispered, "Be on your toes, Peter. I think you are going to be part of this."

Startled, I looked at her. But before I could be enlightened, half a dozen Phuili emerged out of an opening at the side of the room. Their powerful little bodies were clad in togalike garments of various muted colors, their feet in wide-fronted moccasins which made a soft slapping sound as they walked. As they stopped in front of us, one of their number separated and stepped on to a low platform.

"Bertram," Jenny whispered. I nodded. Who else?

"We have wemote see systems at AAs." Bertram's alien voice was harsh in the stillness. "See system at AA Eight-o-zwee saw awival of object and wecorded. Watch."

The room darkened and a concealed projector produced an image of an AA on the sloping front wall. The image rapidly expanded until it seemed the room itself was merged into The Shouter's stark landscape. A few stars were visible in the deep blue of the sky above our heads, and the meanderings of what looked like a dried-up river bed extended into the foreground and disappeared almost at our feet. Huge boulders littered the flat on which the AA stood, breaking its long shadow into patches of light and dark. Suddenly the image flared with an intolerable brightness, giving way to a madly churning maelstrom of dust and debris out of which house-sized fragments ejected in all directions like gigantic pieces of shrapnel. The dust cloud began to thin, revealing the AA like a colossus dimly seen through a swirling brown fog. And then something jagged appeared and expanded enormously . . .

The image flickered and went dark.

"Jesus," someone muttered as with trembling fingers Jenny groped for my hand. I groped back, at that moment needing the reassurance of human contact as much as she did.

"See system destwoyed," Bertram announced. "Now you watch again."

This time the speed of the action was hundreds of times slower, starting a fraction of a second before something appeared from above the AA and angled down to the right of the huge artifact. Still it was almost too swift for the eye to follow, though at the instant of impact we saw the hemisphere of expanding fire caused as the object's kinetic energy was abruptly transformed into heat. Again the image went dark.

I glanced at Jenny. "Boo," she said, her eyes crinkling. A resilient girl, that one.

"Now vewy slow. You pleese watch most close."

The projection this time ran for only a couple of seconds before a gasp of astonishment came from every human throat. "It came out of the light," Dewy whispered. "How . . ."

"Again," Bertram said.

In real time the event had lasted bare nanoseconds. But again we watched it at a rate perceivable to our human senses, and again we were stunned by its impossibility. The AA and its ball of radiance were contained well within the limits of the projection, so there was no doubt from where the rocky missile originated. First it was not there, then suddenly it was—emerging *out* of the light and almost instantly fading behind the shock wave produced as it slammed into The Shouter's atmosphere. Bertram turned off the projection when it was obvious we understood the significance of what we had seen.

"Now humans know what Phuili know. You go back PERU and talk. Zen Clawence and new one weturn here and talk. Good-bye." With a polite jerk of his massive head, Bertram rejoined his companions. The six Phuili then formed into a line and with quaint military precision marched out of the room.

Helda, who was sitting just in front of us, expelled her breath with an explosive, "Well!" Swiveling in her seat, she turned hostile slate blue eyes toward me. "You're the only new one here, Digger. What makes you so bloody special?"

"We will discuss that later," Clarence said sharply before I could respond to the big woman's challenge. He stood up and faced us. "But before we do, I want each of you to spend a quiet, thoughtful couple of hours within the privacy of your own quarters. We will then assemble in Observation at thirteen hundred and jointly try to make some sense out of all of this. Until then, ruminate, cogitate, but *don't* communicate. I want no consensus until you have had time to sort out your individual reactions to what you have just seen. Is that understood?"

Clearly understood. Which was why we were a silent crowd as we rode back to PERU. But as we emerged from the bus, Clarence pulled me aside. "In my office," he said. He nodded to Jenny. "You, too."

I don't know what the others (especially Helda) thought as Jenny and I were ushered away to a cozy little conference. I do know Clarence had more than our colleagues' sensibilities on his mind as he closed the door behind us and said unequivocally, "Digger, you have been on The Shouter for only two days."

I said nothing. There was little point responding to the obvious.

He went on, "Yet during that brief time, you have managed to disturb our Phuili hosts quite profoundly."

I looked at him doubtfully. "I don't know why. All I have done is . . ."

". . . hit them right where it hurts most—in their carefully nurtured egos." The A.R.A. chuckled. "Largely because of you, young man, the Phuili have made the astonishing discovery that we humans are something more than primitives with a technological bent."

"I did that?"

"In absolute innocence," Jenny said soothingly. "Peter, you are the living proof of the value of an untrammeled mind."

"She's right, you know." Clasping his hands atop his indecently tidy desk, Clarence studied me closely. He had the worried air of one who has been forced into a premature decision; hoping he is correct, risking serious consequences if he is not. His jaw firmed. "PERU's central problem has always been the Phuili attitude to humans. To them we are no more than a race of monkeys who know how to build steamboats but still live in trees. As scientists, they find us quite fascinating. As individuals, most Phuili are rather fond of us in a sort of condescending way. Beyond that, to even suggest a human may be something more than a primitive who happens to have a knack for technology, would be equivalent to Copernicus declaring the Earth is not the center of the universe. It just is not done."

"But that's exactly what Copernicus did do," I said, puzzled.

"True."

"He had some pretty strong evidence, though."

"Also true."

I took a deep breath. "Correct me if I am wrong, but are you telling me that with the right kind of evidence the Phuili will accept us as equals? Evidence such as . . ." I swallowed. ". . . a smart monkey?"

Jenny pealed with laughter. The A.R.A. managed not to smile, though I suspect it required considerable effort.

I was more embarrassed than amused. "Clarence, when the Phuili came up with the idea the AAs could be the visible indication of an advanced subsurface civilization, how long had they been on The Shouter?"

He smiled at the apparent change of subject. "About a couple of centuries. Which is quite a long time considering it took you only a few hours to come up with the same notion. Don't you think so?"

I said irritably, "I would rather not comment if you don't mind." I knew I was being stuffy, but at that moment I had the feeling I had been manipulated and it annoyed me. Still with the chip on my shoulder, I went on, "In any case, what has all this rigmarole to do with what happened at Eight-o-three?"

"Later," Clarence said. "When we meet with the others. Right now, Mr. Peter Digonness is the prime subject of this discussion."

I shifted uneasily in my chair. Jenny was watching me anxiously, and I tried not to meet her gaze. The being manipulated part was bad enough, but if Jenny herself was involved . . .

It was a treacherous thought, one I tried to ignore. Unfortunately, thoughts are immune to dismissal, especially those born out of a bruised ego. For my own peace of mind I knew I should challenge Jenny; present my doubts and accept the consequences. But it was not the time or the place. Other questions still needed answers.

"You were, in a sense, primed for this," Clarence said, beginning to answer the unspoken questions. "First by your background, and then by the fact we deliberately withheld from you certain events concerning the history of Phuili activities on this world. The rest was mostly up to you." Leaning back in his chair, he beamed at me. "Believe me, my boy, what started as a long shot has ended up as a near miracle. It turns out you were the ideal catalyst."

No thanks to you, I wanted to say. Instead I turned to Jenny. "Did you know about this?"

"Some," she admitted cautiously.

"Tell me."

"I'd rather Clarence . . ."

"Not Clarence. You."

She looked at me doubtfully. "All right." She turned her face away from mine. "We had to convince the Phuili—against their own ingrained instincts—that we humans are more than bright morons. Simply telling them so was no good because the Phuili would not believe it. They would not *want* to believe it—any more than we humans would want to believe that a bunch of apes are as smart as we are."

I nodded. "So you set things up hoping your new

expediter would come up with an answer it took them centuries to . . ." I stopped. "Dammit, that's no good. The subsurface civilization idea was strictly mine. I consulted with no one."

"Not since college," Jenny said. She turned and faced me again, her expression determined. "'*Space, The Perfect Heat Sink.*' Don't you remember?"

Dumbfounded, I stared at her. "My third year thesis," I whispered. "I'd forgotten."

"Consciously, perhaps. But your subconscious remembered. Put radiators on every mountaintop, you said. Get rid of thermal pollution by projecting it into space. Is it so surprising you interpreted the AAs the way you did?"

"It certainly didn't surprise you," I said bitterly. "Did it?"

She looked hurt, but at that moment I did not care. "And how did you persuade the Phuili I actually did what I did? From what you have told me, it's certain they would not accept any third party explanation. How was it done, Clarence? Did you have a Phuili eavesdrop from the next room?"

"As a matter of fact, yes," the white haired man said calmly.

That stopped me. Astonished, I stared at him. "Bertram?"

He shrugged. "Who else?"

I should have known. I should also have felt angry, but all I could manage was a spark of irritation. "So it was a setup. But how did Bertram know I was not part of the deception? Hell, I could have been acting a bigger lie than any of you!"

"Peter, there is something else you don't know about the Phuili," the girl said.

I sighed. "I'm sure there is. I am also sure you are going to tell me. Whether I give a damn or not."

She ignored my sarcasm. "They have a sort of sixth sense. It isn't telepathy exactly, because they can't read conscious thoughts. But what they *can* read are emotions—which they do with an accuracy barely this side of uncanny. Pain, joy, guilt, and the rest are like a printed page to them, a communication. So, Peter, as you described your theory to Clarence yesterday, Bertram had no difficulty sensing your sincerity."

There was much I could have said at that moment. Even more I wanted to say, especially to Jenny. But the moment passed and so, I think, did some of the innocence of my feelings for her. But as reason became a little less clouded by emotion, I began to realize I was ahead in the game. That, in fact, the pawn was about to become a player.

I made my first move. "Clarence, I want to talk about AA Eight-o-three. *Now.*"

As has already been emphasized, Phuili and humans are very different. Yet in the physical context, they are remarkably similar. Of course it is nature's way to evolve for efficiency, and there is no denying the advantages inherent in an upright four-limbed design with an articulated internal skeleton. Yet it is the differences imposed by vastly dissimilar environments which remain important, the opposites which in this case both repel and attract with a delicate—and unstable—balance.

Man had fought and clawed his way up the evolutionary slope. The Phuili had placidly taken their time; driven by obsessive curiosity rather than by any need to dominate competing predators. By the standards of humankind, the rise of Phuili civilization had consequently proceeded at the rate of the proverbial snail. The Phuili industrial revolution had taken place long before primitive humans erected monoliths at a place called Stonehenge. Yet the first Phuili space craft was not launched until a human called Copernicus was shattering the accepted egocentric view of the universe.

The concept of time was not, however, the only chasm separating the understanding of each species for the other. Of even greater significance, was an abstraction called pride—

Zero minus sixty seconds.

The probe was a modest affair; merely one of our atmospheric sounders with short wings added for horizontal stability. AA One was about ten klicks away; a giant which, if it had awareness, would probably not even notice the pinprick we were about to administer into its bright head.

Zero minus forty-five seconds.

Irv Dewinton (Dewy) had come up with the idea during our noisy buzz session in PERU's Observation Lounge. "We saw that damn rock appear out of nowhere. Right?" He grinned. "So it'd only be poetic justice to throw one back, even if it is into the wrong AA."

My own idea, suggested earlier to the A.R.A., had been that we conduct a series of "bombing runs" in which specialized free-fall probes would be dropped into the sphere of light from a slow moving shuttle. But considering our meager resources, also the fact ground-to-orbit shuttles are not exactly suited for such atmospheric antics, Dewy's more modest proposal made obvious sense. So I swallowed my pride and raised no objections. Neither did Clarence and Jenny, though I sensed the stare of one pair of puzzled green eyes.

Zero minus thirty seconds.

Not everyone from PERU was present for the launching. Despite DeLaforte's protests, Clarence had dispatched the geologist and two assistants to join the Phuili investigation of the new crater at Eight-o-three. Undoubtedly, the three would radiate enough displeasure to be detectable by even the least sensitive of the empathetic Phuili, so I assumed it was the A.R.A.'s way of demonstrating to our hosts that human thoughts do not necessarily dictate human actions.

Zero minus fifteen seconds.

On the other hand, only one Phuili was present as we prepared to poke the eye of AA One. And he, I suspected, was more interested in "why" than "what." Bertram himself had given the clue to his attitude when Clarence and I went to him with our proposal. "If you wait until work finish at Eight-o-zwee cwater, zen you can send pwobe into light fwom where wock came. Yet you do expewiment here, where event not happen. Do not understand."

I bet you don't, I thought with an irritation which was becoming the norm for a lot of Phuili pronouncements. Still, their blind logic was a weakness, a crack in their supercilious hide. If only I could convince Clarence . . .

Zero.

With a flash and a roar the probe bounded aloft, tilted into level flight and sped toward its target. We braced ourselves as it neared the light above the enormous artifact, expecting anything and everything—a flare, a burst of energy, a spectacular happening which hopefully would leave us still on our feet. What we did not expect was that the probe would vanish with as little fuss as a rabit diving down its hole, leaving only the dying thunder of its passing.

We looked wordlessly at each other. Then we looked again at the enigmatic sphere of light. Still nothing. The insistent beeping of a priority signal alarm finally broke the paralysis. *"Eight-o-three calling One. Eight-o-three calling One. Clarence, are you there? Dammit, is* anyone *there?"*

Despite the sputtering and crackling of an unusual amount of electrical interference, the voice on the priority channel was recognizable as DeLaforte's, supposedly at the site of AA Eight-o-three five hundred klicks away. So we shared Clarence's immediate assumption of trouble as he answered, "Okay Jock, I can hear you but not clearly. What's the problem?"

"Problem? More like a disaster! Clarence, Eight-o-three is falling apart! First the light went out, and now the whole damn structure is turning itself into a pile of rubble!"

"Are you Okay? Is anyone hurt?"

"We three are fine. So are all the Phuili, I think, though I can't tell for sure because of the dust. It's already so thick it's like trying to see through a wall. But we can hear the breaking-up noises, and the ground

is shaking like a young earthquake. And the lightning! Clarence, how is AA One? Is this local or is the whole planet going?"

"AA One and The Shouter are both fine, Jock," the A.R.A. replied calmly. "However, I suggest . . ." His voice trailed into silence as he became aware of the frantic gesticulations I was making from my station at the launch control panel. His attention gained, I then repeatedly pointed at the panel. Finally he nodded as he understood the point of my antics.

"Jock, I don't know how much hard data you have on that . . . ah . . . event, but can you at least pinpoint the exact time the light went out?"

For a few moments there was no answer. Just the staccato noises of the interference. Then: *"Eight minutes and seventeen seconds past the hour. Is that significant?"*

"My god, is it ever," I muttered, awed. Though all the test data had been recorded, some figures—including time of telemetry termination—were still registered on the digital display. Clarence could not see the figures from where he was, but he heard me over my open channel. So did Jean DeLaforte.

"Who is that? Is that you, Digger?"

Clarence said, "Never mind." I heard him take a deep breath. "Jock, we successfully launched the probe. Its telemetry terminated when it disappeared—literally— into the light above AA One. I'll let you guess the exact time of that termination."

There was an astonished silence. But the verbal response, when it came, was a cool, *"Guess we'd better book the next flight back to PERU."*

Easily said. Not so easily done. Unfortunately, there was only one aircraft on the planet, and it was not owned by PERU. Though Bertram came over and had the 08:17 indication explained to him, he remained unmoved. "Wingship weturn fwom Eight-o-zwee when work at cwater finish. Maybe in two, zwee days. No need for sooner."

If a rain forest sprouted overnight from the barren

Shouter desert, I suspect Bertram would have taken his time to determine if the phenomenon was worthy of investigation in "due course." And had he been human, I would have called him pigheaded. But he wasn't, so obviously I couldn't. I knew my colleagues shared my sense of helplessness; I could see it in their helmet-shadowed faces. But in the cause of preserving the status quo, we somehow controlled our frustration and settled into a rigid calm. Whether or not Bertram was reading this repressed gamut of emotions I could not tell, but in any case I suspected he would accept it as a normal human reaction which mattered little. I briefly wondered if, by pressing Bertram and forcing a second refusal, I could finally trigger the repressed anger of my colleagues. But I had sense enough to realize this was not the time. That the sudden unleashing of a flood of resentment and wounded pride would be a pyrrhic victory at best. The objective was, after all, to persuade the Phuili to accept us as equals, not to provide what Phuili hardliners would gladly accept as further evidence of human irrationality.

". . . Okay," Clarence was saying, "concentrate on what is left of Eight-o-three and let the Phuili continue their thing in the crater. Meantime, if you can come up with a rational explanation for all this, then for sanity's sake use the radio and save us a lot of headaches. In any case, I expect you back at PERU within two or zwee days."

The A.R.A.'s deliberate parody of Bertram's speech was so uncharacteristic, only Bertram himself—who lacked the human sense of the incongruous—did not react in some way. Fortunately the small alien did not query the assorted noises of stifled mirth, though I suspect he was not unaware of the lifting of tension which followed Clarence's verbal palliative. Certainly Bertram was not his usual garrulous self as he watched us prepare our equipment for transportation back to PERU. Signaling me to turn off my radio, Jenny came over and touched her helmet to mine. "Have we finally made a dent in that one-thing-at-a-time Phuili logic of his?" she shouted tinnily, gesturing at our friend.

I peered into her face, only inches from mine. "If not us, then what we just did," I shouted back. "From now on, I think we're going to have to be pretty damn careful what we do or say when he's around."

She grasped my arm. "Meaning?"

"Meaning an unpredictable Phuili is a combination I, for one, would rather not have to deal with."

"Oh." Jenny's grip tightened. "Digger, talk to Clarence. Have him call another meeting."

"He probably already has that in mind. Anyway, when he does, there is something else I want to bring up."

She stepped back to look at me. Then she came close again and our helmets bumped. "What do you have in that devious mind of yours?"

I grinned at her. "I want us to build a model airplane."

Everyone's immediate acceptance of my proposal was a flattering surprise. The truth was that Clarence's guarded approval, the support of Jenny and my other colleagues, even Bertram's noncommittal, "You do, I watch," made me overlook the idea's real value—that it was cheap and therefore affordable. Even if it failed.

I had been an enthusiastic model builder in my youth, so when Jock and the others finally arrived from Eight-o-three, *Dragonfly* was ready for its test flight. First, however, I was present when Jock reported what the Phuili had found below the crater near the small mountain of rubble which was all that was left of the huge artifact.

". . . was pretty well pulverized by the impact of course, but enough was left to indicate some kind of thrust device and guidance system. I understand the Phuili intend to check out the metallurgy, but I doubt they'll have any more success than they did with the material of the AAs."

"Technology from the same source?" Rhiddian

Felmann hazarded. He blinked solemnly. "Now wouldn't *that* be some can of worms!"

"More than you realize," the A.R.A. said, rising stiffly to his feet and joining Jock at the front of the room. He looked tired, which was not surprising considering his bed had hardly been used for days. "So before we start trying to make two and two equal five, let's look at the facts. To start with, all we know for certain is that the dissolution of Eight-o-three was somehow triggered when our probe disappeared above AA One. It is equally certain we do *not* know how or why an apparently guided object appeared out of nowhere at Eight-o-three. Neither do we have any hard evidence connecting that earlier event with the dissolution.

"So please, my friends, keep your hunches to yourselves and demonstrate to your partners you can be as systematic and logical as any Phuili. Already they have learned we humans are more than we seem, and I think they are slowly coming to terms with that fact. But if we push too hard and further challenge their concept of proper order, I am afraid we run the risk of losing everything we have gained . . . and probably more. Sorry Jock, but for the moment we will have to consider your mission at Eight-o-three as strictly as exercise in P.R. Whatever the Phuili found there must remain a matter for the Phuili only. If and when they want us to become involved, I am sure we will be notified. Officially."

"But we are involved!" Jock protested. "Dammit, we were there!"

"As observers only. As Bertram was at AA One. Mutual diplomatic courtesies, nothing more."

"Horseshit," Irv Dewinton grumbled. "We've as much right as that bunch of . . ."

"Oh, Dewy, shut up," Jenny said crossly, turning in her chair and glaring at the astonished engineer. "For the sake of your stupid rights, would you wreck our chances to learn something about matter transmission?" Suddenly she jumped to her feet and glared at us all. "What is the matter with you people? It's been staring us in the face since that rock appeared out of nothing, and still no one will say it. So I'll say it for you." She took a deep breath. *"Matter transmission!"*

A scientific impossibility, of course. Earth science had declared so long ago, Phuili science centuries before that. But human scientists are not the masters in their house; though they declare, they do not control. In contrast, science on Phuili is a religion, scientists are its hereditary priests, and scientific declarations bear the holy stamp of infalibility. To dispute such declarations is therefore the same as saying the Old Testament prophets were liars. So the awkward silence which followed Jenny's outburst was not so much a condemnation of her daring as it was a symptom of the "don't rock the boat" syndrome which had come to affect our discussions even within the privacy of our own building.

The silence ended as Clarence said quietly, "Thank you for that, Jenny. I am not so sure I agree with you, but we would hardly be true to ourselves if we ignored every . . ." He coughed. ". . . impossibility."

It was typical of him. Though Jenny had seemingly ignored his request to restrain our more radical ideas, his immediate and wry acceptance of the genie being out of the bottle did a lot to clear the air. There was no need for further discussion; we all knew our re-stated awareness would not be unnoticed by the empathetic Phuili. So when we went outside for the test flight and were confronted by Bertram and another Phuili inspecting our flimsy contraption, my immediate gut reaction was a nervous, *He will sense the lie. So how do we avoid the truth?*

Equally ominous was the Phuili wingship squatting only a couple of hundred meters from PERU's front door, obviously moved there while we humans were agonizing within. If the motive was a not-so-subtle put-down, it was effective. Compared with their droop-winged monster, our little model was a crude toy.

When Bertram saw me, he pointed at *Dragonfly*

and confirmed my worst fears with a single word. "Why?"

Clearly he sensed a deception, so I had to respond in a hurry. I tried to avoid the dilemma by stating the obvious. "We will fly it into AA One. Just as we did with the probe."

"Not same." Bertram stooped beside the tube and wire fuselage and pointed to the small camera I had installed behind the power cell. "Zat is differwent."

I swallowed. "Just a slight variation. Optical imaging is an old trick with us. It may not be scientific, but we find the pictures . . . er . . . pleasing."

Alien eyes studied me reflectively. "What you zink you get pictures of?"

A gloved hand gripped my shoulder. "If we knew," Clarence said, "we would not have installed the camera. It would not be logical."

Bertram's jaws flexed slightly. *A smile?* I wondered. "Your pwobe not weturn. Maybe not zis one also. So how you get pictures?"

The grip on my shoulder tightened. "*Dragonfly* will be programmed to fly along a return course."

"Ah." I braced myself, certain the next question would not permit further evasion. Instead, Bertram confounded us all by gesturing toward AA One. "Light is high. Four kilometers above gwound. Little machine must climb hard." His strange features unreadable inside his elongated helmet, he continued, "So I take on wingship. Digger come wiz me and welease little machine when wingship near light. Better, eh?"

I suppose it hit everyone the same way. In my own case, after my stomach recovered from its flip-flop, I weakly thanked my Phuili partner and said something about the need to first run a test.

"No test. Flight now. I take wingship up slow wiz little machine. You welease when you zink pwoper."

At another time the comedy of Bertram's English would have lightened the moment immensely. Instead, the dilemma he was forcing on us was somewhat akin to making us choose between the devil and very deep waters. Desperately, I wracked my brain for an excuse which would persuade Bertram to grant time for a "humans only" consultation.

A thought ahead of me, Clarence tried the direct approach. His tone was deferential. "Bertram, may we be permitted a few minutes to discuss this?"

"I wait," the Phuili replied. "You not take long."

So we hurried back into PERU's main lock. As soon as the status panel indicated PRESSURIZATION COMPLETE, Jenny whipped off her helmet and said angrily, "He wants us to fail! Why else won't he allow a test?"

Wearily, Clarence sat on an empty packing crate. "Why, indeed," he echoed. He looked at me. "Well, Digger, it's mostly your project. What do you recommend?"

I wished he hadn't asked me. There was no clear answer and I was sure he knew that as much as I did. "If we insist on a test," I said, "we are admitting the possibility of a failure. But if we don't test and accept Bertram's offer, we will be using an untried machine with an even better chance of failure."

"So what's failure?" It was Helda, looking belligerent as usual. "Nobody likes it, but it's part of what we do, isn't it?"

Clarence sighed. "In the Phuili context, failure is synonymous with the state of being inferior, and according to official dogma a scientist is *never* inferior. Probably because of pressure from his hardliners, Bertram has apparently decided to use the *Dragonfly* project to force the issue of human status on The Shouter. If, as we claim, we are true scientists, then the project will succeed and our cause will be immeasurably advanced. But if *Dragonfly* does something silly like crashing, or disappearing without returning data, then I am afraid we face restrictions which will probably terminate PERU's usefulness."

"Arrogant little bastards," Felmann muttered.

The A.R.A. smiled slightly. "Look at it from their point of view. They have assumed their exclusiveness for so long, it has become an instinct. Suddenly we humans appear on the scene, creating an unsightly crack in their pristine ivory tower. And when we . . ."

I interrupted. " 'Scuse me, Clarence, but wasn't it already cracked? What about that abortive attempt to prove the existence of a subsurface civilization here?"

Again the smile. "What about it?"

"It was a failure, wasn't it? How did they handle it?"

"They had two choices. Either to accept immediate demotion to serf status, or to remove their embarrassing presence from the universe. To the Phuili Elite that is, of course, no choice at all. So they did what they had to do. All ninety of them."

From the sounds of indrawn breath, it was apparent this was the first time anyone had heard the story. "What did they . . . er . . . ?"

"They boarded their ship and dove it into the sun."

I wasn't sure what this had to do with our present situation, though if I dwelled on it I suspected I would come up with some uncomfortable parallels. So I decided to damn the torpedoes and full steam ahead. "Let's take Bertram up on his offer. If he wants to rub our noses in it, let him work for the privilege. What do we have to lose?"

"Well, don't expect *me* to take a dive into the sun," Allan Phu Wong said darkly. The only Oriental on the team, he had a sense of humor with a disconcerting bite. "But I agree with Digger. On the slight chance *Dragonfly* pulls a rabbit out of the hat, I want to be around when the Phuili realize they have helped us do exactly what they didn't intend—which is prove that we humans are a damn sight smarter than they like to think we are."

"Amen," Jock said fervently.

"Two amens," Jenny said, with an anxious look in my direction. I wondered about her apparent concern, but the chorus of consensus diverted me until Jenny pulled me aside and whispered, "Peter, please be careful. Before we came in here, I saw Bertram hand his Command Disc to his deputy."

"Sorry, but I don't . . ."

"It's the delegation of authority. As Clarence does when he is planning to be away for a few days." Suddenly she clutched my arm. "But not if he's only going for a thirty minute plane ride!"

So it was only to be a short ride. But perhaps the Phuili hierarchy is so rigid it cannot tolerate being without a top "dog" for even a few minutes. Or so I reasoned as I squatted uncomfortably in the wingship, holding *Dragonfly* as firmly as I could against the buffeting slipstream. As Bertram had promised, the ascent was gentle, but even the most advanced technology could do little about the huge volumes of air rushing into the down-swiveled jets. I looked away from the tiny dots of my friends still watching the bat-winged vehicle bearing us skyward, and turned my attention to the flickering enigma ahead. Already we were slightly above AA One's huge dish, and I marveled at the absolute and unrelieved blackness of the dish's inside surface. Nothing reflected from it, not even the sphere of radiance so close above its center. Still we climbed, and now the helmeted head of my small pilot was silhouetted against the light.

"How are you doing up there?" came Clarence's voice. *"From where we stand you look pretty close to launch."*

"Vewy soon," Bertram replied. "First we go closer and higher. Zen I dwop wingship so Digger can welease little machine."

"Good luck to us, Digger."

"We need it!" I muttered, inwardly cursing the strange communications system which allowed only the pilot to transmit. I turned on the bird's power and control systems, felt an increasing tug as the tiny electric turbine whined up to speed. Bertram tilted the wingship over into a shallow dive, and quickly my arms began to ache as *Dragonfly*'s three-meter wings bit into the thin air. The AA's light was enormous, filling half the sky in front of us. Below, the dish was an incredible black lake with no shores, the other half of a whole which was closer to nightmare than reality.

Bertram spoke. "Now."

Dragonfly soared away like a free spirit, and as Bertram slowed our descent I saw her begin a graceful turn, the sensor in one wing-tip aiming her at the target like a moth to a flame. The small wings leveled, and accelerating swiftly . . .

No!

The flash of the laser was an obscenity still fading from my vision as the burned tatters of *Dragonfly* fluttered and dispersed like scraps of garbage thrown into the wind. "No," I repeated, releasing my restraints and clawing my way forward into the seat behind the pilot. If I had been a member of a half savage species such as the Phuili wanted to believe, then at that moment I would have killed Bertram and taken my chances with the wingship's unfamiliar controls. Instead I was only angry, a cold and rational outrage which demanded an answer. I tapped Bertram on the shoulder. "Why?"

For some reason we were rising again, the huge light dropping below the wingship until only its upper edge extended above our visible horizon like a sun peeping over the edge of the world. Bertram did not look back at me as he answered, but even to my inexperienced ears there was a note of strain in the emotionless, alien voice.

"Phuili not like humans to be equal to Phuili. But we accept if humans pwove zey equal. Phuili not accept zat humans better zan Phuili. If little machine go into light and come back, Phuili science bad hurt by beings not Phuili. Not to be accepted. Perhaps to be accepted if Phuili and human do together . . ."

"Clarence, are you listening to this?" I shouted, hoping the sound of my voice was penetrating to the pickup in Bertram's helmet.

"No talk wiz gwound," Bertram said. "I stop."

I sagged back into the seat. So we were alone in the sky; me, a small alien, and ideas as strange to each of us as we were to each other. I had sensed desperate sincerity in Bertram's disjointed explanation, to my surprise I seemed to be detecting mood easier than meaning. A preposterous idea occurred to me. It was that we were two halves of a whole, different only in the sense left is different from right, up from down, past from future. Yin and Yang. Different aspects of the same unity.

I was detached, riding on philosophical wings of thought far more real than the alien wings which were carrying me through The Shouter's sky. That we had tilted into a rapid descent, even that the wingship was drawing dangerously close to the light above AA One . . . these were minor matters. Hardly important enough to interrupt this ecstatic totality of feeling. Had it been suggested I was being manipulated, I would have laughed aloud. This was me, my *real self*. Free at last from the stifling restraints of convention.

Much later I learned Bertram had a stun pistol, that he was prepared to use it if I tried to interfere. But I was so divorced from reality, it was only at the last impossible moment I began to realize what was happening. *Phuili and human do together*, Bertram had said. Now, too late, I finally understood.

Around us, the brightness flared.

I shattered . . .

One wing askew, its forward section crumpled, the wingship lay in a rocky valley between gold-flecked mountains. Enormous spiky-leafed trees, one of which had been our undoing as Bertram fought the wingship down through the heavy air, were scattered along the valley and up the surrounding slopes. Atop the crest of a high pass at the head of the valley, an AA towered into the blue-green sky, its crown of light shimmering among piled white-rimmed clouds. Obviously that bright portal was our way home. But without some means to repair the wingship, The Shouter was as much beyond our reach as the small moon in the sky.

I stared moodily at the prone body of my Phuili companion. At first I had thought he was dead, or at least badly injured. But now I was reasonably sure his color and temperature were normal—as much as I could tell from my limited knowledge of Phuili physiology—and his double heartbeat was as regular as my own. I had removed both our helmets, and despite the hopelessness of the situation I savored the warm, sweet-smelling air.

Had it been matter transmission? Certainly we were not where we started, and certainly the method of transportation had been more than a little traumatic. The tearing sense of disassociation, followed almost instantly by the terrible *squeeze* of reassembly, were memories I would like to forget. But probably wouldn't.

A thought intruded. *This must be a parallel world. Instead of traveling distance as along a line between separate points, we have merely changed realities. The congruity remains the same.*

I laughed. *Like stepping through the frames of a closed picture book? Sorry, but I can't buy that. It just isn't good science to look for far-out explanations when there are simpler ones at hand. A man named William of Occam taught us that.*

So you believe instant relocation across perhaps light-years of distance is more logical than no spacial relocation at all? Strange reasoning, my human friend.

Who said instant? As far as I am concerned, what we think of as yesterday could easily be a hundred years ago. E still equals MC^2.

Ah . . . As the intruding thought faded, I jerked out of my trance and stared astonished at my supine companion. "Bertram?"

I know, I do not understand it either. How, for instance, did you learn to converse in my language? And so quickly?

"But I didn't . . ." As the words faltered in my throat, my bewilderment found an echo. For long seconds, two patterns of confusion whirled within my brain. Then:

I think we have been changed.

Yes. I stared, not seeing.

Unfortunately, my body still resists my will. But I do not believe there is any serious damage. I will regain control soon.

"No hurry," I muttered. "Neither of us is going anywhere."

You are too negative. If my perception of our situation is correct, I believe a return is quite feasible.

"That's nice," I said sourly. "Of course, you have a four-kilometer ladder neatly stashed in that wingship of yours."

A most impractical idea, the thought returned seriously. *But there is a signal device with a vertical range of several kilometers. It contains a small recording unit, plus an abbreviated time transmitter designed to transmit its message at the peak of trajectory. Would you oblige me by retrieving the device from the wingship?*

Despite the impossibility of Bertram's congruity theory, hope lent wings to my feet as I ran to the disabled wingship. I found the device in the undamaged rear section. It was small, bazookalike, with a ring sight and something resembling a trigger at the lower end. Under Bertram's direction I dictated our situation into a tiny microphone which pulled out from beside the trigger. Then I lifted the device to my shoulder, aimed, and fired. There was a slight shudder, and with a whisper of sound something streaked out of the open end and vanished skyward.

After a few seconds, Bertram asked, *Did you see anything unusual?*

"No. Should I have?"

I am glad you did not. After the message has been transmitted, the device self-destructs into a bright and long lasting flare. Because you did not see such a flare, I assume the device has successfully traversed the congruity. Now we wait.

For how long? I wondered bitterly. I voiced my doubts aloud. "For ten years? One hundred?"

Bertram did not answer. In fact he did not communicate again until about twenty hours later, after a night filled with unfamiliar stars. I had just drunk from the glacial stream which trickled down the valley, and was wondering if I dare bite into a yellow-brown fruit I had plucked off a nearby bush, when I heard a weak voice.

"Somezing comes . . ."

It had not been, exactly, a linear transmission from one world to another across a distance which happens to be thousands of light-years. Neither had it been, exactly, a sideways movement to a parallel universe. What it had been, although not exactly, was a composite of both. A transfer through a continuum which, although multidimensional, nevertheless lacks the familiar dimensions of space and time. For those with minds of the scope and power which can understand its unpredictable convolutions, the continuum offers instant access to the pasts, presents, and futures of all places in the physical universe. Also, of course, the ultimate power to influence infinite possibilities. But because it is a universal axiom that intellect must always be balanced by an equivalent ethical sense, a certain race reached out from its doomed planet and created, for the benefit of two younger cultures, a "gateway" to the galaxy.

The bait being set, we/I—the elders—waited.

First the Phuili came, and then man. Warily they coexisted, aware of their differences, unaware of the plan which made those differences complementary. An object completed its long fall from the cometary halo of a distant solar system, and according to the plan entered a nexus above a world long since scorched and rendered lifeless by its errant sun. Within a span of time too small for even theoretical meaning, the object emerged out of "Eight-o-Three" on the gateway world and appropriately terminated.

My/our calculations indicated only within a ninety-seven percent probability what the response would be. But when a primitive missile entered the nexus known as AA One, I/we finally closed Eight-o-Three and permitted our ancient home the dignity of anonymity. Soon, through a few gates and then through thousands, a new duality would spread into the universe.

It would be a good beginning.

. . . and then, like a shadowy echo, Bertram's thought. *Something comes.*

Startled, I turned. Bertram was half sitting up, one arm pointed shakily skyward. I looked toward the light above the AA, just in time to see a colored parachute blossom like a huge and lovely flower. I ran crazily in the direction the chute was drifting, by some miracle not breaking my neck as I dodged rocks and boulders. Finally it bumped to ground ahead of me, a large container covered with Phuili symbols. The chute was still settling downwind as I feverishly snapped back the container's fastenings and pried up the lid. The first thing I saw, neatly taped atop the supplies within, was a note from Jenny.

See you soon, love.

THREE
EARTHGATE

Challenge. Stimulation. Always, there must be another horizon beyond that which is immediate.

Although The Shouter is equidistant between Earth and Phuili and is therefore close to both worlds; to those constrained by a short life and limited technology, "close" defines a neighborhood which is inconceivably mighty.

So it was no small thing when the frail ships crossed the interstellar gulf to The Shouter; from Phuili, and later from Earth. Neither was it a small thing when the first human and Phuili rode a primitive aircraft through a gate; accomplishing together what neither could—or would—accomplish on his own.

Soon, crews from both worlds crossed through other gates. They arrived at planets as unspoiled and untouched as had been their own before technology began to pollute the seas and skies. There were dreams of ultimately populating the galaxy.

Yet still the way was not open—

"We have a problem," Peter Digonness said.

"Don't we all." Gia Mayland was in no mood to be sympathetic. She was still smarting because of the abrupt recall which had brought her from a beach in the Bahamas.

"It's about our search for the Earthgate," the Deputy Director of Expediters went on. "It seems someone does not want us to find it."

79

Gia raised a delicate eyebrow. "Now isn't that interesting."

He frowned. "More than you think. Jules Evien was murdered yesterday."

"Oh my god." Her face white, she sat down. "How?"

"Very neatly. At long range with a laser rifle. Strictly a professional job."

There was a silence. Stricken, Gia was remembering an old lover and a good friend. Then, "Could it have been for another reason? Other than Earthgate?"

"I doubt it. Jules is the third member of the Earthgate team to expire within the last two years. Heidi Jonson fell off a mountain in the Canadian Selkirks. Lynn Quoa died of apparently natural causes in a Denver hospital. Three out of the original seven who drew the assignment." Digonness shook his head. "Pretty long odds, Gia."

"But that makes Jules' murder a pretty stupid blunder, doesn't it? Now you are suspicious enough to wonder about what happened to those other two."

"The murderer was pressed for time. Three days from now, Jules is scheduled for deep sleep aboard the *Farway.* I told him I thought we had been concentrating too much on the Earth end, and he agreed. He was going to set up an investigation on The Shouter."

Brown eyes blank with thought, Gia slumped back in her chair. The Shouter, the instantaneous gateway to nearly twenty thousand destinations throughout the galaxy, was six hundred light-years and twenty-six months travel time from Earth. For Earth's sorely crowded billions, The Shouter was the access to unrealized dreams; a way to empty lands under clean skies and by unpolluted seas. But the waiting time was long; currently nearly twelve years to gain passage on one of the few dozen phase ships capable of making the trip. Millions more would undoubtedly apply if they did not have to wait a large portion of a lifetime just to get on a ship. So as long as that transportation bottleneck existed, the dream of Earth being able to reduce its populations to something less than bearable limits would forever remain a fantasy.

Her eyes strayed to the famous "Earthgate Summary," framed and hung on the wall above the D.D.'s desk. Ornately lettered and presented to Digonness before he was transferred back to Earth from The Shouter, the Summary was a constant reminder that:

Item: *Someone, somewhen, somehow, established the terminal for an instantaneous galactic transport system almost exactly between the home worlds of the only two known starfaring races.*

Item: *It takes more than two years for even the fastest ships to reach The Shouter from either of the two worlds.*

Item: *Of the nearly twenty thousand gates on The Shouter, there are two which do not lead anywhere.*

Conclusion: *That AAs 6093 and 11852 are the gates to Phuili and Earth.*

Questions: *Which of the two is Earth's? On Earth, where is the corresponding "Shoutergate"? And how is the system activated?*

Neat, concise and definitely logical. But like most of her colleagues in Expediters, Gia accepted the Summary as much on faith as on reason—because if there was any justice in the universe, it simply had to be true. If it was otherwise, populating the thousands of available worlds would be comparable to transferring Earth's deserts a few hundred grains of sand at a time.

Out of nowhere and completely irrelevant to her train of thought, a name popped into Gia's mind. "Transtar," she said.

"I beg your pardon?"

Her eyes widened. "That's it. The motive! Except for a few ships servicing the old worlds, Transtar has committed just about all of its resources to The Shouter run. So if Earthgate is opened up, it'll ruin them. The giant of the business will become a corporate has-been overnight! Can you imagine a better reason to stop us finding Earthgate? Even if it involves murder?"

"Frankly, no," Digonness admitted smoothly. "But with a motive that obvious, Transtar—*if* they are guilty—will have concealed their involvement behind false leads and middlemen enough to drown an entire army of investigators for years. So forget it, Gia. I did not bring you here to play gumshoe."

"Neither did you bring me here just to tell me bad news!" she shot back. "Or did you?"

He looked at her. After a few moments, Gia's eyes dropped from his steady gaze. "Sorry. I should not have said that."

"No," he said briefly. "You shouldn't." He did something behind his desk and the room darkened. A circle of light appeared and expanded. In the center of the field, set in a red-hued desert under an infinite sky, a huge saucer was balanced horizontally atop an incredibly slender pylon. Above the saucer, a pale sphere of flickering light. "You know what that is, of course," Digonness said.

Gia smiled into the darkness. "You'd fire me if I didn't. Even kinder-schoolers can recognize a stargate."

"Officially still an AA, alien artifact," he reminded her. "That happens to be AA One, my own favorite."

Gia nodded, although she suspected the fame which had come to Peter Digonness because of AA One was not entirely to the liking of this mild-mannered man. Despite the honors which waited for him on Earth, he had elected to remain on The Shouter while manned and unmanned vehicles began to probe the thousands of worlds beyond the AAs. It was only after months of unrelenting pressure from Expediters Central that Digonness finally, although reluctantly, returned home to take charge of the Earthgate search.

He pointed at the holographic image of the AA. "That is the main reason I am convinced we are wasting our time Earthside. Three kilometers high and two wide—if such a thing exists on this planet, then every human being has been blind for—how many thousand years? Okay, so perhaps it's disguised as something else, though god knows what. A thing that big would have to be concealed inside a mountain. The point is, if we don't know what we are looking for, then what are we looking for? If there is an answer at all, it can only be on The Shouter. Which, young lady, is where you come in. I want you to go in Jules' place."

Gia was not surprised. She and Jules were the only two who had been recruited into Expediters from the World Union Council's Security Service, so it was natural that the Deputy Director would seek her investigative talents. Nevertheless, she decided to play cautious.

"To do what?"

"I would think that is pretty obvious. I want you to find out how to open the Earthgate."

She frowned. "Not what I would call a modest assignment."

Digonness folded his hands together and leaned forward on his desk. His gray eyes were intent, probing. "Believe me, if I could assign this mission to myself, I wouldn't hesitate. I have friends on The Shouter, of both races. But in their wisdom, the powers that be have decided the answer is on this planet, and that I must continue to direct the search. But at least I was able to persuade them to assign one of *Farway*'s sleep tanks to Expediters, so you won't have to put up with two years of boredom aboard an interstellar people-freighter. And because you have no close relatives . . ."

". . . or emotional entanglements," Gia interrupted with a smile. "But you know that, don't you?"

Digonness looked slightly embarrassed. "I could not be sure, of course. But I'm glad you confirmed it."

"That's nice of me," the girl said sadly.

"Dammit, Gia, I'm offering the opportunity of a lifetime! Whoever or whatever put the AAs on The Shouter obviously intended them to be used. Which means that in some logical way there must exist a switch to turn on one of the two blank AAs to Earth. I'm even willing to lay down hard money that that switch is there for the eye to see, in full view. So please, girl, use your special talents to find it, huh? Turn on the Earthgate!"

Sleep tanks were such hugely expensive and complex pieces of equipment, most emigrants to the new worlds still had to suffer through more than two years of confined existence aboard one of the fleet of ships built specifically for The Shouter run. So when Gia Mayland was revived a week before the *Farway* arrived off The Shouter, she was not surprised at the hostility of her fellow passengers. The fact she was an expediter made little difference. That once glamorous profession was now merely respectable, another way to make a good living. But the hostility was not really a hardship. The crew were cooperative, and in any case Communications had a backlog of tachyon-wave messages for her. Most were routine, though the most recent one from the Deputy Director was ominous.

UP TO RECENTLY WE HAVE REMAINED COMPLETELY BAFFLED IN THE MATTER OF EVIEN'S DEATH, Digonness had sent. BUT LAST MONTH'S ARREST OF A KNOWN ASSASSIN ON AN UNRELATED CHARGE HAS VERY DEFINITELY REOPENED THE CASE. NOT ONLY HAS THE MAN CONFESSED TO JULES' KILLING, BUT HE REVEALED ENOUGH ABOUT THE MANNER HE RECEIVED PAYMENT TO LEAD US TO A PERSON NAMED JOPHREM GENESE, WHO IS EMPLOYED BY A SALES ORGANIZATION WHICH HAPPENS TO BE A SUBSIDIARY OF—YOU GUESSED IT—TRANSTAR INTERSTELLAR. BEYOND THAT, THE ONLY INFORMATION I HAVE IS THAT GENESE HAS NOT BEEN SEEN OR HEARD FROM SINCE EVEN BEFORE THE ASSASSIN COLLECTED HIS FEE. SO HE COULD BE ANYWHERE ON EARTH. OR PERHAPS OFF IT.

GIA, AS I REMINDED YOU BEFORE YOU SHUTTLED OUT, YOUR PRIMARY MISSION

CONCERNS THE EARTHGATE. BUT PERHAPS IT WOULD BE WISE TO LOOK OVER YOUR SHOULDER ONCE IN A WHILE, EVEN TO EXAMINE THE LISTS OF YOUR FELLOW PASSENGERS. I HESITATE TO ADVISE MORE, BECAUSE IN THAT GAME YOU ARE MORE QUALIFIED THAN I.

P.D.

It was a complication the young expediter would rather have done without. But she appreciated Digonness' warning to occasionally "look over her shoulder," especially during the weeks until *Farway*'s complement of settlers were shipped out to their various destinations across the galaxy. If nothing untoward happened while the hundreds of families were being processed and prepared for their great adventure, then it was probable nothing would. Unless there is a crowd to merge into after he has earned his pay, a careful assassin would probably prefer to wait for a safer assignment.

The day before disembarkation, Gia determinedly deposited her worries in temporary storage and settled into one of the observation blisters on the side of the orbiting ship. A few hundred kilometers away The Shouter's Marslike landscapes rolled grandly by, the sparks of the stargates resembling randomly scattered tinsel. Even as she watched, she knew aircraft were plunging into those sparks of light and emerging hundreds, thousands, perhaps even a hundred thousand light-years away on the far rim of the galaxy. Or perhaps returning, bearing crews who only minutes before had said farewells to those who even now were turning to a new life under an alien sun.

Sunk in reverie she did not notice the man who quietly entered the blister and joined her contemplation of this strangest of worlds. "Fascinating," he said. "Quite fascinating."

Startled, she turned. It was not, as she exepcted, a crewman. He was a drably dressed civilian; plump, totally bald, and with a wide, pink-cheeked smile.

Incredibly the smile broadened. "They don't like me either. I'm the other tanknaut."

Gia blinked. Tanknaut? Suddenly his meaning caught on, and she laughed delightedly. "So you are the one? I wondered who I have been sleeping with."

He blushed, like a small boy accused of liking girls. "Sorry we were not introduced. Endart Grimes of P.L.S.; Penders Life Support Systems." He added, as if apologetically, "Once in a while we do use our own products."

She accepted his hand. His grip was firm. "Gia Mayland. I'm with Expediters."

"Ah." He looked at her with interest. "Expediters. Wasn't Peter Digonness one when he . . . ?" He gestured at the planet.

"He was. Now he's my boss." Curiously, Gia asked. "Are you heading for one of the new worlds?"

He shook his head. "Unfortunately, no. I am merely an unattached person who can afford a few years away from Earth while I check out a few refinements in our . . . ah . . . process." He frowned. "Too bad it remains so damned complicated and cumbersome as well as expensive."

"Can't that be changed?"

The fat man shrugged. "Naturally, we are trying. Trouble is, the system is not only innately unreliable, it is field unserviceable. So we have split it into eight replaceable modules. With a life expectancy per module of only a few months; that, of course, means a lot of spares. On this trip, for instance, there are thirty such replacement units in the system. *Farway*'s two sleep tanks are, in fact, wired and piped to about one hundred and eighty thousand kilos of equipment. Did you know that?"

"My god." Gia was shocked. "No wonder the colonists are unfriendly!"

Grimes regarded her thoughtfully. "A few days of social ostracism is a small price, I think."

He was right, of course. Twenty-six months of communal living in a crowded steel shell was tough for even the most ardent gregarian. So Gia dismissed guilt in favor of gratitude for her good fortune, and settled down again to watch the unfolding scene.

Grimes said, "I understand it is called The Shouter because the emissions of the stargates make it one of the most detectable objects in the galaxy. True?"

"True," Gia agreed.

"Then why isn't The Shouter detectable from Earth?"

Gia sighed. *The ignorance of some people.* She pointed at a nebula-hazed cluster of stars rising beyond the planet's rim. "The Pleiades. Draw a straight line from here to Sol, and it passes exactly through the middle of those stars. For some peculiar reason, their nebulosity is opaque to the frequencies emitted by the stargates. So The Shouter was not detected until *Far Seeker* cruised out from beyond the Pleiades' shadow back in twenty-four-ought-six, thirty years ago."

Grimes gazed at the legendary star cluster, so familiar despite its reversed configuration of suns. Then, quietly:

"So perhaps the Pleiades is the reason there cannot be an instantaneous transport link to Earth. An Earthgate. What do you think, Ms. Mayland?"

It took eight shuttle trips to ferry *Farway*'s hundreds of passengers down to the surface; which again did not endear Gia to those who knew she had ridden one of the P.L.S. tanks and now saw her assigned to the first flight. But she had become used to their resentment, though she wished she was free to disclose her mission so she could turn some of that hostility into friendship. Even Endart Grimes, despite his affability, had seemed oddly distant—a bland exterior which did not match what she sensed was behind the man's pale blue eyes. In any case he was not on the shuttle, so she supposed he had surrendered his priority so he could tinker within the maze of plumbing and electronics which served the two life suspension chambers.

A few minutes after the shuttle rode its jets down to a gentle touchdown, two pressurized buses coupled to the exit locks and everyone cautiously filed into the transparent-topped vehicles. As her bus began to bump along the graveled road toward the semi-underground complex of the Colonization Authority's Reception Center, Gia gazed across a rocky plain at the domes and pyramids of the Phuili base. Some of those graceful structures were centuries old, yet they all gleamed a crisp white under the light of The Shouter's distant sun. About halfway between the base and the Center, incongruous in its straightlaced economy of construction, the four-story home of PERU rose slab-sided against the sky.

Somewhere there was a throaty roar, and suddenly a broad-winged shape rose into sight from behind the Center. It accelerated swiftly, climbing higher and then banking toward the sun. Shading her eyes, Gia saw the incredible structure toward which the aircraft was heading; the vast saucer, the almost line-thin pylon which supported it. The sun was too bright for her to see the sphere of light which was the actual stargate, and for the same reason she did not see the aircraft enter. But the rumble of jets ceased as if cut by a switch, and Gia knew yet another load of passengers had arrived at a distant world.

"Where did it go?" shrilled a child's voice. "Mamma, where did it go?"

"To a place called Serendipity, dear."

"Is that where we're going?"

"No, dear. We are going to New Kent."

"Why aren't we going to Serendiddy?"

"Because it's not New Kent," the mother replied testily, and left it at that. But in her mind, Gia continued the explanation,

Because Serendipity was the first world to be reached through a stargate, humans and Phuili jointly decided that it would remain as they found it, unsettled and unspoiled. Scientists were on that aircraft, perhaps a few media people, and even some tourists. But they will not be allowed to stay. In weeks, or at the most, months, they must re-emerge out of AA One just as Peter

Digonness and his Phuili companion did eighteen years ago. It's not such a bad trade, really. One world for thousands . . .

Genevieve Hagan, the Assistant Research Administrator of PERU, was a small woman with intense green eyes. Rumor was that she and Peter Digonness had had something going during his years on The Shouter, and somehow Gia thought that quite fitting. Aside from her undoubted charm and keen intelligence, the A.R.A. also possessed an outgoing femininity which would have been the perfect complement to Digonness' reputed reserve.

After instructing the new arrival always to address her as "Jenny," the A.R.A returned behind her desk, shuffled a few papers and shyly asked, "How is Peter? Is he holding up behind that Earth-bound desk of his?"

"He's trying to. But he did tell me he would prefer to be on The Shouter."

Jenny nodded. "We wish he could be." Gia noticed the unconscious emphasis of "We." *I think she still misses the man. Even after more than three years!* Abruptly the softness firmed and the green-eyed woman became the cool professional. "Now, then. You received Peter's message about Jophrem Genese?"

"It was given to me after I was revived."

"Then you understand why I ask this question. Did anyone aboard *Farway* seem particularly interested in you?"

Gia smiled. "The other tanknaut."

"Tanknaut?"

"The man in the other tank. Endart Grimes of P.L.S."

"Oh, I see. Yes, I know about Grimes. But I was thinking more along the lines of someone connected with Transtar."

Gia frowned. "That's a bit unlikely, isn't it? If Transtar wants to stop us finding the Earthgate, their agent is hardly likely to advertise his connection by being listed as one of their own."

"He'd have no choice. Other than Grimes and yourself, the only people from the *Farway* who don't work for Transtar are the colonists. And they will be confined to the Center until they are shipped out."

"So if Genese—or whoever—was aboard, he has to be a member of the crew. Is that it?"

The older woman pushed a file across the desk. "Here are the idents of all fifty-two crew members. Also a likeness of Jophrem Genese, facsimiled from Central a few months ago."

Gia flipped open the file. On the top, a head and shoulders picture of a thin-faced man with dark skin and slightly protruding eyes. She leafed through the rest of the sheets, each a single page summary with a small picture of the person described. The only one who even slightly resembled the thin-faced man was a female crew member.

"Not much help, is it?" Jenny said.

Gia closed the file and handed it back to the A.R.A. "I am here to find the Earthgate," she said firmly. "I don't intend to be diverted by some hypothetical mystery man."

Thoughtfully, the A.R.A. studied the young expediter. "I'd take Peter's warning quite seriously. Whatever else he is, he is definitely not the paranoid type."

"I know. And believe me, I intend to take all the basic precautions. But beyond that, I will be working full time on my primary assignment."

"Well, it's your decision, of course." Jenny balanced the file in one hand for a moment, then dropped it into a drawer and closed the drawer with a slam of finality. "Now that's done with—I hope—let's get down to specifics. How can PERU help Gia Mayland find the Earthgate?"

"For a start, Gia Mayland needs updating," Gia replied promptly. "I have been somewhat out of touch during the last couple of years."

Jenny chuckled. "So you have. Okay, two words. Nothing new."

Gia was astonished. "Nothing? Nothing at all?"

"What did you expect? Digger continues to spend government money looking for what he knows cannot be found, while on The Shouter we don't have the resources even to start looking. But I am glad you are here, because I also happen to agree with Digger that the answer—if there is one—is on The Shouter. Which is, I am afraid, my devious way of telling you not to expect too much from us. With all the teams going out from here, PERU is already spread far too thin."

Gia shrugged. "Which means we'll do what we can with what we've got, I suppose. Which is . . . ?"

"Use of our T-Com facilities, of course. I have already arranged fifteen minutes of open channel for you once every day at sixteen hours. It's expensive, but at least you will be able to keep in touch with Peter and the rest of the high-priced talent at E Central. Further to that, I have assigned someone to be your guide and helper. Meet Galvic Hagan."

He must have been waiting outside, because he walked in almost before the A.R.A. had released the key on the intercom. He was young, sturdy, and red haired. And his grin was infectious. "Is this the lady, Ma?"

The A.R.A. sighed. "Don't you think that joke's getting a little thin?" She looked apologetically at Gia. "He is not even related. But somehow he has got half the people here thinking I am his mother." She shuddered. "God forbid."

"Poor lady doesn't know what she's been missing," the young man said, shaking Gia's hand. He stepped back and eyed her critically. "Have you eaten lately?"

Gia knew what he meant. "The sleep tanks are not one hundred percent efficient," she explained. "I guess I lost a little weight."

He nodded. "Then I suggest we go down to the commissary and put some substance back on that nice bod of yours. Between mouthfuls you can ask any question you like, and if we're both lucky I may come up with some right answers."

"Good idea," Jenny agreed. "Gia, take it easy for the rest of the day. Have Vic show you around the facility and introduce you to people. And then get a good night's sleep. Tomorrow, you will meet David."

"David?"

"Oh, didn't I mention him? He is your Phuili opposite number here. His job is to find the Phuiligate."

"David" was short and humanoid, with a pink-fleshed canine head. Gia's held reaction to the little alien was to be nervous and at the same time curious, though negative feelings soon evaporated under the scrutiny of the large eyes, which were violet in color with a hint of humor in their depths. Also, the clasp of the rough-skinned hand with its two fingers and two opposed thumbs, was friendly. "I am Davakinapwottapellazanzis," he announced in a rapid flow of syllables. "But to human fwiends, I am David."

Gia licked her lips. *How does one make conversation with a being who looks like an upright bull terrier?* "Er . . . have you been on this assignment very long?"

"Since five of your monz. I come to Shouter after not finding gate on Phuili."

"Do you think there is a gate on Phuili?"

"If zere is gate on Shouter, zere is gate on Phuili. But not get much help on Phuili."

For a moment Gia did not understand. Vic looked just as uncomprehending, while Jenny merely shrugged and allowed herself a slight smile. They were in the A.R.A.'s office, the alien perched awkwardly on a low stool brought in to accommodate his dimunitive short-legged frame. Trying to ignore the two interested spectators, the expediter looked directly into the violet eyes. They stared back unwinkingly. "Do you mean that other Phuili are not interested enough to help? Or that there was direct opposition?"

David looked puzzled. At least, it was the impression given by a slackening of his flexible muzzle. "Not understand. What mean opposition?"

Gia carefully explained. "If the Phuiligate is found, there will be no further need for the ships and crews which journey between your world and The Shouter. Wouldn't those who run the ships want to stop you?"

The "puzzlement"—if that was what it was—deepened. "If gate found, ships go ozer places. Cwews go where ships go."

Is greed peculiarly human? Gia wondered, ashamed of her race's larcenous instincts and envious of Phuili innocence. But romantics do not make good expediters, and she quickly realized that simplistic judgments are self-defeating as well as downright silly. Because the Phuili were subject to the same natural laws as humanity, then somewhere down the line they had undoubtedly learned the same lesson; that angels are for the next universe, not the harsh realities of this one.

It was as if David was reading her thoughts. "Phuili develop over long time. Phuili young few, so planet still have much woom. Old ways not need to change. Yet gate will change old ways because much will come in fwom outside. Humans cwowded, zey need new worlds. Not Phuili. We go only to look. Not to stay."

Even Genevieve Hagan was surprised. In her years of dealing with the Phuili, never could she remember such a confession of unease; like a hermit fearing his castle of solitude is about to be invaded by hordes of tourists. Undoubtedly, David's "much will come in fwom outside" was a reference to humans, those—by Phuili standards—unpredictable beings with their unholy devotion to change. At the same time, however, the little alien's disjointed statement was also a contradiction.

The A.R.A. was not the only one who recognized the contradiction. "If the Phuili do not want the gate," Gia said puzzledly, "then, why, David, do you seek to open it?" Even as she asked the question, she sensed distress where earlier there had been humor. It was a strange feeling. Even with people she had never been able to sense mood like she seemed to be doing with this little alien.

David's reply echoed the mood. "Humans use gate even if Phuili not," he said sadly. "Soon zis zen become human galaxy. Maybe Phuili ways saved, but Phuili people lost."

Phuili people lost. Perhaps it was his awkward use of the human language, but nevertheless it conjured a poignant image of an ancient race relegated to a galactic backwater. Gia was beginning to appreciate the dilemma faced by the Phuili, the "go" or "no go" situation which was almost Aristotelian in its terrible simplicity. Either to accept the challenge offered by the gates and as a consequence endure the shattering effects of change on the fragile underbody of their monolithic society, or to turn inward and eventually be humbled into obscurity by a species which was still living in caves when the Phuili culture had already matured into something resembling its present form.

The expediter moved closer to the Phuili and the mood of distress intensified. It surrounded him like an invisible aura, a form of communication as alien as he was. Telepathy, she wondered? *David, do you understand me? Can you read what I am thinking?*

There was no answer. Only the sorrow.

Despite Vic Hagan's protests, Gia borrowed a runabout and went out on her own the next day. After bordering the shuttle landing complex, the graveled road terminated a few kilometers farther on below the huge bowl of AA One. The bowl was supported by a three-kilometer pylon which was so slender it seemed barely capable of supporting itself, let alone the mass which loomed incredibly overhead. For a while Gia sat in the artifact's shadow, not thinking of anything in particular but letting impressions soak gradually into her brain. At this stage she did not expect to learn anything scientists on at least three worlds did not already know, but she knew this small pilgrimage marked the true beginning of her mission. Finally she clambered out of the runabout and wandered around for a while, uncomfortable in her pressure suit but happily enjoying the same feelings of awe Peter Digonness had undoubtedly experienced when he first came.

It was difficult to think of appropriate superlatives. The sheer scale of the enormous artifact was such that though the pylon seemed incredibly frail from a distance, the close-up sixty-eight meters across its base suggested the comfortable solidity of a concrete monument. It had already been explained to Gia that the faint marks impressed on the smooth gray surface up to about the three-meter level, were, in fact, as much as Phuili science could do in an attempt to remove a material sample for analysis. It was while she was marveling at this unbelievable resistance to even the sun-heat of a laser torch, that Gia became aware of a second vehicle parked near her own, and a stolid human figure trudging toward her. She waited, irritated at this intrusion yet curious as to the stranger's identity.

"How do you do," a familiar voice puffed in her helmet phones. "Guess we're both doing what all the new people do when they first come to The Shouter. Right, Ms. Mayland?"

She smiled. "Right, Mr. Grimes. When did you come down?"

"On the early morning shuttle. And please call me Endart. Or even En if you like to be so informal. I don't mind."

Is he kidding? "And I'm Gia," she said politely. She waited as Grimes stared at the AA, then agreed as he voiced an appropriate expression of awe. Suddenly something reminded her of a remark he had made yesterday, in the *Farway* observation blister. Strange it had not registered before, but how in blazes had he known about the Earthgate? She asked him.

The question puzzled him. "Why is Heaven called Heaven? You may not believe in it, but it has to have

a name just so you can identify what you don't believe. Right? Anyway, I know I saw 'Earthgate' mentioned somewhere. Or heard it. I'm a bit of a sucker
for that kind of thing, you know. Ghosts, Atlantis,
UFO's, even the Bermuda Triangle. Nonsense, of
course, but fun. Guess I'm a bit of a romantic at
heart.''

It was a very human explanation. Not too glib and
therefore having a ring of truth. So Gia decided not to
pursue the matter. In any case, Expediters did not own
title to the somewhat unimaginative term "Earthgate,"
which to the uninformed could mean a lot of things,
real or otherwise. It seemed Digonness' warning about
the mysterious Jophrem Genese had affected her more
than she realized, and she wondered if she was becoming paranoid.

Not if I can help it, she told herself grimly.

However, the subject was not so easily dropped.
Grimes' curiosity had been piqued. "Why did you ask
that? Is it possible there is such a thing as an Earthgate?
Are you somehow involved?''

Gia tried not to overreact. "Of course not. As you
said, it's nonsense. My job is to expedite, not to spend
public money chasing fantasies.''

He seemed relieved. "How glad I am to hear that.
So what are you currently . . . ah . . . expediting?''

The man was becoming a nuisance. "Not very much
at the moment. We're waiting for one of the teams to
come in, from Gaylord. It's apparently one of the
better worlds, though no decision to colonize will be
made until we have evaluated the team's report. Believe me, Endart, being a sort of scientific mediator is
only part of my work. The rest is mostly dull routine,
as in any profession.'' Gia began to walk back to her
runabout, and after a moment's hesitation Grimes hurried after her.

At the vehicles, he turned again to the towering
AA. "Such a shame, really," he murmured. "All those
thousands of worlds, as accessible from The Shouter
as stepping through a doorway. While on our poor,

overcrowded Earth . . ." Shaking his head, he clambered into his runabout, waved, and drove off. Like a careless tourist he had forgotten to turn off his transmitter, and his muttering remained even after he was no more than a cloud of dust.

". . . such a shame. Such a terrible, *terrible* shame . . ."

Gia asked for photographs. Of AA One, and of 6093 and 11852. Galvic Hagan delivered them to her and watched curiously as she spread the prints in three groups on the library table. "Comparing?" he asked.

"No, I just like looking at pretty pictures," she replied irritably after she had arranged the collection to her satisfaction.

"It's already been done, you know."

Gia picked up one of the prints and held it closer to the light. "So?"

He spread his hands. "So nothing was found. Every AA on this planet is exactly the same as every other AA. Same dimensions, same markings, even the same spectral signatures."

"Hmm." Though she was not about to admit it, Gia knew the young man was right. She had slept badly the previous night and was feeling physically and mentally sluggish. At that moment fresh ideas seemed as rare as a Sahara iceberg. Again she looked at the print in her hand. It was of 6093, one of the two nonfunctioning AAs. "Vic."

"Yes, ma'am?"

She pointed at the light above 6093. "Have you flown through that? Or through the one above eleven-eight-five-two?"

He nodded. "Several times. Through both."

"What does it feel like?"

He shrugged. "Same as any other AA. We just didn't get anywhere, that's all."

"Vic, I have only heard Digger's description of the sensation. I want to know if it is the same for everyone. So let me repeat the question. As you are transported through a stargate, what does it *feel* like?"

"Okay. Now I get you." Vic considered a moment. "It's being torn apart and then squeezed together again. That's what it feels like. But like everything else you get used to it."

"Are you a pilot? I mean, of an aircraft?"

He blinked at the abrupt change of subject. "Sure. Where do you want to go?"

She glanced at the wall map. "To six-o-nine-three I think. It's the closest, isn't it?"

"A tad under six hundred klicks. About seventy minutes flight time."

"Arrange it as soon as possible. For tomorrow, if you can. I would also like to take David along."

Vic shook his head. "Sorry. Both ships are already booked for tomorrow." He glanced at his watch. "But what's wrong with now? There is still time to give you two or three hours of daylight at the site." As he spoke, he turned to the com unit and punched a three-digit number.

"Phuili," said an alien voice.

"Is that David?"

"Not David."

"This is Hagan. I am about to fly Gia Mayland to six-o-nine-three. She wants David to come."

"David come." There was a click as the Phuili broke contact.

"Just like that?" Gia asked, surprised. "Don't they even think to ask him if he's free?"

Hagan chuckled as he held the door open. "That is something else you'll have to get used to. Though to us the Phuili may act like individuals, sometimes they seem parts of one organism."

She stopped close to him. Though he knew she was at least ten years older, he felt a sudden protectiveness. He swallowed. "They're aliens," he said.

She nodded, thoughtfully. "As we are to them."

David met them as they pushed the aircraft out of the hangar. Clad in a silvery pressure suit with an elongated helmet, he looked more like a cuddly space toy than a member of a species older than man's. But his assistance as he and the young human male unfolded and locked the wings was that of an experienced professional. Which was not surprising considering the machine was a human adaptation of an original Phuili design. Finally the ill-assorted threesome strapped themselves into the narrow cockpit, and with a surge from its jets the *Eloise Three* floated smoothly into the thin air.

Seemingly a frail assembly of tubing and stretched plastfilm, this was actually a rugged and durable craft which had already proved its worth in hundreds of flights. Nevertheless Gia found herself breathing a little easier as they approached the slender column below AA 6093. "Can we spiral downward from the bowl?" she asked the pilot as she readied her camera.

"No problem," Vic replied, resetting the controls. As they entered into the enormous bowl's shadow, he tilted the machine into a slow descending circuit. Gia started taking her pictures, carefully spacing the shots to encompass all four sides of the pylon from bowl to base.

"You zink you find what ozers not find after doing same?" David asked interestedly from the rear seat.

"The pictures I have seen were all taken from the ground," Gia said, clicking away. "Nothing from this close, or from this angle."

"Still same," the Phuili commented.

He was probably right. Though the camera was the state of the art in electronic imaging, Gia suspected the ground-based holograms contained as much information in four shots as she could obtain with dozens. But such was the strangeness of this world, she had decided that yesterday's truth is not necessarily today's. Digonness' own early experiences on The Shouter had demonstrated the fragility of several rigidly-held absolutes, and Gia was immodest enough to allow the possibility she could also fracture a few. Especially if she found the Earthgate.

As they finally sped away from the pylon a few meters above the barren ground, Vic guided *Eloise Three* into a wide climbing turn. "Do you want to go through the light?"

"Of course. It's one of the reasons we're here, isn't it?"

"Okay. But be warned. For first timers, it ain't pleasant."

"I'm aware of that." Gia remembered how Digonness had described it. *It's being exploded apart, spread all over the universe, and then being imploded together again.* She turned to the other passenger. "Have you done this before?"

"Not wiz zis one. AA One only. Because zis AA not work, I wonder if hurt same. I come to compare."

Still same, Gia was tempted to say facetiously, having already been told by just about everyone in PERU that the "hurt" was equally unpleasant whichever AA one went through. But that was only the human experience. Perhaps to Phuili senses there would be a difference, though how that knowledge could help the search was problematical. In any case, how does one describe a subjective impression to an alien? She doubted David could do that any more than she could.

Again she remembered Digonness. *I'm willing to bet hard cash the switch is there to see,* he had told her. Well, maybe. But if he was right, then something had recently changed. Otherwise, she did not doubt the magic toggle would have been found long ago. She patted the camera. So perhaps her picture-taking made some sense after all.

They were above the bowl now, about a kilometer away and turning toward the pale radiance which shimmered above it like concentrated electricity. The bowl's inner surface was the most intense black she had ever seen; an effect infinitely more than a mere absence of light. Despite her heated suit, Gia shivered. Nevertheless, even before Galvic Hagan's exuberant "Tally Ho!" as he dove *Eloise Three* into the light, she was already taking more shots, hoping the camera could cope with the incredible contrasts of the unreal scene. Her concentration was so intense, it was almost unexpected when everything vanished in a sudden blaze of radiance.

". . . ohhhh . . . !"

Seconds, minutes, or perhaps years later—her confused senses seemed momentarily flung aside from time—AA 6093 was behind them as the aircraft hummed smoothly through the thin air. Digonness, and more recently Vic, had tried to describe how it felt, but Gia now knew that words would always be totally inadequate to describe what she had just experienced. In real space and time, she supposed they were a few kilometers and two or three minutes beyond the gate, in the same sky and above the same desert where they had entered. But deep inside herself Gia knew without doubt that they had been *elsewhere*, that within the span of a moment they had journeyed beyond the universe and returned.

"Shall we do it again?" Vic asked cheerfully.

"Yes," Gia replied, surprising herself. "Yes!"

He swung around in his seat, and even behind the helmet visor she saw his astonished face. "You're kidding!" Then, plaintively, "Aren't you?"

"I too want do again," David said. "But also I zink we stop inside light for while. You have auto?"

Even Gia was shocked by the request. To extend that ultraschizoid splitting to a virtual infinity of moments would be worse than the most malevolent concept of hell. That the Phuili could be such a masochist . . .

"When we in six-o-nine-zwee, we go ozer place and come out again. No time between, so in and out one moment. But if auto stay us, zen in and out separwated by short time. Hurt not differwent, just two smallers. We twy?"

. . . or on the other hand, a useful friend to have around. We need a few of his kind in Expediters. Her thoughts whirling at David's penetrating logic, Gia asked, "Can it be done?" *My god, perhaps the other place is Earth. Deputy Director Digonness, are you in for a surprise!*

The pilot began setting switches. "In, stop, hover for about fifteen seconds and then out again. If I could set it for as low as five seconds, I would. At least she'll stay on an even keel for a while, long enough for me—hopefully—to regain my senses. Dammit David, are you expecting this to be the quick way back to Phuili?"

"Iss not logical? But if human world, not matter. Ozer AA zen lead to Phuili."

Fifteen minutes later *Eloise Three* was parked on the desert a few kilometers from AA 6093. Aboard the aircraft, its pilot and two passengers sat quietly. But their thoughts crackled like lightning.

. . . *telepathy for God's sake!*

. . . *it is what happened to my next level ancestor after he and the human named Digonness first went through AA One.*

. . . *David! It was your father who was Digger's companion?*

. . . *it is true. It is also true the thought-speak faded rapidly after they returned to The Shouter. So I suggest most strongly we exchange our impressions before we are also returned to the inadequacies of speech.*

. . . *I agree. Question. Where were we?*

. . . *God knows,* the pilot thought. . . . *but it certainly was not any place I know. Or am likely to.*

. . . *Galvic, dear, it was just too easy to persuade you. Which makes me suspect we were being influenced even before we reentered the gate.*

. . . *damn right! By every standard I can think of, what we did was insane. But we survived, and now we're yakking like three animated radios.*

. . . *did you see anything? Feel anything?*

. . . *see anything, no. Feel anything? Well, it's hard to say. I do know I received a pretty lucid message from . . . whoever. For some reason, I am to examine Eloise' tail section.*

. . . *interesting. Do you know why?*

. . . *I only know I am supposed to do it before we*

take off again. Would you believe it, they even knew I'd ground her after reentry.

. . . *it seems they know a lot of things.* David pondered a moment. *Gia, do you agree there were other entities?*

. . . *absolutely. I even tried to . . . er . . . converse with them.*

. . . *yes?*

. . . *I asked about Earthgate.*

. . . *how strange. I asked about the gate to Phuili.*

. . . *ah ha! Did they answer you?*

. . . *with an image. Very strong, very clear. It was of a pair of human hands framing a circle. They were smaller hands, smooth. A female's, I think.*

. . . *mine?*

. . . *it would seem logical.*

. . . *all I got was an impression of a white dot.*

. . . *nothing else?*

. . . *I did not understand it either. It seems we . . .*

It was not as if a switch had been opened. At least, not exactly. But with breathtaking suddenness the three found themselves returned to their separate shells; their few minutes of warm sharing a fading memory. Galvic Hagan descended from the aircraft and began to inspect the wires and struts of its spidery rear section.

"Am glad it not last more," David said at last.

Gia turned in her seat. "Why?"

"At moment zis one not happy at loss of zought-speak. But zis one also know time make normal. If zought-speak last longer than did, zen I zink time not make normal. Me and you and Hagan stay always in loss."

"I see." Indeed, Gia did see. Like sex, their intimate sharing had been a sweet agony. Literally, a "high." Much longer, and it would have become an addiction for the rest of their lives, like a potent drug with no antidote except the drug itself. And that, she knew, was gone forever.

Her wistful reminiscence was interrupted by an exploded epithet. "Well, I'll be . . . !" Muttering angrily, Vic came forward to the cockpit and handed up to her a puttylike blob about as big as a thumb nail. "Bloody murderer!" he snarled.

Gia rolled the substance between gloved fingertips. Her throat was tight. "Explosive?"

"And how! See those little gold flecks? That means it's denzonite, a plastique normally as inert as a stone until it's zapped with a precisely tuned radio signal. It doesn't need a receiver, or a detonator. It's its own trigger."

"Take it, please," Gia said, feeling slightly sick. She flinched as she watched him grind the ugly substance into the ground with his boot heel. "We're Okay, I hope?"

"We'd better be," Vic said as he returned behind the controls and turned on the power.

"Wait a minute."

He turned. "What now?"

"We took this flight at a moment's notice. Right? So how could—whoever it was—have known? Even which of the aircraft we would use?"

The jets whined and *Eloise Three* surged upward. "He didn't have to know," the pilot replied as he banked the machine in a wide circle about AA 6093 and then set the course toward home. "Presuming you are the target—which seems entirely likely—it required no great feat of the imagination to figure out you would sooner or later need one of the aircraft. So our nasty friend simply took advantage of an early opportunity and attached a package on both Eloises. By now he certainly knows you are on a flight somewhere, so I presume he and his button are just waiting for us to sail gracefully over the horizon." Vic chuckled. "You know, I feel real bad about how we're going to disappoint him."

"Maybe assassin Phuili," came a quiet comment from the rear seat.

The two humans were astonished. The aircraft wobbled as in his surprise Vic twitched the controls. "Phuili don't do things like that," he said. And then his doubts surfaced. "Do they?"

"Not before," David replied. Sadly, he added, "But zis time Phuili life can change much. I zink some might twy kill to stop change."

It was an astonishing admission. But at that moment Gia was thinking of beings who were neither human nor Phuili. Perhaps it would be easier to think of them as gods; all-seeing and all-powerful, as much cognizant of the rules which guide the universe as they were of a sabotage device aboard *Eloise Three*.

The mysterious entities beyond the AA were apparently benign beings. But if human and Phuili were being manipulated—even for their own good—where did that leave free will? The joy of achievement and discovery?

Behind them the sun sank below the horizon as the aircraft raced over a shadowy landscape rapidly deepening to blackness. Stars were appearing in numbers and brilliance far beyond that which could be seen from under Earth's dusty skies, but the mind of the human female was being turned inward, away from the external world.

Whatever their powers, they are nevertheless mortal.

Coming from within herself though not originating with herself, the statement was a true one. Gia did not know why she knew that, but she had no difficulty accepting it as incontrovertible fact. It had a corollary; that because the entities were physical beings, then like most life forms they had originated in the organic soup of some primeval ocean. They had traveled the same road man and Phuili were now traveling, so knew the value of the painful learning experience which is true progress.

Then why their intercession?

Because for us, there were no others.

The rise to intelligence of the entities had been a freakish circumstance during the dawn eons of the galaxy. Life should not have happened but did, on a world on which evolution somehow avoided the sidetracks, dead ends, and natural catastrophes which make normal evolution a spasmodic sequence of fits and starts. So when they looked for their peers among the stars, they found they had arrived too soon; that only a mere handful of primitive life-bearing worlds existed among literally thousands which were still condensing from the accretion discs of countless young solar systems.

With "others" there could have been a new viewpoint, an exciting consensus of opposites. It was a special mathematics in which *two* is infinitely greater than *one*—an equation which for the entities was tragically incomplete. So a decision was made. If they could not be part of that equation . . .

. . . they would become the mathematician.

The equation was now—finally—almost complete.
Man plus Phuili.
The new duality.

"Interesting," the A.R.A. said after Gia had finished.

Gia nervously bit her underlip. "Don't you think it's a bit more than that?"

"Perhaps." Green eyes thoughtful, the older woman leaned back in her chair. "Well, Galvic? What do you have to say about all of this?"

The young man shrugged. "I'm not so sure about the last part. But the rest I can vouch for. Especially the telepathy. That's how they told me about the denzonite."

"As I said. Interesting." Jenny held up a speckled blob. "This was found in the tail section of *Eloise One*." She grinned. "Don't worry. It's been neutralized."

"It had better be!" He took the blob and looked at it sourly. "I don't know how much you know about this stuff, but even a few molecules are pretty potent."

"Oh, yes." Wickedly, "The scorch marks on your aircraft prove that."

Vic stared. "Then he . . . it . . ." Abruptly he subsided. "Oh, what the hell."

Gia shared the sense of narrowly avoided disaster. "They saved our lives, you know." She shivered. "Wish I knew who. Or what. And who did . . . ?" She gestured at the substance in Vic's hand. As if it had suddenly acquired legs and a sting, he threw it down on the corner of the A.R.A.'s desk. It adhered obscenely.

"Second question first," Jenny said. She produced a photograph. "Gia, do you remember this person?"

The girl studied the picture. "You showed this to me before. Isn't she one of *Farway*'s crew?"

"That's right. Carmen Klaus is the one with a family resemblance to Digger's mysterious Mr. Genese."

"Now I remember." Gia looked up. "So?"

"A few hours ago, Klaus booked out a runabout and was last seen heading toward Pock Hill."

"Yes?"

"Pock Hill is an excellent vantage point in the direction of six-o-nine-three."

Gia's stomach did a flip. "Interesting," she said, in unconscious parody of the A.R.A.'s recent reaction. Not so restrained, Galvic let out a long whistle. "A woman, by god!" He spread his hands wide. "And why not?"

A good question. Gia felt she could kick herself for overlooking the possibility. History was, after all, full of accounts of women impersonating men and getting away with it, sometimes for years. So it seemed one riddle (and presumably its accompanying threat) was finally about to be exorcised.

The A.R.A could be excused for her air of satisfaction. "I have already dispatched a security patrol," she said, anticipating the obvious question. "I think that is one lady who is about to be withdrawn from circulation for a while."

"Provided she is the assassin, of course," Gia said, still faintly tasting sour grapes. She rose to her feet.

"Going somewhere?"

The expediter nodded. "I need to think for a while."

"About how to tell illusion from reality?"

Gia hesitated. "Something like that."

"Your description of the beings' history, their promotion of a 'duality' between us and the Phuili. Why didn't Vic pick that up?"

"For the same reason I did not get the message about the denzonite, I suppose," Gia said. "It depended on who was being talked to."

Galvic blinked with surprised realization. "Say, that's right! Whatever was said to us, it was never via an open three-way . . ."

Gia laid a restraining hand on his arm. "Vic, it's not what happened on the other side of the gate which bothers me. It's what happened on *this* side, during the return flight. If I was not hallucinating, then we and the Phuili are on the verge of something pretty incredible; right? But if I was merely the victim of an over-stimulated imagination, then how do we avoid proving to the Phuili hard-liners what they have always preferred to believe—that we humans are not only inferior, but unstable?"

"Did you discuss this with David?" Jenny asked.

"Would you?" Gia retorted.

The A.R.A. regarded the younger woman thoughtfully. "Put yourself in David's shoes. If he picked up the same message, and had the same doubts, do you think he would have discussed it with any human before he talked to his own kind?"

Gia's jaw dropped. "You think . . . ?"

"*You* think about it," Jenny said.

She was studying the pictures she had taken of 6093, when the little alien entered the lab and watched her for a moment. Then, "I speak Jenny."

Gia turned and looked at him. "About what, David?"

"About ozers ozer side of AA. About humans and Phuili togezer being more zan humans and Phuili not togezer."

Gia had a sinking feeling. "She told you."

"Not twue. I told her." The jaws flexed in the Phuili equivalent of a smile. "Zen she told me."

In her excitement the expediter knocked some of the prints off the table. "Glory," she whispered. "What a day this has turned out to be."

"I wish not tell you until I say to ozer Phuili. After I say, I am told human female perhaps hear same. But not tell me for same weason I not tell her." The large eyes twinkled humorously. "Perhaps humans and Phuili should more twust ozers of each."

"Yes," Gia said fervently. "Oh, yes."

With the rolling gait characteristic of his short legs and splayed feet, David walked across the room and picked the prints off the floor. As he handed them to her, he pointed to the top one. "I see zat before."

Putting the others aside, she looked at the print. Showing the bowl as seen from above, it was the one she had been studying when he came in.

"Put picture on table," the Phuili instructed. "Hold wiz hands as you just doing."

Puzzled, Gia did as he asked. "I don't understand . . ." Wide-eyed, she stopped. The thumb and index finger of each hand had automatically spread apart, holding the print down by the corners and framing the image of the bowl between. *A pair of human hands framing a circle. Smaller hands, smooth* . . . It was part of what she would never forget, part of the warmly silent communicating they had shared and then lost. And there was something else.

"A white dot," Gia whispered. "They showed me a white dot."

David nodded. "Me ask about Phuili gate, zey show me circle. You ask gate your world, zey show little dot. What means?"

Gia was staring at an enlarged photograph on the wall of the lab. Apparently put there either as a measure of frustration or because someone had a peculiar sense of humor, it was a rectangle of unrelieved black. She pointed. "I suppose you know what that is."

The alien nodded. "We have same, zough we not waste spaces on walls wiz pictures we know show nozing. Many pictures taken fwom above bowl AA

One to twy find twansmitter fwom where energy come. Zat picture and many more taken by wobot flyers vewy close to middle of bowl. Much time waste."

"Perhaps because they were examining the wrong AA," the expediter said, pulling the sensing head of the projection magnifier toward her and carefully inserting the print of AA 6093. She turned on the magnifier, and as the room lights dimmed she began to rotate the zoom control. The round black image swelled beyond the edges of the lab's two-meter screen, causing the room to become stygian as The Shouter's brighter landscape was swallowed beyond the frame. Suddenly, at the center of the screen, a point of light appeared and then diffused as the magnification limit was exceeded. Gia reversed the zoom until the light contracted to a sharp, bright point. "The white dot!" she said triumphantly.

It was more than an hour since Galvic Hagan had dropped out of *Eloise One*, the jets of his harness brilliant until he vanished beyond the rim of the bowl. Commentary from the pilot of the circling aircraft remained spasmodic, as he flew in as close as he dared to watch Vic's progress, then as he retreated to a distance where his signal was not completely blanked by 6093's radio interference.

"*. . . crawled almost up to the edge of the bowl, slow as hell but sure. Seems those adhesion pads really work, huh? Whatever gizmo he found must be pretty small; his abandoned lift harness looking a lot more conspicuous there in the center. Going back in now . . .*"

Undoubtedly he saw Vic step off the edge, but by the time he was able to transmit the news, everyone on the ground was already watching the tiny figure drift downward under its huge canopy. It took time to descend three kilometers of vertical distance, and when Vic landed it was amid a crowd. But by prearrangement everyone held back to allow one human and one Phuili to approach the parachutist.

"Please don't expect me to do that again!" Vic said

breathlessly as he returned Gia's hug and clasped David's extended paw. "The harness worked fine, the chute worked even better, but getting up the slope of the bowl . . ." He shuddered. "Now I know what frictionless means." After discarding the suction discs attached to his knees and elbows, he reached into the voluminous pouch on the front of his suit and withdrew a glittering object about thirty centimeters long. "Here, lady. It's your bauble."

Gia gasped in wonder as she held it. A flat-ended cylinder of material which refracted light in brilliant colors, its translucent heart contained a tiny three-dimensional image of an AA. "It's beautiful. But what does it do?"

"S'for you and David to figure that one out," Vic replied with ill-concealed smugness as he watched her pass the object to her Phuili colleague. "But I lay you a hundred-to-one another one of those is in the bowl of eleven-eight-five-two."

"Zat is logical," David agreed as he examined the crystal-enclosed miniature.

By this time the mixed group of humans and Phuili had crowded around, and exclamations of human astonishment were interspersed with Phuili gutturals. David returned the object to Gia and fired a burst of syllables to an attentive member of his own team. Immediately the other Phuili turned about and trotted toward a tiny single seat aircraft parked apart from the other machines. "He weturn base and awange Phuili mission to ozer AA," David explained to the humans. "Soon we know if same in zat bowl."

"If it is, which I do not doubt," Genevieve Hagan said as she took the object from Gia and held it up to the light, "then our mysterious benefactors will have put two rabbits into the hat." She looked at Gia. "You know, of course, this pretty paperweight was not there a month ago?"

The expediter nodded. "I've looked at the last series of photographs. Clean as a whistle." Gia turned to David. "Do you mind if we take this back to PERU?"

"You take," the Phuili agreed. "I come talk later."

By this time *Eloise One* had spiraled down to a dusty landing, and Vic immediately persuaded the pilot to return as passenger on another machine so he himself could fly the two women and the "gizmo" back to PERU. Not unexpectedly nothing was solved during the seventy-minute flight, though Gia and Jenny exchanged the trophy at least a dozen times as they attempted to fathom its purpose.

"We'll just have to see what the lab can do with it," Jenny said finally as the cluster of buildings rose over the horizon. She sighed. "Gia, presuming this is Digger's 'key'—in full view, as he said—now what? I have an uneasy feeling that instead of an answer we have uncovered an even larger question. And right now, my dear, more questions are what I don't need."

The A.R.A.'s foreboding was not misplaced. Two hours later they met in her office and heard a harassed-looking technician describe a scientific impossibility.

"Whatever it is, it certainly isn't matter as we know it," he reported, staring at the object with distaste. "It doesn't chip, it doesn't scratch, and it reacted in absolutely neutral fashion to every frequency I could throw at or through it."

"Solidified energy," Gia murmured, intending to be facetious. Galvic started to chuckle, but subsided as the technician said angrily, "Why not? Tell me Earth's moon really is made of green cheese, or that the universe is smaller than the head of a pin, and right now I won't argue. Because that . . . that . . . *thing* has screwed up scientific logic in a way nothing short of shameful!" Still red faced, the man stamped out of the room and slammed the door behind him.

"Well," Jenny said after a moment.

"The poor chap was almost violent." Vic picked up the object and hefted it. "Energy? Green cheese?" He put it back on the desk. "Shameful!"

The A.R.A. smiled, but faintly. "Gia, have you contacted Earth yet?"

"Haven't had a chance." Gia hesitated. "Aside from the fact there has not been enough reason."

"Well, there is now, isn't there? And there is the matter of the late Carmen Klaus."

Vic started. "Our denzonite suspect?"

"More than a suspect, I think. She apparently blew herself to bits as you flew over Pock Hill. One of the bits—her hand—was still holding a button transmitter."

"I don't understand . . ." Gia began.

"I think I do," Vic said. "The stupid broad must still have had some denzonite with her when she tried to blow us out of the sky." He shook his head in disbelief. "Even the best of us make mistakes. But . . . *that?*"

It had been an awful death, even for one whose trade was bringing death to others, but Gia experienced a lifting of spirits as she realized she was finally free of a disturbing threat. Later, as she sat before a T-Com console, fingers aching from ten minutes of unaccustomed typing, she wondered if she had been out of the security game too long. Expediters were not, after all, supposed to be risk takers, yet for days that ancient bony finger had not been far from her shoulder.

Suddenly a new pattern of lights swept the console and Digonness' reply began tracking across the display:

JOPHREM GENESE BEING A WOMAN CERTAINLY EXPLAINS THE EASE WITH WHICH SHE ELUDED ARREST. AT LEAST WE ARE WELL RID OF HER, THOUGH IT IS TOO BAD HER DEMISE HAS EFFECTIVELY SEVERED POSSIBLE LEADS TO HER EMPLOYER. I KNOW WE HAVE OUR SUSPICIONS IN THAT REGARD, BUT SUSPICIONS ARE NOT EVIDENCE. SO PLEASE KEEP THAT PART OF IT TO YOURSELVES FOR NOW.

"Agreed," the A.R.A. murmured. Squeezing into the seat alongside Gia, she typed, THIS IS JENNY. ANY IDEAS WHAT TO DO WITH THE GIZMO?

SO FAR, IT SEEMS ABOUT AS USEFUL AS A BOOKEND.

WHAT ABOUT THE PHUILI? HAVE THEY RETRIEVED A SECOND UNIT?

NOT YET. BUT I AM CERTAIN IT IS THERE.

IN THAT CASE, SUGGEST TO THEM THEY KEEP THEIR UNIT ON THE SHOUTER. THEIR LAB IS LARGER AND BETTER EQUIPPED THAN PERU'S, SO IT IS LOGICAL THEY TACKLE THE PROBLEM USING THEIR SHOUTER-BASED FACILITIES. MEANWHILE SHIP YOUR UNIT OUT ON THE FARWAY. IF THAT THING REALLY IS A KEY, IT IS STILL POSSIBLE THE LOCK IS HERE ON EARTH.

Galvic whistled. "But we'll lose two years! The Phuili could be off and running while the *Farway* is still this side of the Pleiades!"

MAKE THAT FOUR YEARS, Digonness came back. BECAUSE IF THE ANSWER IS AT YOUR END, THE UNIT WILL HAVE TO MAKE THE ROUND TRIP. NEVERTHELESS, I AM CONVINCED WHAT I SUGGEST WILL SERVE THE GREATER GOOD. THINK OF THE PHUILI AS MEMBERS OF A PARALLEL SCIENTIFIC TEAM, NOT AS COMPETITORS.

"What a nice idea," Jenny said. She chuckled. "Now if we could just persuade the Phuili to think the same way."

Later they met with David. The two units, one labeled *6093* and the other marked with a Phuili hieroglyphic, stood side by side on the table. They were identical; the same shimmering yet nonreactive substance of the cylinder, the same tiny AA replica embedded within. Jenny had passed on Digonness' proposal and the response was an extended exchange of gutturals between David and his two Phuili colleagues. Finally,

"If we find before ship weturn your world, Phuili gate open much sooner."

"We accept that possibility," the A.R.A. said.

David nodded. There was approval and a hint of respect in his large eyes. "In short time zis way perhaps better for Phuili. But in long time I zink it better for humans and Phuili togezer. Zerefore we agwee."

Just like that. Gia thought her mixed-up feelings were hidden, but she had forgotten the legendary empathetic sense of the Phuili. For the sake of interspecies harmony, Peter Digonness and his Phuili opposite number had long ago concluded an agreement in which the Phuili would respect the human need for emotional privacy, in exchange for human acceptance that "haste" is not in the Phuili lexicon. By definition the human side of the agreement was the more difficult, especially considering the dragging pace of most joint projects. So to say Gia was surprised at David's alacrity in accepting the proposal, is an understatement. Equally unsettling was the inescapable fact that once the unit from 11852 disappeared into the Phuili research lab, her own role on The Shouter would become redundant. David, recognizing the human female's aura of confusion and apparently deciding this was a moment to bend the rules, was sympathetic.

"Gia, you not like zis. You not zink we do wight?"

Gia blinked at the little alien. Perhaps it was innate or perhaps it was a residue of what they had shared beyond the AA, but she had no doubt he knew her feelings. And the fact she knew he knew, hinted at a still open two-way. But she did not mind.

"You are doing what must be done," Gia told David sincerely. She turned to the A.R.A. "It's just that as things start becoming interesting, I find myself sort of . . ."

". . . out of it?" Jenny queried, her eyes twinkling.

The expediter shrugged. "As far as Earthgate is concerned, anyway."

"Well, you are wrong," Jenny said.

Gia was revived as the *Farway* reentered normal space three days travel time from Earth. After thirty minutes of painful exercise, followed by an even more painful experience of being required to swallow an evil tasting high-nutrient concoction, she was released, as the medic humorously put it, "under her own recognizance." Forcing unsteady legs to carry her in the direction of the bridge, her steps echoing hollowly along the silent corridors of the nearly empty ship, Gia finally entered inhabited territory in the deck immediately below the cavernous space vessel's humming Control Center.

Suddenly she was startled by a pair of strong arms and a hug. "Vic!" she said, astonished.

Galvic Hagan slackened his hold and grinned. "Welcome to the land of the living."

"Where . . . how . . . ?"

He chucked her under the chin. "Came aboard right after they turned you into a corpsicle, dear." His grin broadened. "By the way, the difference between our ages has narrowed a couple of years. Care to take me on?"

Placing both hands on his chest, she pushed herself away. "Boring couple of years, huh?"

"Not so much. I'm returning home to go back to school. Done a lot of studying."

"Subject?"

"Planetology."

"A good choice," Gia said approvingly. "You already have the field experience, so you should have no trouble . . ."

"Bless my soul, she's awake!" Beaming, Endart Grimes trotted over and grasped Gia's hand. "Galvic my boy, why didn't you tell me?"

"You didn't ask," the younger man sighed.

"And you, young lady. How do you feel after your second long rest in four years?"

Gia noted the fat man's apparent good health. "Not as up to it as you, I suspect. How do you do it?"

Grimes chuckled. "No miracle. There is still much work to do on the equipment, so I had myself revived several weeks ago." He patted his stomach. "I have had time to catch up."

"But between meals he is always in his workshop," Vic said. "Gia, you should see it. I bet he could build a phase converter if he wanted to!"

Grimes blushed. "Please. I am just a mechanic performing a few modest modifications." He added sadly, "Unfortunately, there is still no way I can repair a sour module."

"Don't be so bashful, man. You're an artist!" The fresh voice was that of a large, middle-aged man with a lined face and twinkling blue eyes. He went directly to Gia and kissed her soundly. "You look well, Ms. Mayland."

"And so do you, captain," Gia returned fondly. It was no secret they were old friends, though Captain Joel Greshom's personal relationships were matters he normally did not discuss with his professional associates. Firmly holding her arm, he steered Gia across the deck to the door which led to his private quarters. Once inside, he sat her in the most comfortable chair. Then he called up the steward and ordered a light meal.

As she relaxed, she looked around the big room. At the simulated antiques, old leather-backed books, the handsome Turner reproduction above the realistic stone fireplace. "If the colonists had known about this . . ."

He laughed. "Girl, you're barking up the wrong tree. Many have supped here, and without exception they all felt sorry for me. I remember one farmer solemnly informing me that a few creature comforts are no substitute for a wide landscape under an open sky. He was right, too."

"You haven't been planetside since my mother died, have you?"

For a moment the captain looked bleak. "Never felt like it." He went to a trophy case, and from among the memorabilia of a dozen worlds lifted out a glittering cylinder. "Here. Forget about my past and concentrate on your own. A little something to refresh your memory."

It was like a tonic. Gia felt a restoring glow as she

held it up to the light and examined the delicate structure contained within. "It's not a matter of memory. For me, it was yesterday when I brought this on board. Anyway, why isn't it in the safe? I don't think you realize its importance."

Again the big man laughed. "What would be the point? The person in charge of the safe also happens to be a loyal employee and shareholder of the outfit which is apparently the prime suspect behind your troubles. So why would I go to the trouble of protecting that bauble from Transtar's evil machinations—whose loyal employee and shareholder is me? Hmm?"

He was, of course, making fun of her. But the point was well taken, though Gia did not immediately abandon her concern. "So everyone knows about this? What it means and where it is kept?"

"I suppose. My officers, of course, who often visit me here. And young Hagan. And certainly Endart Grimes."

"Oh, yes. Endart Grimes." Gia reluctantly replaced the tiny AA in the trophy case and closed the door.

The captain eyed her curiously. "Don't you like the man?"

She shrugged. "I hardly know him."

"Which is the problem, I suspect. He acts like a fond uncle and you resent it. Right?"

"You are very discerning."

"Not really. I just know you too well. Anyway, he's not such a bad fellow. A little lonely, perhaps, but he has his work to keep him company. He is very dedicated to what he does, you know."

"So are we all," Gia said moodily, reflecting on the fact that in her own job it was going to be difficult to sustain the interest and excitement of The Shouter assignment. When Jenny had suggested she belonged with the crystal-enclosed artifact right through to its hoped-for solution on Earth, it had made a lot of sense at the time. But in the cold light of reason, it was more likely the harried A.R.A. had had better things to do than invent work for an expediter who was better at detecting than expediting.

"Penny for your thoughts," the captain said.

"Nothing important," Gia lied. She forced a smile. "I think I need to resume an interrupted holiday."

She was serious about the holiday. A few days of relaxation might do much to revive her flagging spirits, especially while the artifact was being examined in Expediter's labs. But thoughts of sun and sand were put firmly aside by the first ground-to-orbit call to the huge starship. "I want you down on the first shuttle," Peter Digonness told her, his four-years-older screen image tight with suppressed anticipation. "If what you have is what I hope it is, then from now on you can select your own assignments with my blessing. If it is not, then you and I will probably end up sharing the same terminal in the computer pool."

Gia nodded. She knew the Deputy Director was not exaggerating the consequences of failure. "I am not really worried," she said. "The artifact was placed where it had to be found. So it has to have a purpose."

Digonness agreed soberly. "Perhaps. We do know that so far the Phuili have accomplished nothing with their unit. So it is just possible that bringing ours to Earth is the right approach. After all these years, I wonder . . ."

They were separated by millions of kilometers, their images relayed via a communications net encompassing ground and space. Yet suddenly the two shared a rapport far beyond the linking ability of lasers and microwaves. Gia had felt it before; she welcomed it gladly and then felt a sense of loss as it faded as abruptly as it came.

Digonness' astonishment was replaced by a dawning realization, and then by an introspective calm. He said softly, "It seems, my dear Gia, there is somewhat more to communicating than I realized."

It turned out that the first shuttle was not designed to carry passengers. The space below the flight deck was cramped, with Gia, Galvic Hagan, and Endart Grimes squeezed into a space not as wide as a standard ground car. Behind them, most of the thirty-meter cargo bay was filled with two disassembled life suspension chambers and four unused modules, all destined for modifications at the P.L.S. plant in Seattle.

The artifact had been stowed in a compartment next to her seat, and as soon as the maneuvers of separation and retrofire were complete, Gia retrieved the crystal-enclosed model and turned it over in her hands.

"Some souvenir," Vic commented seriously.

"True," Gia agreed, peering at the delicate miniature within. Somehow her enthusiasm was diminished, making her wonder if she was a victim of overload—too much, too fast. Subjectively the rapid pace of events on The Shouter had happened only yesterday, and not even twenty-six months in stasis could relieve the effects of accumulated stress. Yet it had been only hours ago in real time that the feel of this ice-silk surface had kindled within her a soaring sense of accomplishment. There had been no doubt, no doubt at all, that the dream of Earthgate was finally on the verge of realization.

Now, she felt nothing. The dream was dormant.

Suddenly Gia stopped rotating the model. She upended it and peered along the bottom edge of the crystal cylinder. She carefully traced her thumb along the edge and then looked again. "This is not it," she whispered.

"It isn't what?" Galvic asked curiously.

She turned to him. The young man flinched at the shock in her eyes. "My god, Gia, what . . . ?"

"It's a fake," the expediter said. Abruptly she grasped his hand and dragged it, palmwise, across the cylinder's edge. "Look. Is it bleeding?"

He pulled his hand free and glanced at the fading impression on the skin. "No, it's not bleeding. Should it be?"

"You would have been sliced to the bone if this were the genuine artifact! See the little nick on the edge? Not even a diamond should be able to do that. Compared to the original, this is putty!" Gia looked across at the other passenger. "Isn't that right, Endart?"

The fat man, who had apparently been dozing, half roused himself. ". . . ah . . . I beg your pardon?"

"When did you make the substitution, Endart?"

"Now just a minute!" Astonished, Vic looked from one to the other. "Gia, what are you getting at? What substitution?"

"Ask him!" she flashed. Leaning forward, Gia met Grimes' heavy-lidded gaze. "Endart, what is your actual connection with P.L.S.?"

Grimes lowered his head modestly. "Founder, Director of Research, and Chairman of the Board." He looked up. His face was still jovial, but the pale eyes had become aware. And cold. "Endart Penders Grimes. That is my full name, you see."

"Oh my lord." Galvic Hagan shook his head in disbelief. "Move over, Transtar."

"You'd better believe it," Gia said. "P.L.S. is a small one-specialty outfit heavily dependent on government grants to improve a product which Earthgate will make obsolete overnight. Now *that* is a motive! The woman once masculinely known as Jophrem Genese was working for Grimes all along. It was no accident she blew herself to kingdom come when she pressed the button which was supposed to blow us out of the sky. One insignificant blob of denzonite, tuned to the same frequency as the denzonite Genese herself had concealed aboard our aircraft, and Grimes almost had it all. No us, no witnesses, hopefully no Earthgate, and no hired killer. Do I have it right, Mr. Grimes?"

The Chairman of Penders Life Support Systems was regarding his accuser thoughtfully. "Very ingenious. But, of course, absolute nonsense. For instance, why would I substitute for something which never existed in the first place?" He pointed at the artifact. "Where was it really made, Ms. Mayland? In the workshops of PERU, perhaps? It seems to me that your scheme to save your own reputation at the expanse of a poor fat man who has never done you harm is most reprehensible. I am sorry, but after we land I intend to report this whole sordid matter to the proper authorities."

It was an amazing performance. Despite herself, Gia felt a reluctant admiration for the mental agility contained within that polished skull. But Grimes was clearly on the defensive, so she determinedly pressed her advantage. "Go ahead. Report. Meanwhile, I am sure an analysis of material samples from your workshop will find something with an interesting similarity to material from this." Gia held up the artifact. "Or don't you think so?"

Grimes was unimpressed. "I use common enough substances. So make your analysis. It won't prove anything."

"It won't get us Earthgate either!" Vic said angrily, swiveling in his seat and grabbing the front of a voluminous tunic. "Tell us what you did with the original you bastard, or, by heaven, I'll . . . *oof!*"

He gasped and released his grip as Gia thumped him between the shoulder blades. "Vic, you are a jackass," she said coldly. Her voice softened. "The artifact is indestructible, so he has to have concealed it somewhere. Probably, I suspect, aboard the *Farway.* We'll simply make sure nothing is shipped to ground until the ship is searched. Even if it takes weeks."

"Or years?" Grimes asked slyly as he straightened his rumpled tunic. "So the charade continues, eh, Ms. Mayland?" He smiled. "You will find nothing, of course. But we both know that, don't we?"

And he's probably right, was Gia's gloomy realization as she thought of the enormous volume contained within the living decks and storage spaces of the three-hundred-meter starship. But whatever the outcome of the search, one thing was certain. Grimes had to pay for what he had done. If she could not see him put away in one of the orbital prisons, Gia was sure she could filter enough evidence through to the P.L.S. stockholders to firmly exclude the stout executive from any of the financial fruits of his crimes. Which would certainly damage his pride, as well as his bank account.

Damn him!

All the punishment in the world could not compensate for the loss of Earthgate. Staring miserably in front of her, Gia barely noticed the flare of a steering jet through the side window, and then the dropping away of Earth's horizon as the shuttle's nose came up for reentry. She heard a slight thrumming as the thick wings began to bite atmosphere, felt a gradual increase of weight as deceleration pressed her into her chair. As the shuttle slid down its narrow track of safety toward denser air, the thrumming increased and became a vibration. Reacting to computer commands, control surfaces extended from their housings. There was a coughing roar as ramjets fired up . . .

"Explosion aboard!"

Even from the lower deck they heard the pilot's shout as the shuttle shuddered and then began to break apart.

"Emergency separation!"

There was a bang and then breath was gasped out of their lungs as something shoved with enormous force against the rear bulkhead. Looking like a larger version of an ancient Apollo capsule, the separated nose section immediately flipped over to reentery attitude, and for a moment Gia saw the crumpling shuttle fall away behind them. Haloed with a flickering blue light, the discarded stub-winged craft was falling in on itself.

It's imploding!

The moment was barely enough for astonished uncomprehension before there was another jolt as the drogue chute snapped out behind them and steadied the jarring motion of their fall. Somewhere a relay closed and the huge main canopy shot out after the drogue, again ramming their bodies deep into restraining cushions as the shroud lines snapped, stretched, and then held.

"Is everyone okay down there?" the pilot shouted.

Apparently the intercom was gone, along with just about everything else.

"I think so!" Vic shouted back. "What the hell happened?"

"Something cut loose in the cargo bay, that's all we know. Thank god this is an old prototype model with capsule separation. Otherwise we'd be part of the mess back there. Anyway, brace yourselves. We're going to hit!"

They did, violently. After the first bounce the capsule hit again, tilted, then rolled completely over until it stopped with a shuddering jar and a screech of riven metal. It took only a moment to trigger the latches of the escape hatch, and not much longer for the three passengers and two crewmen to scramble out of their dented confinement. They found themselves on a sandy slope with sparse patches of coarse grass struggling for existence amid eroded rock outcroppings. The sun was low, the sky clear, and the air cool. For a minute or so it was good to relax, to breathe deeply and to marvel at the fact they had all come through the experience with nothing more serious than a few scrapes and bruises. Even Endart Grimes, despite being older and overweight, looked almost content as he surveyed the scene. "Where are we?"

The pilot noted the position of the sun, then looked at his watch. "It's mid-afternoon and we were approaching Kennedy along a polar orbit. So I would say sixty degrees north or thereabouts."

"Canada," Vic said. "Some landing pad, huh?"

A wind began to blow up the slope and it seemed the sky was darkening. Gia thought she heard distant thunder. "Hope we're not in for a drenching," she commented as she and Vic climbed up to the top of the slope. Already the wind was fiercer, so they crouched low until they reached the edge of a cliff which overlooked a very stormy sea. Winded, Gia sank down on her knees. "If we had come down in that . . ."

". . . we would not be breathing now," Galvic said,

his face pale as he realized how close they had been to eternity.

There was a crunching of feet as the others joined them. By this time the wind was so strong everyone had to shout to be understood. Gusts of stinging sand beat on exposed flesh and sea birds squawked alarm as they flapped laboriously inland toward safety.

It was a strange kind of storm and it was becoming stranger.

A few kilometers out from the shore, a roiling dark cloud seemed suspended over the water. Lightning flickered in and around the cloud and thunder rumbled incessantly. The wind had increased to a frenzy, forcing the five to flatten themselves prone on the ground. Gia thought the assistant pilot shouted something, but his words were swept away in the roaring cacaphony.

What is it out there?

The question was obvious, the answer was not. For the first time in her life Gia felt a genuine fear of the unknown, like a child abruptly abandoned in a dark room. The wind whipped and howled toward the thing over the water, toward the frothing column which had reared up into the base of the cloud like a liquid pedestal. Within the cloud itself there was something shadowy; a vagueness which slowly rose upward until, just below the summit of the cloud, it began spreading into a gigantic T.

"It can't be," Gia whispered. "It just can't be."

But it can be, a voice mocked in her mind. *It is!*

Along with realization came a sound of laughter, high pitched and with more than a hint of hysteria. The wind was beginning to subside, enough that Endart Grimes, between paroxysms of mirth, was able to gasp, "Don't you see, girl? Don't you see? I've given you Earthgate!"

"He has what?" Vic asked with astonishment, trying to look both at the cloud and at the wheezing executive. "What is the man blathering about?"

"I think it is pretty obvious," Gia replied stonily,

her eyes fixed on the now unmistakable shape within its stormy cocoon.

"I didn't want even the slightest chance of it being found," Grimes went on hoarsely. Hands clutched against his stomach, he was rocking back and forth as if he was in pain. "So I hid it in one of the P.L.S. suspension chambers, just before the equipment was dismantled and loaded aboard the shuttle. I mean, how could I know it wanted Earth's atmosphere to feed on? That it was, in fact, nothing more than a template?" The fat man gave way to another wracking paroxysm of laughter. "Just think about it! If what you had with you in the cabin had been the real thing, we would not be here now, would we?" Wheezing horribly, he pointed shakily at the thing over the sea. "Instead, we'd be part of . . ."

He did not finish the sentence. Eyes bulging, Endart Penders Grimes toppled slowly on his side, quivered once, and lay still. After a moment, Gia checked his pulse.

There wasn't any.

The place was Akimiski, a large island in James Bay. North of the island, James Bay widened into Hudson Bay, the ocean in a continent's heart. Ten kilometers off Akimiski's shore, a *seed* had reached for, and found, millions of tons of matter. Starting with a couple of hundred tons of spacegoing machinery called a cargo shuttle, it then began absorbing from the gas-liquid interface at the planet's surface. Like a mini black hole it was impartial; along with air and water it took in huge numbers of fish and birds, a few seals, a couple of beluga whales, and one polar bear. It would have made no difference wherever it landed; ocean or desert, mountain top or city, it only needed matter. Unlike a black hole, however, the *seed* was not insatiable. It was, as a dying man pointed out, merely a template, a means to recreate itself on an incredibly larger scale.

Which it did.

*   *   *

Exactly two hours and thirteen minutes after the implosion began in the shuttle's cargo bay, the process of transformation was complete and a new AA towered over the shallow waters of James Bay. The vortex was no more, air and sea were calm, and a rescue heli-wing accomplished a smooth landing near the four survivors.

At plus two hours and thirty-two minutes, even as the heli-wing was climbing away from Akimiski, a huge sphere of flickering light suddenly appeared above the AA. There was no accompanying heat or noise, and the air remained calm.

At plus thirty hours and three minutes, a broad-winged aircraft appeared from the south and quietly vanished into the light. Roughly a tenth of a second later, *real time*, the same aircraft emerged above an AA locally known as "6093" and shortly thereafter alighted on the dusty surface of a hurriedly prepared runway. Six hundred light-years had been traversed in less time than it takes to draw a breath.

Two passengers emerged from the aircraft. One, a young woman, held back as her older male companion walked hesitatingly toward a mixed group of humans and aliens who were waiting nearby. One of the group, a human, came forward and met the man halfway. They clasped hands and studied each other. Finally, a smile.

"Welcome home, Peter," Genevieve Hagan said softly.

FOUR

JOINT ACTION

They were intelligent, prolific, and savagely antagonistic to all life other than their own. If there is such a thing as race insanity, they were its victims. They were also beyond cure.

Because of their antilife crusade, their planet had become a sterile world of steel and concrete. Nothing swam in the oceans, walked, hopped or crawled on the land, or flew in the sky. Even clouds were anathema; orbiting solar mirrors burned them away as fast as they formed. Nothing was allowed to contaminate the pristine purity of what they had created. Food, adequate but dull, was synthesized from raw elements. The oxygen in the air was replenished by fusion plants scattered around the ocean shores.

Already their ships were swarming between the thirteen planets and countless minor bodies of their solar system. In an accident rare in nature's lottery, a second planet had supported an efficient though primitive life ecology. But ships bearing radioactive dust had fallen like metal rain out of space, and within days not even a living cell remained. The race was thorough.

There was no doubt what the future held. They had studied the stars and were aware of the possibility of countless solar systems with life-bearing planets. It would take generations, of course, but they were an immensely patient people to whom time was never an enemy. So the Great Work began.

It is fortunate that for every disease there are antibod-

ies; even against a disease which threatens the mighty organism which is the galaxy. So it was not entirely coincidence that even as scientists of this mad race fiddled strings of mathematical formulae toward what was known elsewhere as the phase-shift star drive, an actual phase ship came undetected into their system—

"*Jase, you are to go to Phuili and take up the post of Resident Expediter in our legation there.*"

"*But that's crazy! I'm a security agent, not an expediter!*"

The shuttle was racing northward over the Canadian Shield. Rocks, trees, water, and sky were the prime components of this rugged land, one of the last wild places on Earth. Hopefully it would remain wild, now that Earthgate was open and the galaxy beckoned. Ahead, the spreading glint of Hudson Bay. On the horizon, beyond the large island known as Akimiski, something flickered. The P.A. cleared its throat.

"Transfer in four minutes. Please take your queltabs and make sure your seat restraints are secure."

The flickering had become a pulsating sphere of pale light. Just below it, something enormous.

"*I know what you are. This desk and the four walls of this room know what you are. But to every human in the legation, and especially to the Phuili outside it, you will be an expediter. Anyway, what is so magical about expediting? It's more mediation than science, so you will be all right. Meanwhile, I want you to do your damnedest to find out which of the legation staff is trying to screw up Earth-Phuili relations.*"

Director Kreinhauser of the World Union Council's Security Service was known as something of a hard-nose, a reputation which he himself had carefully fostered. The truth was he was a gambler who so far had demonstrated an uncanny knack for holding the winning hand. But Jase Kurber, conscious of his own not too scientific background and more than a little doubtful of his ability to fool the dozen or so scientists who worked out of the legation, was convinced that this time the Director had gone too far. If I belly flop on this one, Kurber reflected, it'll be more his head than mine. The lanky investigator popped the green queltab into his mouth, swallowed it with an effort, then braced himself as the thing sent searing waves of hot and cold through his system. *Damn gut convulser. This so-called cure is worse than the disease!*

The light, actually not much brighter than the background sky but somehow pulsing with a vivid contrast, now loomed a few kilometers ahead of the shuttle. Below the light, balanced delicately atop a frail looking pylon thousands of meters tall, was an enormous bowl with an inner surface of intense, mind-stunning black.

This was Earthgate.

Kurber had transferred often and was prepared. But even the easing effect of the queltab did not disguise the brutal wrench of splitting and reassembly which assaulted every nerve at the moment the shuttle entered the light. As his stomach unknotted and his eyes cleared, he became aware that the sky beyond the window was suddenly a much deeper blue. Then the shuttle shuddered as its jets roared and the wings extended to gain lift in the thinner air. Kurber's mind knew that within a breath the shuttle had somehow traversed six hundred light-years, to a destination beyond the Pleiades. But even after having made the same trip a dozen times, his body and instincts still denied the fact. It was a normal reaction which he knew would be over within minutes. But he was also uncomfortably aware that of all the medical people who traveled through the gates into the galaxy, psychologists remained a stubbornly tiny minority.

The landscape below was all desert, varying shades of red splashed across flatlands and eroded highlands, occasionally fading to a dim fuzziness under the swirling sandstorms which were common here. This was a planet almost the twin of Mars; a dry and unprepossessing little world of a type common in the galaxy— big enough to have a tenuous atmosphere, close enough to its sun its temperature extremes could be handled with only a modest technology, but not friendly enough to host even the most primitive life-forms. Yet this was The Shouter, and a few kilometers behind the shuttle was Alien Artifact AA 6093, one of the remarkable structures which had given the planet its name.

A few hours' flight time around the curve of The Shouter was AA 11852, the portal to Kurber's ultimate destination on Phuili. First, however, was the mandatory stopover (for most of the shuttle's passengers) at the Colonization Authority's Reception Center. For Jase Kurber, it was at PERU, the Permanent Earth Research Unit, on this way station to the stars.

Ninety minutes later, the shuttle rolled to a dusty stop on a hard-pack runway. Two pressurized buses instantly coupled to the hull and began to absorb its load of chattering colonists and their families. Their destinations, after processing in the Reception Center, could be any of nearly ten thousand worlds assigned for human colonization: from Hubris, a mere three hundred light-years from The Shouter; to Farhome, a garden world thirty thousand lights beyond the hub. Not that it made any difference how far or how close. The mere act of walking the length of the shuttle's main cabin took more time than it did to transfer to the galactic rim.

Kurber had to suit up so he could be driven to PERU aboard an open six-wheeled vehicle which was definitely not intended for passengers. After loading half a dozen crates from the shuttle's hold onto the vehicle's flatbed, the taciturn driver accelerated in the direction of the blocky four-story PERU building as if his air supply was about to run out. His passenger—apparently just another package—was eventually delivered, flustered but unharmed, into the presence of PERU's Deputy Assistant Research Administrator.

"Sorry about that," Esham Pitte apologized after wincing at Kurber's blistering complaint. "Budgetary restraints have forced us to use PhD's as errand boys,

and one or two are quite hostile about the situation."
He shrugged. "Truth is, the A.R.A.'s much better at
soothing ruffled feelings than I am."

"Where is she?"

"With Peter Digonness on Van Buren's World. Something big, apparently."

Doesn't have to be that big to get those two together,
Kurber mused. The relationship between Genevieve
Hagan and the former head of Expediters was well
known. And, in the current situation, awkward. "Dammit, I have to see her!"

"I don't think so." The Deputy A.R.A. grinned.
"You know, I am rather enjoying this. It's not every
day I get the chance to assign a cloak and dagger
man."

Kurber was too experienced to react to this unexpected turn. He merely propped his chin in one hand
and inquired gently, "Oh?"

"I know you are an S.S. operative assigned to Phuili,
that I am to use this office to give you legitimacy, and
that I am supposed to transform you into the semblance of an expediter before the next Phuili shuttle
leaves." Pitte glance at his watch. "Which is in about
twenty-three hours."

"I see." Kurber paused for a moment, his thin face
thoughtful. Then he shrugged. "Okay, so you are my
contact. As far as turning me into an expediter is
concerned, is that so impossible? Some of Expediters'
best people came from Security."

"One or two only. And if you have the example of
Gia Mayland in mind, you are barking up the wrong
tree. Even she had to submit to a couple of years of
field training after she transferred out of the S.S."

"Just do your best, huh?" Kurber asked, thinking of
the woman who had gone from Security to Expediters,
and then on to fame as the one who had opened up
Earthgate and eliminated twenty-six dreary months of
travel time between Earth and The Shouter. "Ah . . .
I beg your pardon?"

"When were you last on The Shouter?" Pitte repeated patiently.

"About nine months ago. I was passing through from a job on Markov Four."

"Hmm." Pitte rubbed his chin. "That means there are a few still here who might remember you. Okay, we'll conceal the truth behind a half truth—to the effect that you are following in Gia Mayland's hallowed footsteps from Security to Expediters. You are still a trainee, of course, which explains your lack of experience. How am I doing?"

"Pretty good," Kurber said, surprised. "Is it possible you yourself came out of Security?"

Pitte sighed. "You don't have to go that route just to learn deviousness. I can hardly remember the time when an expediter's job was simply to 'expedite' communication between scientists of varying disciplines. Now we are also required to function as diplomats and lobbyists, as well as paper shufflers. It's one reason why Peter Digonness got himself assigned to Van Buren's World, and why Jenny is with him right now. Those two are pretty close, you know."

"So I have heard." Digonness and Genevieve Hagan were famous for their role in the discovery of the purpose of the AAs, and for many people they still exemplified the true meaning of expediter. Kurber was beginning to realize this was one role he would not find easy. "Perhaps it would be better," he said, "if you simply gave me a few pointers on how to expedite."

During the next several intensive hours, as the Deputy A.R.A. drilled him on the history, objectives, and procedures of Expediters, Kurber began to understand the frustrations of those who currently belonged to that organization. Originally a communicator, with enough basic knowledge of several scientific skills he could meld a quarrelsome mix of specialists into a coherent scientific team, the typical expediter was now—as Pitte had sadly pointed out—anything but. The idea behind Expediters had been a good one, and indeed the demand for its services was as strong as ever. But science as now taught in Earth's schools was not as parochial as it used to be, and the current crop of graduates did not need middlemen to help them interact constructively with each other. But they still seemed to need someone through whom they could interact with the "outside" world; especially if that someone had the ability to be as much at home with a research project on the far side of the galaxy, as he was seeking increased grants from politicians or peacemaking between man and Phuili.

The caninelike Phuili had already been on The Shouter for centuries when the first human ship ventured out of the Pleiades' shadow and detected the screaming radiation source a couple of hundred lights beyond that nebula-hazed star cluster. Fortunately, the Phuili were by nature an obsessively curious people, so they allowed the setting up of a human research station on The Shouter so that their own scientists could in turn study these clever primates. Instantly, the issue of human "intelligence" became a controversial one, cutting to the heart of the mystical concept of Phuili exclusiveness in the galaxy. The result was a schizoid compromise in which individual humans were accepted as equals, while humanity was condescendingly regarded as a lesser species which happened to have an unusual aptitude for technology.

The potential for conflict was consequently a factor from the beginning, setting human pride and assertiveness against Phuili pride and conservatism. But those who had created the AAs—though long departed from the physical universe—reached out from across eons of time and infinity of distance, to nudge the two species toward a kind of awkward compatibility. It was understandably a precarious relationship, resting uneasily on a substrata of bigotry and mistrust. Nevertheless, among individuals of both species, there developed a reluctant realization that in many ways human and Phuili complemented each other; that as far as the exploration of the galaxy was concerned, the sum was showing evidence of being greater than its parts.

But there were those, human as well as Phuili, who remained implacable in the hostility to the infant duality. Hence the reason for the increasing diplomatic role of Expediters; the only human organization having enough influence with high-level Phuili to prevent minor grievances attaining crisis proportions. But in cases involving deliberate trouble-mongering, diplomacy as a healing process could not be applied until the cause was expunged. "Which," Jase Kurber explained, "is where Security comes in."

"Comes in for what?" the Deputy A.R.A. asked, puzzled. "What is happening on Phuili anyway?"

"Are you familiar with a publication called *Universe Realities*?"

Pitte nodded. "I've heard of it. Makes the Jew-hating propaganda of Hitler's Nazis seem amateurish."

"Translated copies are currently being circulated on Phuili."

"My god." Pitte's eyes widened with shocked disbelief. "How the hell did that happen?"

"It's easy if you consider that one microchip can hold the text of a dozen issues. Someone in the legation is smuggling the chips in from Earth, then passing them on to a Phuili group with the rather unsubtle title of 'The Human Eaters.' The Eaters in turn handle readout, translation, and distribution. The poison is slow-acting, but it is apparently working. If it is not stopped, and damn soon, Earth-Phuili relations are going to be right back to square one."

"Talk to the leaders . . ."

"We have. And we think they understand. Trouble is, they are bound by a code which was old when our ancestors were still huddling in caves. According to that code, any form of slander against their ancient society is what they call a 'supreme crime.' I'll leave you to guess what the punishment is. At the same time, however, the Phuili are solemnly committed to the protection of human lives and property on their world. The dilemma for them is obvious, and ultimately has only one solution."

"Kick all humans off Phuili."

"Exactly. My job is to find the mole and get *him* off Phuili while there is still time to defuse the situation. I can't go in as a cop because he will simply suspend operations until after I have gone. But if I am just another expediter . . ."

"Give me your ident," PERU's Deputy Assistant Research Administrator said. He accepted the small disc and handed over another. "I guess we're one up on you, friend. This was coded directly from Earth even before you made the transfer." He smiled and extended his hand. "Jase Kurber, welcome to Expediters."

Sensors extended and computers humming, the ship floated inert in the ring system of the sixth planet. Within the long hull, the complement of Phuili scientists studied the incoming data with emotions ranging from excitement to apprehension. The presence of intelligent life in this system was obvious, the advisability of contact not so. There was a strangeness about this new race and its swarming ships; about the slagged planets, moons, and asteroids which were being exploited with ruthless abandon.

Increment by minute increment, the visitors were painstakingly deciphering the signals being exchanged between the smog-shrouded second world and the hundreds of outposts scattered throughout the system. There was frequent reference to the "Great Work," a mysterious activity somehow tied in with the mad plundering of the system's resources. There was statistical information, dealing with mundanes such as shipping requirements and production quotas. At no time or on no frequency could the Phuili detect the subtleties of culture or entertainment. Not even messages from home—those tenuous links of personal contact surely so necessary for warm-blooded beings with roots in the soil of a home world.

The Phuili were uneasy, especially as they garnered further disquieting facts from the remains of a big-brained, silver-furred and undoubtedly warm-blooded biped they had retrieved from the wreckage of a small spacecraft on a nearby moonlet. To the logical Phuili, the contrast between this graceful being and its compact, efficiently designed spacecraft on the one hand, and the senseless rampage of its species through the system on the other, was too much akin to a flawed computer program which defied analysis.

There was menace here; subtle, unexplainable, yet as real as a slumbering carnivore. So the visitors withdrew to the edge of the great dark, where they prepared their ship for phase-shift into multilight.

But only milliseconds before the PS drive unleashed the tremendous energies necessary to thrust the ship and its contents beyond the constraints of normal spacetime, one of its hull sensors detected and recorded an event near the second planet . . .

"Welcome to Expediters," the Deputy A.R.A. had said. A happy if not unexpected phrase to the ears of one who has spent years preparing for the great moment. But Jase Kurber was not one of those; the plan had merely required that he act like an expediter—not actually be one!

He snapped the ident disc out of his wrist bracelet and looked at it. A small marvel of technology; imprinted with his personal history, health status, retinal identification patterns. And now his membership number and classification in Expediters. The situation on Phuili had to be drastic for Security and Expediters to go to such an extreme. Ident discs were sacrosanct, guaranteed, and accepted by every military and law agency in human space, and they were not changed easily. In fact, they were hardly changed at all. No temporary expedient, this. Kurber was now, and for the foreseeable future, an expediter.

How did they get Kreinhauser to agree to it? the former security agent wondered. Some pretty persuasive arguments must have been used to get the old Director to agree to the permanent transfer of one of his own to a rival agency.

How do I feel about it?

Actually, not bad. Despite Pitte's lament about how things had deteriorated since the old days, Expediters remained a prestige outfit right out there on the cutting edge of human progress. Nevertheless, Kurber felt an uneasy twinge as he thought about the humans on Phuili who would undoubtedly seek his "special" talents. And which of them was the mole? Though he had been briefed by Pitte, those people were still only a collection of names to him. All seemed competent in their field, none were extraordinary enough to stand out—which, of course, a good mole never does.

"Entry in two minutes," the P.A. said. Kurber glanced through the shuttle window at the rapidly advancing outline of AA 11852, popped the queltab and braced himself. Later, as his insides rearranged themselves back to normal and his eyes cleared, he looked down on a broad blue-green plain and a city. He had barely time to notice the almost mathematical regularity of the city's alternating rings of towers and parkland before the shuttle banked steeply and glided to a gentle touchdown on a broad, smooth runway.

As soon as they stopped rolling, a ground tug hooked on to the shuttle and towed it alongside a pillbox-shaped structure rimmed with circular ports. A boarding tube extended from one of the ports and thumped against the hull at the forward air lock. After a few seconds the inner door swung open and a thin, harried-looking human entered. "I am Barton Hale from the legation. Please follow me." Without waiting for a response the man disappeared back into the tube. The shuttle's eleven passengers obediently lined up and shuffled after him into a circular room about five meters across. The walls and floor of the room were heavily padded.

"You are aboard a car of the local subsurface transport network," Hale announced. He was sitting on the floor, his back pressed firmly against the wall padding. "It is not a gentle ride, so I suggest you all assume this same position."

With varying degrees of difficulty everyone accepted Hale's advice, and hardly had the last one—a plump diplomat in an old-fashioned jumpsuit—groaned himself down, when the floor abruptly fell away from beneath them. After about five seconds of headlong descent, the vehicle deaccelerated, rotated, then surged in a horizontal direction. Kurber sprawled against his neighbor, who laughed and pushed him upright. "Is this your first time, Mr. Kurber?"

He looked at her. In her early thirties, neat and slim, with wide-eyed almost elfin features, she was not the type one would easily forget. "Do you know me?" he asked.

"Of you," she corrected. She held out her hand. "My name is Gia Mayland."

Her handshake was firm, impersonal. "Well, I'm damned," Kurber said. Then he laughed. "I'm sorry. Honest, I won't ask for your autograph."

"Good. And I won't volunteer it," the woman once popularized by the media as the "Earthgate girl" replied. She went on, "I understand you recently saw our former boss. How is the old gentleman these days?"

"Fine," Kurber replied, wondering how much she knew. "He . . . ah . . . sent you his regards."

"I doubt that," she came back primly. "Director Kreinhauser was not exactly pleased when I told him I was transferring to Expediters. And now you have followed along the same course, I doubt he likes you either."

Kurber was beginning to feel like an actor who had been thrown into a play without first seeing the script. "Yes, but I . . ."

"It's a bit unusual for one with your lack of experience being assigned to an important post such as Phuili, but I'm sure you can handle it. In any case, I will be around for a while, and will be available if you need me—which I hope you won't. I am not on Phuili to expedite."

Because she was speaking in a conversational tone, audible to any of the others aboard the vehicle should they choose to listen, Kurber suspected Gia Mayland was not talking to him alone. She seemed, in fact, to be cleverly reinforcing his cover as the new Resident Expediter, though that was hardly proof she knew the real nature of his assignment on Phuili. "Why are you here?" He asked. "Or isn't that a proper question?"

She shrugged. "I'm here to renew a friendship. A Phuili I once knew as David."

"David?" And then an explosion of consonants: "Davakinapwottapellazanzis?" It was the plump diplomat, bearing a look of smugness on his apple-cheeked features as he came over and settled his broad rump next to Gia. "Forgive an old man's intrusion, but I know David quite well. In fact, it is because of his tutoring that I may be the only human alive who can properly pronounce a Phuili name."

"True enough," Gia agreed. "But who cares?" She turned to Kurber. "This rather large gentleman is Mason Dewitte, the legation's trade specialist. Mason, this is our new R.E., Jase Kurber."

"Splendid." The fat man beamed at Kurber. "And don't worry about your lack of experience, young man. The people here get on very well together, so I doubt there will be much demand for your services."

"That is nice," the recently appointed expediter commented, unsure if he should be grateful or disappointed.

"We're almost there," Hale called. "Brace yourselves." The vehicle shuddered, swung about, and then shot vertically upward. As it lurched to a stop, the padded entrance door slid aside to reveal a concrete walkway rimmed with slender, spike-leafed trees. The outside air was cool, damp, and so unpleasantly pungent it caused several people to gasp. "You'll get used to it," Hale said cheerfully. "If it's any consolation, the Phuili find Earth's air equally as offensive."

The legation was housed in a modest tower behind

which others towers rose in serried ranks against a sky which was a paler blue than Earth's. Though the Phuili did not seem to have much use for windows, the skyline was not unlike that of many modern cities Kurber had seen. The only obvious difference was the lack of noise. They could not even hear their own footsteps—the "concrete" walkway had a gentle resilience like good turf. So it was almost a relief to enter the comfortable human environment of the legation, to view the uninspiring furniture and decor of the entrance lobby.

A prim-faced woman appeared at Kurber's side. "Are you Jase Kurber?"

"That's right."

"This way, please."

"See you later," Dewitte called as Kurber followed the woman across the lobby. He looked around for Gia, but she had already disappeared. He was shown into a small room containing nothing but an ident unit on a small table. "Disc, please," the woman said.

So that's it! How the Phuili legation had suddenly acquired this Pri-A1 classification was a mystery, but it did explain why a mere impersonation would have bounced Kurber back to The Shouter even before he had a chance to draw breath. He fingered the release on his bracelet. "Isn't this a bit unusual?"

"It is required." The woman held out her hand. "That is, if you do not wish to return on the next flight."

Kurber chuckled as he handed over the I-disc. "Succinctly put." He leaned over the machine and peered into the eyepiece. There was a wink of light and he stood up. Then the woman slid the disc into a slot at the side of the machine. A light flashed green, and then another.

The woman returned the disc and watched as he snapped it back into the bracelet. Her lips twitched as he asked politely, "So my particulars check out, huh?"

She pointed to a door on the far side of the room.

"You will wait in there." The twitch became a stiff smile. "Please."

Feeling he had made a conquest of sorts, Kurber smiled back. "Of course." Then he entered the next room.

He was not overwhelmingly surprised to find Gia Mayland waiting for him there. But it required a trained reflex of deadpan as he saw her companion.

"Gweetings, Kurber," the Phuili said.

The being was a little more than a meter in height, humanoid, with a pink-fleshed canine head which reminded the man of the bull terrier he had grown up with as a child. Large, beautiful eyes regarded the newcomer quizzically. "Please to sit," the Phuili invited.

Kurber sat, with a side glance at the woman. She smiled encouragingly.

"I am David," the Phuili said. "Once I work wiz Gia when we look for gates."

"Ah. You are the one who knows Mason Dewitte."

The long head inclined. "He zink he know how speak Phuili."

Recognizing sarcasm, Kurber wanted to laugh. Instead, "Why am I here?"

"About weason you come to Phuili. About need to stop bad information going to Human Eaters."

Again, Kurber looked inquiringly at Gia. "There are no secrets here," she told him. "David and I know you are on Phuili to smoke out the human who is causing this trouble."

Helplessly, he looked at the two dissimilar individuals. "But why me? Gia, you are ex-Security . . ."

She laid her hand on his arm. Her touch tingled. "Aside from being out of practice, I am also too well known." Suddenly, a brilliant smile. "Besides, you happen to be good. If I had remained with the outfit, I don't doubt you would have been my sector chief by now."

Kurber frowned. "I am an expediter. I take that seriously."

"So you are—and should. But you should also know

that it was Giesse Frobert who clamped Pri-A-one on this legation. The matter is serious, Jase. More than you realize."

Kurber was astonished. The Chairman of the World Union Council was known for his disdain of anything other than what he constantly referred to as "the larger picture," so would hardly have intervened unless it involved far more than even a threatened debacle on Phuili. "Look, I understand how damaging the material from *Universe Realities* is to Earth-Phuili relations. But enough to get the Chairman involved? And why Pri-A-one anyway? There's no . . ."

Gia said, "There is another space-going race."

Kurber stared. *So it has finally happened!* "My god," he whispered. Then, "Has there been contact?"

"No. And we pray there will not be." Gia turned to the Phuili. "May I tell him? Time is limited, and we do share a common tongue."

The Phuili said gravely, "You tell. It best he know pwoper."

"Thank you, David." Gia produced a photograph of a graceful, silver-furred humanoid. The skull was obviously crushed, but enough remained to indicate a braincase of impressive proportions. "Pretty, huh? He was found by a Phuili expedition operating out of Groombra Four, about two thousand lights rimward. Millions of those beings are swarming about their solar system like maggots on a corpse—literally devouring everything from dust up to planetoids in an apparent lust for astronomical quantities of raw materials."

"Materials for what purpose?" Kurber asked, his attention diverted from the picture.

"God knows. The Phuili commander sensibly decided to pull out before he was discovered and wiped out. You see, enough had already been deciphered from the local radio traffic to determine that this new race represents a threat of awsome significance." Gia tapped the picture. "Jase, these lovely beings are antilife!"

"It iss zeir holy mission," David explained, his alien

features intent and solemn. "To zem, life not zeir own must be destwoyed. Alweady zey have stewilized zeir own world and anozer which once had life. Soon, zey look to stars."

When he was only five years old, Jase Kurber was accidentally locked in an unlighted basement for more than seven hours. He had not thought about it for years, but suddenly it was there like yesterday—a child's eternity during which he cowered in a corner and waited for unimaginable things to errupt out of the dark. Now, from the greater dark . . .

Kurber sternly quelled his racing imagination and commented reasonably, "Looking to the stars is one thing, getting there is another. Neither of you have said anything about them having that kind of capability."

"Jase, what do you know about the history of the P.S. drive?" Gia asked.

"Other than that it was a long and very rocky road between theory and practice, not much," Kurber replied, wondering what this was leading to. "I know there were some pretty spectacular accidents along the way, including the addition of a fair-sized crater on Luna farside." His eyes widened. "Wait a minute— are you telling me such an event was observed from the Phuili ship?"

She nodded. "A burst was detected just before the ship phase-shifted. What it signifies is not definite, of course, but it's a pretty strong indication."

"A bloody powerful one, if you ask me," he muttered.

"So now you know why your assignment here is so important. The Silver People have to be stopped before they start, Jase, which certainly won't happen if we and the Phuili are squabbling with each other instead of acting against the common threat." Gia added passionately, "The supplier of that xenophobic garbage has to be found and neutralized!"

Where to start?
There was no doubt there was open resentment at

the presence of humans on the planet, but that was nothing new. Phuili life was largely ritualistic, based on a complex set of rules in many ways similar to the Jewish *Talmud*, though much older and certainly more extensive. Add a class structure even more stratified than the ancient Hindu caste system, and the potential against the freewheeling humans was not only explosive but increasingly probable—as Kurber was reminded each time he tried to leave the legation on his own.

Mason Dewitte explained, "Old hands like myself must always be present to make sure nothing is said or done to offend any of the local people, while at the same time we expect the newer ones—like yourself—to perhaps recognize openings that in our caution we may have overlooked." The fat man had joined Kurber on one of the latter's first excursions into the city, a rather obvious chaperoning which Kurber accepted only because he had to. Dewitte continued, "It's like a sparring match with the other side having all the advantage: their rules and turf, our ignorance. Until recently we humans seem to have held our own, but with that crud from *Realities* seeping in . . ."

"I heard about that," Kurber said cautiously. They were crossing an open area in which booths were set up in the manner of a street market. Buyers were circulating about in abundance, but there were no sellers. Instead, purchase seemed to be a matter of selecting an item, looking at its price, entering something into a counter-mounted keyboard, and then walking away with the item. It was an awesome display of honesty which further emphasized the gulf between Phuili and human. Equally disquieting was the lack of sound to accompany the visual bustle; an occasional Phuili guttural only intensified Kurber's sense of being a male Alice in an unreal wonderland. He winced as a Phuili family—an adult and two smaller ones—hurriedly moved away as the humans approached. "Did you see that?"

Dewitte nodded. "Sub Elites." He indicated the bright colors worn by the three. "I guess you'd call them upper middle class. Moderately educated, economically comfortable, stalwart adherents of the ancient traditions. If they get stirred up enough, they are the ones who will get us kicked off Phuili—and the Elites won't argue."

"Elites?"

"The top brass; scientists mostly. Great theoretical people but slow on application—which is hardly surprising if you consider the built-in inertia of this ossified society. I suppose that is why the Elites are so uncharacteristically garrulous when they are dealing with us humans; our constant adaptation to technological change must be pretty startling by their standards. David is an Elite of course, as are most of the Phuili you will meet. Nominally they rule, though always *by* the rules. The Subs make sure of that."

"Elites. Sub Elites. Then what?"

"Everyone else. The proletariat or 'prols' if you prefer. Generally they are not too bright, programmed to a hereditary trade, conditioned to acceptance of their lowly lot. The most stable labor pool you can imagine."

"So the Czar thought before nineteen seventeen."

"Not the same, my boy, not at all the same. You see on this planet, there is no cross-class migration. None! Over hundreds of generations, the Phuili have consequently evolved to fit their roles; mentally as well as physically. The Elites have evolved brain power, the Subs into natural administrators, the rest into machinists, farmers, shoemakers, and so on. It's a helluva system, Jase, and until we humans barged into their universe, it was one that worked."

Implying, Kurber supposed, that the mere presence of humans had thrown a wrench into the machinery. But as he continued to watch the activity in the market, he somehow doubted that. Every Phuili in sight was, in fact, going about his business as if the two beings from another world did not exist. For Kurber it was not a pleasant experience to be so thoroughly ignored. The reaction of the three Subs, who had shown their dislike of the humans in the most obvious way, was at least understandable. But the absolute nonreaction of these others . . .

He stepped aside as half a dozen of the drably clad prols passed close by, their large eyes blank and unwavering. Dewitte chuckled. "Don't worry, they won't walk over you. They are simply ignoring what they don't understand. In their well-ordered little minds, humans don't compute."

Kurber looked at the other sharply. "You speak as if they are biological robots."

The fat man shrugged and did not comment. But his silence said enough.

It was clearly apparent that Kurber had to be far more than just a tourist to unlock the Phuili enigma. Gaining the confidence of the "natives" was not in the cards for any human, at least not for the immediate future. Certainly the enormous bottom tier of the Phuili hierarchy did not care; for that ninety-five percent of the population, what humans did, said, or wrote simply did not matter. The "flat-faces" were entirely peripheral to the scheme of things. Like the stars from which they had supposedly come, their effect on the ancient routines was no more than a container of water spilled into the ocean.

Conversely, the Elites knew what was happening, and cared. But in their way they were as much bound by tradition as the masses, and would have no hesitation in ordering the humans off Phuili if the Subs demanded it.

Which, like an endless circle, always brought the problem back to the Sub Elites. Jealous guardians of the Phuili universe, their only reason for not objecting to the establishment of a human legation on Phuili was simply a restatement of the principle: "the devil we know is easier to handle than the one we don't." The extremists among them, since formally established as the "Human Eaters," had, of course, gladly accepted the opportunity to circulate translated copies of the Earth publication *Universe Realities*; to prove beyond doubt what most Subs wanted to believe anyway—that humans and their inferior ideas represented an evil which had to be expunged, starting with the removal of every flat face from Phuili itself.

For once, the massive inertia of Phuili society was beneficial for the beleaguered humans; what had already been accepted would be difficult to turn around. But unless the flow of Earth-originated hate propaganda was stopped, what had at best been reluctant acceptance would inevitably degenerate into active hostility—and the malevolence currently germinating around a distant sun would, in the perhaps not too distant future, extract a terrible price.

Gia read, " 'All thinking beings will protect what is theirs. Okay, that is natural for anyone with the concept of personal property. But what if that property is in dispute? What if one party has arbitrarily declared that *all* property is his, who refuses to change his mind even after another legitimate claimant comes on the scene?

'I am, of course, referring to the Phuili. You all know that. They maintain that the galaxy is theirs, that we humans are a lesser species who happen to live on their property. They find us interesting in a condescending sort of way, they even humor us by permitting minor scientific and diplomatic exchanges. But they also study us; intently. And when they finally realize the truth—that we humans are not only equal but are perhaps a superior species, they will act. They will attempt to destroy us!

'My friends, I hate to use the term "pre-emptive strike." It has too many ugly connotations from our turbulent past. But I do say we must prepare for the worst, that when the attack comes—as it must—we will be in a position to give the dog-faces a lesson they will never forget!' "

Gia disgustedly tossed the sheet aside. "And so it goes on, ad nauseam. Lector Fraser, number one bigot, recorded verbatim within the doting pages of *Universe Realities.*"

"Which he owns." Kurber looked at the sheet of paper on the floor with distaste. "Is it all like that?"

"Not all the time. Sometimes the lord and publisher of that muckrag sounds forth on his second favorite subject; creationism. I remember one issue in which he used only a few thousand words to say that man, being the exclusive creation of the Supreme Being, is therefore destined to occupy the universe."

Even David recognized Gia's sarcasm. "Same wiz Human Eaters." Sadly, he shook his long head. "Iss why some alweady pweach *jihad.*"

Startled, Kurber looked at the little alien. He did not know how David had picked up the Moslem word for holy war, but neither did he think to question its use. He had learned enough to be quite certain the Eaters would sacrifice themselves as well as half their world if they could be sure those who were left would resume the purity of the old ways. The same was probably true of the fanatics who belonged to Lector Fraser, though because of the diversity of human society . . ."

Kurber had an idea. "David, can you take me to the Human Eaters?"

The reply was prompt. "Not possible. Human Eaters not talk wiz humans."

"Then how do the *Realities* chips get to them?"

"Ozer Sub Elites make twansfer."

Gia nodded. "None of the Subs like us, but a few occasionally have business at the legation."

"Then assemble those few for me. I bet at least one will be a contact."

"What do you have in mind?"

"Communication," Kurber said.

"*Zey must stopped before weach gate on Toomis.*"
"*Toomis?*"
"*What humans call Gwoombwa Four. Light twavel fwom zeir system, forty year.*"

"That close? That's only six weeks with a P.S. drive!"

"Iss twue. Zey not yet have phase shift, so still westwicted to zeir own system. But our ship see one P.S. expewiment, so I zink not long to first starship."

"If they find that gate and figure out its function . . ."

"Many die. Worlds die."

"So we stop them. Do you know how?"

"Wiz sun seeds."

"Sun seeds? What . . . ?"

"Known by Phuili long time. Two pwobes dwop into sun. First twigger weaction under photosphere, vewy big flares. When weaction at peak, second pwobe make sun nova. Not big, just enough destwoy life on close planets. Outer colonies die wizout support fwom home world."

"My god, what a weapon!"

"But must be done quick. Human Eaters gwow stwong, soon not allow work wiz humans."

"Anything to stop that madness escaping into the galaxy! What do you want from us?"

"Two human ships and cwews. Ships go Toomis gate and zen to sun of Silver People. Dwop seeds and come back."

"I don't understand. Human ships . . ."

"Destwuction of whole wace not possible for Phuili. Humans have big wars. Easy for you."

"Like hell it is! It's because of those big wars and what they did to us, no government would dare to even consider such a thing! Anyway, we honor our treaties. What happens in that area of space is strictly a Phuili affair."

"In zis case, not twue."

"Oh, I think so. You see, I was at the signing. Only Phuili . . ."

"Only human . . ."

"No . . ."

"No . . ."

Kurber had not heard of the deadlock, only that high level discussions were being held on The Shouter.

But even if he had, his approach would not be any different. The menace of the Silver People was still in the future, the widening schism between Earth and Phuili was now.

He had already spent a couple of monotonous days studying the legation's personnel records, solaced by the occasional presence of Gia Mayland who had somehow obtained the printouts without arousing the suspicions of the dragon lady at the front desk. Not that the records, despite their considerable content, told him anything beyond what he had already learned from Esham Pitte's briefing during the stopover at PERU. Seventeen people from varying but unstartling backgrounds, individualists, healthy extroverts, each extremely good at his or her specialty, none with apparently the slightest reason to want to upset the delicate status quo which existed between the two races.

Aware that even during quiet times an expediter was supposed to remain visible to his potential clients, Kurber made a point of taking his meals in the small dining lounge, sharing complaints at the uninspiring quality of the prepackaged food and sympathizing at the frustrations caused by the agonizing slowness of the local Phuili bureaucracy in answering requests to travel beyond the city.

Gia reacted with a smile when he told her about the frustrations. "Jase, you are the Resident Expediter. So why don't you expedite?" Then, seriously, "But you have other things on your mind. I will take care of it."

Two permits arrived within hours, and Kurber had to hide his embarrassment as the grateful recipients thanked him. Would they be as friendly if they knew how much he was into their professional and private lives, he wondered? Then he castigated himself for dwelling on irrelevancies. Other than Kurber himself, there was only one person attached to the legation who was not what he—or she—seemed to be, and that individual was buried so deep under one of seventeen increasingly familiar personae, Kurber was seriously beginning to doubt his chances of being able to identify the culprit by any conventional means.

So it was a relief when he answered a call within his quarters and heard Gia say cheerfully, "Remember you told me you would like to see a typical Phuili home? Well, it has been arranged. David and I will pick you up in one hour."

Kurber had not made any such request. But he had no difficulty translating, *"We have set up a meeting with the Subs. Coming?"*

"Great," he answered. "I'll be ready."

When he entered the lobby an hour later and found Gia and her Phuili friend chatting with Mason Dewitte and the prim receptionist, it seemed so innocent that for a moment he wondered if he actually had asked to meet a Phuili family. But as soon as they left the building and climbed into a Phuili ground car, he knew immediately this was not to be a social call.

"Three Subs are waiting for you in a residence unit a few klicks from here," Gia told him as David steered the low slung vehicle into an automated laneway which led directly toward the towers at the city's center. "We suspect at least one of them is a link between the legation and the Human Eaters, though if you challenge them with that possibility I doubt you will get any reaction other than a polite silence. Believe me, these people are conservative in a way that make our right-wingers look like Marxists."

"My mind is already made up," Kurber quoted. "So please do not confuse me with the facts."

"You have hit the nail on the proverbial head. And by the way, Jase, don't let on you are anything other than an expediter. If word of this meeting gets back to the legation—as it probably will—you are simply using your position as R.E. to try to counteract the effect of damaging, Earth-originated propaganda."

Kurber chuckled. "Don't worry about that. One thing I like about this assignment is that I *am* an expediter. So what is there to hide?"

Gia frowned. "You know what I mean," she said crossly.

It was an uncomfortable ride, sitting knees-up in a vehicle designed for riders the size of human children, so Kurber was not fully attentive to the passing scenery. But he did comment on the scarcity of street traffic.

"Day of Unforgetting," David said. "No work, people stay home and zink of Phuili way. Happen everwy twelve-day."

Gia explained. "It's the equivalent of our Sabbath, a sort of rededication using a common set of rituals at the same day and hour, all over the planet. It hasn't changed for thousands of years."

David nodded as he turned the vehicle into a parking area next to a slender tower. "More zan knowing." He added flatly, "Iss!"

One monosyllable encompassing an entire racial philosophy, though it took a few minutes—the time to reach a dim room on the tower's ninety-third floor—for Kurber to realize he had just heard the hard-core difference separating his own race from that of his small host. Belief, as humans know it, is a transient thing; gods became God, Zeus became Yahweh, unthinking subservience to invisible spirits became that modern cop-out known as agnosticism. Not so for the Phuili. For them, what had started as belief had with time hardened into fact, and as the centuries and then the millennia rolled by, into a knowledge literally encapsulated within the genes.

Realizing the impossible task he had set himself, Kurber wished he could exit the cramped elevator and even the planet, perhaps to find a place where security is the responsibility of the sheriff and where expediting is something done by the local mayor. It was too late for that, of course, much too late. So as he entered the dim room, it was with a certain grim determination.

The three Sub Elites were sitting behind a low table at the far side of the room. Introducing them as Paul, James, and Edward, David said, "I twanslate," and also sat at the table. David's one-piece garment of soft gray was in dignified contrast to the garish colors worn by the Subs. Also noticeable, even in the subdued light, was the fact that compared with his compatriots, David's head was longer and his skin of a lighter shade—seeming further confirmation of the evolutionary divergences wrought by this rigidly ancient culture.

Gia whispered. "It's your party, Jase."

Kurber shuddered. "I know." What followed, though not entirely fruitless, proved to be one of the most difficult interviews of his experience. Speaking through David, the three Subs could just have easily been one.

"I understand you all regularly visit the Earth legation," Kurber began.

"Yess."

"Also that you know of the bad writings which have been obtained and circulated by the group known as the Human Eaters."

"We know."

"Will you please tell me which of the humans brought those writings to Phuili?"

"No."

"I know the Human Eaters have no direct dealings with any human, so it has to be another Phuili who receives the microchips and delivers them to the Eaters. Is that Phuili one of you?"

Silence.

"Then I will examine the legation's records to determine which of you has the least reason to call there."

It was a long shot, and for a moment it seemed that the one known as Edward had shed his apparent indifference enough to betray a nervous tightening of his jaws. But in the bad light it could also have been a trick of Kurber's imagination, so the man continued,

"Actually it is not important which human and which Phuili is involved in this matter. What is important is that all the Phuili recognize the writings for what they are; the rantings of one human who certainly does not represent his kind. As a people we do *not* believe the Phuili are any threat to us, and we know we are not a threat to the Phuili. Neither does humanity and its leaders have any kind of plan to rule the galaxy. Such an idea is absolute nonsense, and can only be the product of a sick mind."

The reaction was immediate. "What one Phuili say, all Phuili do. What one human say, all human do. One sick, zen all sick. Human wace dangerwous. All must go back home planet fwom Phuili and Shouter. Phuili make galaxy safe."

The statement was so outrageous that for a moment Kurber was at a complete loss for words. Counter arguments raced through his mind, including the one in which he would describe the incredible variety of the human species; from Pygmy to European, Marxist to Monarchist, Technocrat to Mystic. But remembering a remark of Mason Dewitte, Kurber was quite sure anything he said would be rejected by the inflexible Subs because it "does not compute."

Damn you, I'm not done yet!

Kurber took a deep breath. "What about the builders of the AAs? Where do they fit into your scheme of things?"

The reply was bland. "Zey gone long time. Galaxy Phuili now."

Kurber felt he would strangle. Gia sensed the pent-up pressure and laid a hand on his arm. "It's not worth it, Jase. Don't play into the hands of the Eaters."

She was right, of course. Kurber took several deep breaths, letting the tension drain from him with each expelled lungful. "I think we had better go," he said.

It was only a straw, yet it was all he had. Kurber spoke about it as the still apologetic David drove them back to the legation. "Those three don't like humans, yet they were willing to talk to us. On the other hand, the Human Eaters feel soiled even if they see a human from a distance. Doesn't that suggest the Subs are not such a homogeneous group after all?"

"It only suggests they are not machines, Jase." Squeezed beside him in the ground car, Gia was an attractive antidote for Kurber's depression. "Sure, there are differences, though nowhere near to the same extent that we have on Earth. In fact, it is that fine balance between the Phuili norm and extreme which makes the *Realities* material so dangerous. In this society, push can all too easily become shove."

The sky was fading into evening. Ahead, the more modest towers of the city's perimeter were hard-edged shadows against a pink sky. In many ways Phuili was an attractive world, and now that Kurber's nose was becoming adjusted to its strange odors, he thought he understood why most of the humans stationed here were into their second two-year terms.

David had remained uncharacteristically silent as he guided the ground car through the darkening and silent streets. But the continuous flexing of his large ears indicated he was listening closely to the conversation of his human companions. He finally broke silence as they turned into the legation's approach lane. "Iss vewy bad. If Subs inwoke law, Elites must go wiz same. Only way is for bad information to stop."

Sorry, guys, it's in your court now. I sympathize, but the law is God and God is the law. So what can I do?

Not much, Kurber supposed bitterly, his brief consideration of the attractiveness of this world evaporating under a surge of anger. Yet, in a sense revitalized by his indignation, he wasted no time after he entered the legation in finding a computer terminal.

"Records," he said.

RECORDS, the machine replied.

"List all items imported from Earth, by the Phuili, during the past twelve months."

LISTING.

He was impatiently drumming his fingers on the console when Gia entered the room. After watching a moment, she said quietly, "Jase, I do not know you too well, but I think I recognize the symptoms. You are mad as hell and ready to pounce on every anomaly in sight."

"Okay, so you've been there. What did you do about it?"

She chuckled. "The same as you, I suspect. Fire random shots and hope one of them finds a target." Gia frowned as she peered over Kurber's shoulder at the rapidly scrolling display on the screen. "What are you looking for?"

"What I should have looked for as soon as I got here. The Phuili may have an advanced technology, but that doesn't make their computer systems compatible with ours. I'm guessing they have imported enough hard and software to analyze us humans right down to the last byte. I want to know what, when, and where."

"For readout and translation. Of course!"

"Of course," Kurber echoed, his smile sardonic. Not too successfully, he was trying to ignore Gia's proximity and the faint yet powerful subtlety of her fragrance. "This could be the lead to whoever in the legation is delivering what chip, to which Phuili, who in turn is taking it to any one of god knows how many establishments that have imported Earth-side equipment." He added dryly. "Our primitive technology is much in demand, it seems."

"Primitive is the word all right." Gia pointed at the screen. "Just look at that stuff. My young nephew was on to better things when he entered grade school."

"You sound surprised."

"Shouldn't I be?"

Kurber grinned. "You'll agree that most Sub Elites, though not as extreme in their views as the Human Eaters, are certainly sympathetic to the antihuman crusade. Right?"

"I don't see what that has to do with . . ."

"Fraser and his extremists probably number no more than a few hundred. But also there are thousands of borderline xenophobes, outwardly decent people who carry on their lives just like the rest of us."

Gia looked at the man puzzledly. "What are you saying?"

"Only that I suspect it would be quite revealing if

we had access to the background files of a few people in the licensing division of the Off-World Export Office."

Gia was startled by the idea. "My god, if that is true . . ."

His attention still largely occupied by the information rolling across the screen, Kurber went on absently, "Despite their infinite wisdom, however, those same bureaucrats still have not realized how much their restrictions have played into the hands of the Phuili hard-liners. Admittedly, the low level hardware they let through is adequate enough for simple readout, even for basic word-to-word translation. But for the hard-liners, the advantage is that the imported equipment *is* primitive; in effect being a further illustration of human inferiority."

"Damn and double-damn!" Gia took a deep breath and added angrily, "Jase, it's all so bloody stupid!"

"Sure it is. A sort of mutual, self-reinforcing paranoia." Suddenly Kurber's eyes widened and he jabbed the key which halted the flow of data. He touched another key, reversing the display by a few lines. "Now why," he wondered aloud, "do they need that particular item?"

The Great Work was nearly done. All that remained was the transfer of millions of beings, and then the final order from the Apex in his tower above a smog-shrouded sea. The other work would continue, of course. What once had only been hypothetical was now a distinct possibility, and teams were already being diverted to the orbital research stations. Either way, the race's holy mission would continue until all things were pure and matter itself was returned to the rigid matrix of the Giver's Law.

Nevertheless the Apex was worried. He had seen the reports of the strange burst of energy from the outer system, the similarity of its spectral components to the explosion which had destroyed Station Eighteen and which had required him to order the termination of the hundreds of thousands whose usefulness had been compromised by the lethal rays.

He did not doubt that life existed among the stars. Time after time, the possibilities had been demonstrated by those who studied the enrichment effect of novae and their shock waves on the interstellar medium. What was in doubt was the nature of that life—was it merely a crawling scum on the bottom of shallow seas, or had it learned to manipulate matter to the extent of building ships that could violate the Holy Void? In which case, what had been the nature of that incredibly concentrated burst of energy? A random natural happening? Faulty detectors? Or had there actually been . . . ?

The Apex dismissed the awful thought and sent for the Deputy Eight. "According to the current arrangements, when can I issue the Order?" he asked.

The Eight bowed. "At the Crossing of The Moons, your words will be the instrument by which every adult and lesser will at last know our race's holy destiny."

The Apex nodded, his gray-furred face thoughtful. "It would please me if it could be sooner. Indeed, much sooner."

Though the Eight was surprised, he did not show it. "It will be difficult. Already every available ship is committed. At each rendezvous there is so much to be transferred, so many to be prepared for . . ."

The Apex gestured impatiently. "That is only because we are organized for a simultaneous activation. Instead, what if we divert the ships to service only fifty of the Units?"

The Eight was shocked. "But the Day! The Knowing . . ."

"Is a ceremony, nothing more. That need not be changed. Nevertheless, I happen to know it will serve The Giver's purpose if a few circles of time are sacrificed so that fifty can be activated . . ." The Apex glanced out at two patches of light in the mud-colored sky. ". . . at the Opposite of The Moons."

Committed by holy oath to make the necessary changes, the bemused official finally bowed his way out of the room. The Apex remained in the darkness, his eyes glittering with an ancient hate as his thoughts pulled back the smog to reveal the lights of other suns. "Perhaps you are not there," he murmured softly, "in which case we will be a little premature. But if you are, very soon you will have much to fear . . ."

It had taken several days of intense negotiating to set it up. Though all the humans were cooperative, the idea of Phuili Subs participating in such a meeting was so startling it required the direct intervention of David and other Elites before Paul, James, and Edward were at last persuaded to attend. Noticeably the three Subs separated themselves as much as possible from the humans, who chatted in subdued tones as they tried to ignore the unusual presences at the far side of the lounge.

At exactly nineteen hours, Kurber, Gia, and David entered and took their places behind a small table. Gia started the proceedings.

"First," she said, "I will not waste time with the obvious. You all know about the written trash from Earth which has been circulating among the Phuili, and you are certainly knowledgeable enough to realize the damage it is causing. Anyway, Earth judged the matter serious enough to send an investigator . . ." Gia held up both hands in a gesture for silence. As the noise died down, she lowered her hands and smiled. "Yes, it is Jase Kurber. No, he is not Security. He *is* the Resident Expediter—with the additional mandate to identify and arrest the human who is responsible."

Mason Dewitte heaved his large bulk upright. "Young man, how long have you been an expediter?"

"Not long," Kurber admitted cautiously.

The fat man nodded. "I did not think so. All right, second question. Have you identified the miscreant?"

"I have."

"In that case Mr. Kurber, the floor is yours." Dewitte beamed and sat down.

Even the three Subs showed signs of interest, in that

sense being one with the humans. *You'd think I was about to announce who shot J.R.,* Kurber thought, remembering a recognized though obscure expression that had been in vogue during his college days. Looking at his audience of curious faces, human and alien, he prayed he was not about to transform some of that curiosity into hostility.

He cleared his throat. "Memory chips. That seemed the obvious means by which the Human Eaters have been acquiring extracts from *Universe Realities.* It was also apparent they could not be getting that material via the obvious route through the Phuili legation on Earth. The legation's staff is, after all, exclusively Elite, and will certainly refuse any order aimed against the interspecies relationship the Elites themselves helped to create. That is why my instructions are to find a human who has the motive and opportunity to smuggle the chips through this legation on Phuili."

"You're wasting your time," Barton Hale interrupted from the floor. Kurber had had very little contact with Hale since the hair-raising ride in from the shuttle terminal, though from what he had heard of the exobiologist's love of the put-down, he was certain he was about to experience that particular irritation. Deliberately taking the bait, Kurber asked mildly, "Why am I wasting my time, Mr. Hale?"

"For the obvious and simple reason that our psychological profiles say so," Hale retorted. "My god, even a storefront operator can recognize a xenophobe, and we were examined by the best psychologists in the business. Sorry, Mr. Kurber, but perhaps you should go back to expediting!" To the sound of scattered applause, he smiled smugly.

Kurber waited for silence. Then, "Who said anything about anyone being a xenophobe?"

"You did! You are the one who implied . . ."

"Mr. Hale, do you like the Phuili?"

"What kind of question is that? Of course, I do. I'd hardly be here if I didn't."

"How do you rate the Phuili against humankind?"

"I don't. As far as I am concerned, the Phuili are neither better or worse. They are simply . . ." Hale shrugged his thin shoulders. ". . . different."

"Very good, Mr. Hale. You have just expressed a sane, middle-of-the-road attitude that is undoubtedly shared by most of your colleagues. However, there is one person here who goes a lot farther than merely liking the Phuili; who idolizes them to the extent of believing—exactly as the Human Eaters—that humans are indeed a threat to an ancient and perfect society. Now I do not know if the psychologists have a name for that aberration, but I suspect it is one they either overlooked or considered unimportant. Which do you think, Mr. Hale?"

Hale did not reply, though Kurber felt a small glow of satisfaction at the man's obvious discomforture. Returning his attention to the main audience, Kurber continued, "I admit I was as surprised as anyone when I realized we were dealing with the opposite to a xenophobe. But for me, that was only the second surprise. The first was something I discovered just before I identified the person we have heard described as 'miscreant.' " Kurber signaled, the lights dimmed and data began scrolling across the big monitor at the front of the lounge.

"Most of you have seen these lists before; itemizing hardware the Phuili have brought in to further their studies of Earth and human society. You will note there are at least a dozen institutions that now have the capability to read imported memory chips, which seems to support the theory that that is how *Realities* is getting to the Human Eaters. There is, however, a problem. Since Pri-A-one was imposed a few weeks ago, everything shipped to this legation has been examined and cleared by a special unit assigned from the Security Service."

Expecting a reaction, Kurber paused. What he did get, instead of indignation, was a stony silence; unexpected though illuminating. It seemed he had underestimated the intelligence of these people, who clearly had anticipated the intervention of the S.S. as soon as they heard of Pri-A1 and the reason for its imposition. Feeling uncomfortably like an adolescent trying to lecture a group of adults, the expediter sighed and continued,

"Okay, we know two things. First, that someone here is the source of the *Realities* material. Second, that there is apparently no way for illicit chips to get through Earth's security check, let alone to the Eaters."

"So perhaps it ain't chips," someone suggested helpfully.

Despite himself, Kurber chuckled. "How right you are." He turned to the monitor. "What fooled me and everyone else is the use of a technology that predates computers." He pointed. "Optec Reader one-nine-nine-zero VX, delivered to Institution Three in this city. In plain language, I-Three has an optical microscope rigged for amplification and projection. An ideal instrument for reading microdots."

"I'll be damned," Mason Dewitte said.

Kurber looked inquiringly at the fat man. "Something familiar?"

"Speaking as a devotee of twentieth century mystery fiction, darn right it's familiar!" Dewitte raised his voice so everyone could hear. "A microdot is a piece of high resolution optical film, small enough it can be disguised as the dot at the end of a written sentence." Dewitte wagged a stubby finger. "Jase, I think you are a nice fellow. But if you do not make the rest of it short and snappy, I may be tempted to revise that opinion."

Kurber chuckled. "Short and snappy it is." He held up a slim magazine, typical of a type of specialist publication that had held its own despite mass electronics. " 'Social Impact of Extra-Terrestrial Relationships,' " he read from the title page. "This little mag and others like it are also imported by the Phuili, though in this case they do not have to order through their people on Earth. Instead they arrange for photocopies of issues brought in by the legation's staff for their own use. So it's no problem for the person who makes those copies, to attach a microdot according to a prearranged formula—such as the end of the seventh sentence on page four. By the way, Ms. Doerker, how do you get the microdots in the first place? Letters from home?"

The only human who did not react sat with prim disdain among the stares and exclamations of her colleagues. Finally, as the excitement died down, Elise Doerker, the legation's receptionist, said calmly, "That is very clever of you, Mr. Kurber."

It was not quite the hysterical denial Kurber expected, and before he could respond there was an explosion of gutturals from the back of the room. No longer silent bystanders, the three Subs were at their full diminutive height as each in turn fired a verbal barrage at the Elite who shared the platform with Gia and Kurber.

David translated, "Zey not wish human female harmed. She fwiend of Phuili who agwee humans bad for Phuili ways. Zey say Human Eaters not act more if female stay and numbers of humans on Phuili not incwease."

The offer was so unexpected that for a moment Kurber wondered if it was an implied threat rather than the concession it seemed to be. But it was a fleeting thought, dismissed in favor of the more probable explanation that the Subs were making the best of a bad situation. Without Doerker's active support they could no longer receive and pass on the grist for the Eaters' propaganda mill, and without effective propaganda the Eaters themselves were no longer a problem.

How about that. I have successfully completed my first assignment as an expediter!

Under normal circumstances Kurber knew he had reason to be at least a little euphoric. But there was still the fact of the Silver People, and from recent dispatches he knew that the human and Phuili negotiators on The Shouter had come no closer to agreeing on a course of action to end the threat. If humans and

Phuili had anything in common at all, it was the incredible inertia of their bureaucracies—which permitted representatives of the two races to argue in useless circles while the margin between threat and disaster was becoming perilously narrow. Ethics are fine, an abhorrence against genocide a must for any civilized society, but against true savagery there can be no diplomacy. Humans, with their Caligulas, Hitlers, and Katryn Gervaks should know that. So should the Phuili. It was a Phuili expedition, after all, that had returned with the evidence of this horror in the making.

Perhaps there is another way.

With a rashness belying his natural caution, Kurber got David to ask the Subs, "Do you know if the Human Eaters believe that the human race should be destroyed?"

The reply, though indirect, was vehement. "Iss wong to destwoy wace!" Then, guardedly, "Human Eaters want humans not anywhere except planets of human sun. Human Eaters say galaxy Phuili."

"What if there is a third race, a race dedicated to the destruction of all life other than its own?"

"If attacked, Phuili defend."

"But if the Human Eaters knew of such a threat, would they wait to be attacked? Or would they move to destroy the attackers?"

If the Subs were human, Kurber did not doubt the provocative nature of his questioning would by now have involved him in a shouting match. But he was gambling on the higher flash point of the Phuili temperament, as well as their natural curiosity to know where he was leading. Nevertheless, the delay in the answering of this last question made him nervous. Finally,

"Perhaps Human Eaters not wait. But Human Eaters not destwoy wace."

"What if the responsibility for such a preemptive act can be shared? What if others, equally threatened, offer cooperation?"

Gia hissed at him. "What others? Jase, you know

damn well the government will never sanction such a thing!"

"Who said anything about the government?" Kurber asked innocently. To the Subs, "Well? If they are not required to do the job entirely on their own, would the Human Eaters do what is necessary to save Phuili and the galaxy?"

This time, mercifully, the Subs took only a few seconds to reply. "Wiz help," David translated, "we zink . . . yess."

Kurber took a deep breath. *Bingo!*

It was clandestine but it had precedents. Historically, Earth nations had often used "client" states or revolutionary movements to wage war while staying clear of the conflict themselves, and though the Phuili did not have that tradition they did seem willing to tread in Machiavelli's well-worn footsteps. The separation of one ship from the inventory of each fleet was a minor matter, as was the disappearance of several of Lector Fraser's followers from their usual haunts, and a similar number of Human Eaters from Phuili. The removal of a pair of sun seeds from storage was not even explained, though if any Phuili chose to query the records he might wonder about a proposed experiment to induce instabilities in a minor star beyond the galactic hub.

After a short but intensive period of ship familiarization and training, the two dissimilar space craft lifted off from separate island continents on the planet Groombra Four and flared into the super-light condition known as phase-shift. Forty years later, observers on Groombra Four (since renamed Harmony), saw a faint star become a little brighter and then slowly fade back to its original magnitude. The time gap was, of course, due to the forty light-years of distance, and two of the observers had been present those four decades earlier, when one of the ships returned to its base on the Second Continent. The two observers remembered that the men and women who emerged from the ship had been strangely subdued . . .

"Did everything go as planned?" Kurber asked anxiously.

The Captain's smile was tired. "Exactly. The dog-faces went in first with their egg, then we with ours." His face brightened. "My god, you should have seen that sun flare!"

"The Silver People . . ."

"The home planet is a cinder. There are still a lot of outposts, of course, but they won't last long. No way they can recreate the necessary technology."

"So why the long faces?" Gia asked. "Have you discovered it's not so easy to obliterate a race after all, even one as unpleasant as the Silver People?"

The Captain held out a hand. "Look. Steady as a rock. No guilt here, lady, or with any of the crew."

"So what is the problem?"

"You won't like it."

"Try us."

The Captain turned his eyes skyward, toward an insignificant speck amid the evening's dusting of stars. "I know we destroyed a hornets nest," he said quietly. "But I am not so convinced that we got all of the hornets."

On the First Continent, the Phuili commander said to Davakinapwottapellazanzis, "Our instruments detected the event as we were preparing to leave. It had all the characteristics of a ship going into phase shift."

"It must have been the humans."

The Captain shook his head. "We had just exchanged location data with the flat-faces. Their ship was on the other side of the system."

They had not had time to develop phase shift to an interstellar capability. But what they did know was enough to sling-shot the fifty units to a distance of half a light-year. They almost didn't make it: the last of the fifty flared out of normal space even as the home world burned and the outposts prepared to die.

The Apex had been right. Although the garden was destroyed, the wisdom of his planning had ensured that enough of its seeds were safely dispersed into the Holy Void.

Now they were spread across the surface of an expanding sphere nearly a light-year across. Inert and totally subject to the laws that move stars and galaxies, each was enormous; a complex of metal and rock, of concrete made from space dust and powdered moonlets, and of hundreds of needle ships anchored to the surface like bristles on a brush. Deep under the surface, thousands of beings lay like death in great stasis chambers, waiting only for the signal that would prick their bubbles of timelessness and allow them to continue the Great Cleansing.

It would be more than a century before even one of the silently drifting arks came close enough to the triggering warmth of another sun. But space is so huge, a few tens of years was not much time in which to find and destroy those dormant seeds—before they sprouted and began to spread antilife into the universe.

For the xenophobes of Groombra Four, what was done had only been the beginning . . .

FIVE

INTENT OF MERCY

The righting of a wrong is always a difficult process. Even if the wrong was originally perpetrated for the loftiest of reasons, there remains a pain which cannot easily be catharsized. It is therefore necessary to accept what cannot be changed, and proceed as if from a new beginning.

Unfortunately, if those who were wronged are incapable of recognizing the extended hand of peace—

The meeting was extraordinary. At the head of the table was the ancient man who by a combination of tenacity and sheer genius had retained the Chairmanship of the World Union Council for almost six consecutive terms. Also present was Director Kreinhauser of the Security Service, as well as his opposite from Expediters. Completing the unlikely four was Jenkins, the Phuili Ambassador to Earth.

Gia Mayland entered the room with apparent calm, though she had not the faintest idea why she had been summoned to join these representatives of power. As she accepted the proffered chair, she was comforted by Peter Digonness' warm smile. "Good to see you, Gia. How are you?"

"Apprehensive," the expediter admitted. She inclined her head to the Chairman. "I am honored, sir."

"Likewise," Giesse Frobert rumbled. He looked at the slim woman appraisingly. "I have heard good things about you, young lady."

171

"Not so young," Gia said with a faint smile.

The rumble became a deep chuckle. "My dear, from where I stand you are a mere youth." Abruptly, the broad face smoothed into an expressionless mask. "Anyway, to business. Director Digonness, if you don't mind . . ."

"Of course." The head of Expediters touched a control and the room darkened. Above the table an image formed. At first ghostlike, it edged toward apparent reality as a hidden holographic projector focused billions of bits of digital data. It was as if a window was opening into the universe. Suns speckled the darkness, gigantic dust clouds straggled across the light years, globular clusters and distant galaxies were faint patches above and below the glory known to humans as the Milky Way. In the foreground was a drifting mountain, its rough-hewn outline peculiarly jagged as if it was covered with sharks teeth.

The mountain enlarged and gained detail. Finally Gia gasped with astonishment as she heard the Chairman murmur, "I was briefed earlier, of course, but I still find it hard to believe. You are certain there is no other possible explanation?"

Digonness shook his head. "I doubt it, Mr. Chairman. That asteroid is carrying something like two and a half thousand small spacecraft."

"I don't understand," Gia began. "Who . . . ?"

Digonness said quietly, "The Silver People. Remember them, Gia?"

"Oh, god, no." Horrified, Gia stared at the slight graying man who to a large extent controlled her life. "Are you sure?"

"As much as I am sure of anything," Digonness replied sadly.

Gia shivered; the chill of an old nightmare revived. The Silver People had been a mad dog race utterly dedicated to the elimination of all life other than their own. A joint human-Phuili military expedition had already sterilized an entire planetary system to prevent the germinating antilife plague from making the quantum jump from its own system to the stars. But not, it now seemed, with absolute success.

With dry tones belying the terrible nature of his revelation, Digonness continued, "Let's not forget the main point of the Groombra reports; to the effect that traces of phase-shift emission were detected soon after seed activation of the Silvers' sun. What you are seeing is proof of what has long been suspected; that at least one of their ships escaped the nova."

"I am not convinced," Kreinhauser said flatly. His voice permanently hoarse from four decades of authoritarian use, the grizzled Security Director added, "That thing, and whatever is stuck on its surface, can be from anywhere. The galaxy is still a mighty unknown."

Chairman Frobert nodded. "My old friend has a point. And because the Silvers' system is still under quarantine, there is no way we can compare that vessel with abandoned sister ships which may still be in the system."

"I zink we not need compare." The Phuili Ambassador, a short pale-skinned being resembling an intelligent bull terrier, had been examining data which scrolled with incredible rapidity across a portable reader. "Data show asterwoid less zan light year fwom system of Silvers. Wesidual velocity is movement still wadiating away fwom seeded sun. Zerefore ship is Silvers."

Gia took a deep breath. As a participant in the events which had led to the scorching of the Silvers' system in the first place, she now knew why she was here. Jase Kurber should also be present, except she had heard he was on assignment on one of the newer colony worlds. She addressed the little Phuili. "Mr. Ambassador, it has been four years since the seeding. If any of the Silvers escaped the subsequent nova using phase-shift, then surely they would be hundreds of light-years away by now." She looked again at the image. "When was that recorded?"

"You are looking at real time." Digonness smiled at her obvious surprise. "Since that thing was discovered, we have been able to assemble a young fleet out there with collectively enough power to punch a lot of information through tachyon space. And I do agree with Ambassador Jenkins that that monster is a Silvers. The reason it is not halfway across the Spiral Arm is, I suspect, because the Silvers were only into first generation P.S. technology. Though such a drive works after a fashion, it allows only one surge before complete meltdown. I doubt, in fact, there is anything more than a pool of slag in what is left of a drive room."

Gia asked reasonably, "So why don't we board and find out?"

"For several reasons," the Chairman said. "Of which, Ms. Mayland, only two need concern you. The first is that the ship is probably heavily defended, or at least boobytrapped. The second reason is political." At this point the old man beamed at the Phuili representative. "Ambassador Jenkins, why don't you tell her the rest?"

"Yess." Two large, faintly glowing eyes turned to the human woman. The alien projected friendliness to the entity he knew had had a long association with his kind. Gia felt that friendliness, recognized it, and welcomed it. Her last couple of assignments had been on human worlds; she missed the unusual but satisfying relationship possible between individuals of the two races.

"Human and Phuili togezer destwoy system of Silver People." The Ambassador's voice was high-pitched and rasping, like a child with a bad cold. "But now know all Silver People not destwoyed. Human and Phuili must zerefore again togezer, zis time not to destwoy. Perhaps be ozer ships escape sun seeding, only chance find out is maybe on zat ship." The Ambassador paused, seeking words in a language which fitted awkwardly on a tongue and palate designed for very different sounds.

"May I?" Digonness asked understandingly.

The alien gestured. "Pleese. It best."

"Thank you." The Director of Expediters turned to the woman he considered the best field agent he had.

"The Chairman said it, Gia. Politics. We need someone in charge out there; someone who not only represents the interests of Earth and Phuili enough to be fully acceptable to both, but who can also make decisions for both. The Ambassador has already been in touch with his home government, and has been told they will accept anyone jointly selected by him and Chairman Frobert. So they decided . . ."

"With your recommendation, no doubt," Gia interrupted dryly. Not burdened with false modesty, she knew exactly where this was leading and did not like it. "Damn you, Digger . . ." Suddenly remembering where she was, Gia blushed and rephrased, "Mr. Ambassador, gentlemen, I am not an administrator and never have been. There must be others who are better qualified."

The Chairman said softly, "All right, Ms. Mayland. Who do you suggest?"

There was a silence, during which Gia realized there was no way she was going to wriggle out of this one. It was her unique rapport with the Phuili they wanted, plus the fact she was well known enough that she could probably order a few humans around without causing too much resentment. Though, she observed somewhat caustically, she did not doubt she would get plenty of advice.

"But of course you will get advice." Digonness seemed puzzled by her reaction. "In fact, I understand the teams out there have already determined several options. You will probably be briefed about them after you arrive."

Gia smiled. "Oh, I am sure of that."

"Then you accept the assignment?"

Gia sighed.

Groombra Four was Gia's first stop. A planet in Phuili controlled space, it was the one closest to the Silvers' system bearing a terminal of the instantaneous galactic transport network which had been created by a race long since departed from the known universe. It was from Groombra Four that two ships, one human and one Phuili, had departed bearing the "sun seeds" which would turn the sun of the Silver People into a small nova.

Toomis (as the Phuili called it) was a not unattractive world, with a breathable atmosphere and native flora and fauna appropriate to its semiarid climate. The terminal towered over a narrow valley on one of the two continents which covered most of the northern hemisphere. There was a Phuili settlement not far south, but Gia's shuttle, as it emerged out of the flickering sphere of pale fire centered above the terminal's enormous bowl, turned east toward the second continent. Ninety minutes later it landed at Fraser's Town, a compact human community of about one thousand souls. At the far end of the landing field was the ground-space shuttle which would take the expediter up to the phase ship she knew was waiting in orbit above the planet.

Gia had looked forward to a few hours' R and R before the next stage of her journey. But the uniformed man who was waiting for her as she emerged from the Earth shuttle, had different ideas. He ushered her into a small ground car which he immediately steered in the direction of the other shuttle. "I am sorry, but my orders are explicit. The *Century* is ready to go, and will phase out just as soon as you are aboard."

Gia's lips tightened in frustration, but she did not object. Though a few hours was not much compared with the forty-two days it would take to reach the vicinity of the Silvers' ship, she realized that even minutes could count if the alternative was hordes of virulent antilife rampaging the universe.

The shuttle was designed for minimum payload and maximum accleration. So by the time it docked with the enormous *Century* and Gia unsteadily emerged from the transfer lock, she hoped she could at least get a little rest. But even that promise was denied, as she was met by a crewman who immediately escorted her through echoing corridors to the ship's Control Center.

The *Century* was one of the interstellar transports built before Sol's third planet was opened up to the galactic network. It could support eight hundred colonists in a spartan though adequate environment for up to three years, so was necessarily of impressive dimensions. But with nearly ten thousand worlds now instantly available from Earth, there was little need for this giant and her sister ships. Now they were usually in parking orbits above various colony worlds, until perhaps needed to ferry people or supplies to destinations not part of the network. The ships were too big to be efficient, but at least they were there. So, though only occasionally, they were still used.

The Control Center was almost as impressive as the old *Century* herself, containing rows of consoles in a vaulted chamber resembling a temple of worship rather than the working heart of a spaceship. Psychologists had insisted on this diversion from the appearance of state-of-the-art technology because, they insisted, the colonists needed to have confidence that those who were operating the ship could take them safely to destinations beyond a sea of suns. In the cathederallike Center, the captain and his officers became High Priest and priests of a religion whose mysterious technological rituals were very comforting to the sturdy farmers whose lives had always been encompassed by the land and the unpredictable sky on the one hand, and their faith on the other.

Gia knew this, and indeed was a skilled technical pragmatist who understood the functions of most of the flickering displays. Nevertheless something inside her was touched by the aura of controlled power as she carefully followed her guide between the consoles until she found herself before the High Priest himself.

"Hello, Gia," the captain said. "How long has it been? Three years? Four?"

Startled, she looked at him. "Uncle Joel!"

"Himself," the captain said fondly as he enveloped

Gia with a rib-creaking hug. Large, ruddy-faced and white-haired, Captain Joel Gresham had always regarded Gia as the daughter he never had, at the same time retaining a healthy respect for her considerable talents. "Take over, please," he asked his First Officer as he gestured Gia to follow him to his quarters behind the Center.

The main room was large and comfortable, containing the furniture and display cases Gia had last seen aboard his previous command; Transtar's *Farway*. A thin-faced man in an unfamiliar black uniform rose from a chair as they came in. "Is this the expediter?" the man asked coldly.

"The lady's name is Gia Mayland," Captain Gresham replied, his voice equally frigid. "Gia, this is Major Harald Gostorth of Gostorth's Guards."

"I am not familiar . . ." Gia began.

"The Guards are necessary to protect Fraser's Town against encroachment by the infidel." Gostorth's face as well as his voice was wooden, humorless. "The universe is a hostile place, Expediter Mayland. Humanity must always remain vigilant."

"Of course," Gia said politely, though she had recognized the fanaticism in the major's pale eyes. Urging Gresham to the far side of the room, she whispered urgently, "That man's a walking threat! Why is he here?"

The captain's reply was blunt. "Because he has the right. Because, my dear Gia, we also carry a representative from the First Continent."

Gia was incredulous. "A Phuili? One of their xenophobes on *this* ship?"

"There was no choice. Every available Phuili ship is already at Silvers One." The captain chuckled. "By the way, it's a female. Uses the name Mary."

Gia whistled softly. "Where did you put her?"

"If you are thinking of the direct approach, forget it. By her own request, Mary is in quarters as far from the human occupied part of the ship as possible." The captain glanced at the dour, black uniformed man from Fraser's Town. "Naturally."

Naturally.

Such was one of the legacies of the genocide committed by a permanent strike force which officially did not exist—although it would forever haunt the diplomatic shadows of the two governments who had clandestinely set up the force in the first place. The humans and Phuili of Groombra Four had been chosen because they were paranoid racists; perfect shock troops against anything "alien" threatening their respective puritanical concepts of what the universe should be. Safely separated by an ocean, the two communities scrupulously ignored each other; accepting cooperation only when certain coded requests were delivered from both home planets.

The destruction of the Silver People had been their first joint action. Now, as evidenced by their representatives aboard the *Century*, it seemed the two communities expected that their services might be required a second time.

Gia went back to Gostorth. "Are you aware there is a Phuili on board?"

The major nodded. "Of course. Considering the circumstances, it is to be . . . ah . . . expected."

"But from your point of view, not desired. Isn't that so?"

"We all have our cross to bear," the major retorted stiffly.

"The Phuili's name is Mary. Do you know of her?"

"I understand she is competent. For one of her kind, that is."

Gia turned to the captain. "Captain Gresham, I believe this calls for a conference." She pointed at the major. "Including him." She then pointed at the com unit. "And of course your other passenger."

"No problem." The captain punched a three-letter code and the big screen illuminated with the alien features of a Phuili. "Captain, I give you gweetings," the being said solemnly.

Gia moved before the screen. "My name is Gia Mayland and I am a member of Expediters. Your government and mine have given me command of the combined fleet at the asteroid known as Silvers One. Do you accept that authority?"

The long head inclined. "It iss wequired."

"What about you, Major Gostorth? Do you accept?"

"If it is absolutely necessary . . ." The major shrugged. "If you insist. Anyway, it is obvious I have no choice in the matter."

"Damn right you don't," the expediter muttered.

Phase shift, the P.A. announced. . . . *five . . . four . . . three . . . two . . . one . . . shift!* The deck trembled, there was a slight blurring of the senses, and then it was over. The *Century* was now enclosed within a bubble of multilight, heading to a destination forty light-years in distance though only days in time.

Gia asked the major to sit near the com unit, then moved herself so that she was facing both the major and the Phuili's screen image. "I want you both to understand," she began without preamble, "that I am not going to that asteroid to supervise its destruction. My purpose is knowledge; about the ship itself, its propulsion systems, and especially its passengers—if there are any. Mary, if you wish to transfer to one of the Phuili ships after we arrive, I will have no objection. Major, you may similarly transfer to any human-manned vessel. But neither of you will be allowed aboard any investigatory probes, and certainly not aboard the Silvers' ship itself. Even if boarding does prove feasible."

Mary said quaintly, "If Silvers on ship, zis one not wish go." The alien voice hardened. "But zink you wong. You should destwoy. Not take chance."

"For once I agree," Gostorth said harshly. "I was there when we sun-seeded the Silvers system, and I remember how we rejoiced when we thought we had destroyed that festering evil. Expediter Mayland, perhaps you have forgotten it only needs one microbe to start a plague."

"But what if there are many microbes, Major? Will it stop the plague if we kill only one?"

The captain coughed. "Until they asked me to bring the *Century* out here, like most people I had never heard of the Silver People and what was done to them." His face became bleak. "My god, to hear about such an act in this day and age . . ." He shook his head. "Anyway, my briefing did include the evidence suggesting at least one of their ships got away as their planets were frying. But what if that was not a one-shot? What if there were others? Dammit, how many Silvers are tucked away just to man the more than two thousand spacecraft that *one* monster is carrying? What are we up against? A fleet? A fleet of fleets? We need answers, and from where I stand there seems only one place where we even have a chance of getting them. And that is inside the guts of that asteroid!"

Gia went to the old man and hugged him. "Captain, I could not have said it better."

Mary asked sensibly. "But how you get on asterwoid?" With Phuili understatement, she added, "I zink Silvers not want you on asterwoid."

The captain chuckled. "Good question. Good comment."

Major Gostorth's eyes glittered. "I think, madam expediter, this is one time you will regret not bringing my guards."

Gia did not try to hide her contempt as she looked at the black-uniformed man. "Major," she said succinctly, "you are a fool."

The *Century* arrived and took up station in a void as apparently empty as would be expected in the almost-nothingness between the stars. But on the big ship's detectors, this was a busy area indeed. Roughly encompassing the surface of a sphere thirty thousand kilometers across, sixteen spacecraft of assorted types orbited about an object currently known to the twenty one hundred entities aboard the ships as "Silvers One."

This was an overwhelmingly Phuili fleet, which was natural enough in this predominantly Phuili-settled part of the galaxy. It also explained the choice of a human operations director. The Phuili, being an obsessively logical race and not desiring to take on more than their fair share of what was, after all, a joint human-Phuili problem; had balanced the equation by acknowledging the authority of a human. Expediter Mayland was therefore not particularly surprised at the two-to-one ratio of Phuili over humans when she was introduced to her advisory staff aboard the bulbous vessel which was the fleet's command center.

What did surprise her, and pleasantly so, was the Phuili who came to her and took one of her hands in a very uncharacteristic gesture of friendship to one not of his race. "I zink you and I are souls of one body," Davakinapwottapellazanzis (known to humans as David) said seriously.

Gia politely concealed her pleasure. "This is not a coincidence, is it David?"

The long head inclined. "Iss difficult. But I awange."

Gia doubted the difficulty. Aside from his high status in the Phuili hierarchy, David's own part in the Silvers affair had given him formidable leverage. Though she was uncertain if gratitude should be the proper response for her place in this uncomfortable hot seat of responsibility.

Of the three humans on the advisory staff, one was also an old friend—whose embrace hinted at perhaps a little more than friendship. Pushing him to arm's length, Gia laughed delightedly. "Jase, it is just like Christmas homecoming! How in blazes did you finagle this one?"

Jase Kurber grinned as he ran fingers through his thinning black hair. "I didn't. Believe it or not, Digger assigned me here a couple of months ago."

Gia's eyes widened in astonishment. "The devil he did!" So even as she attended the meeting with Giesse Frobert and the others, Expediters' Peter Digonness had already set the wheels in motion to renew a previously successful partnership. Not that she minded the director's intervention. Gia, Kurber, and David had proved their compatibility. Still, there was a hint of forces beyond her control which made Gia uneasy. But for the moment dismissing her doubts, she said briskly, "Okay, I was brought here in a hurry so let's not waste further time. What can anyone tell me that perhaps I do not already know?"

The Phuili version of an "operations" room in which Gia and her advisers were located was low, curved, and slightly claustrophobic to the humans who were considerably taller than their small alien colleagues. But claustrophobia became vertiginous agoraphobia as the unoccupied half of the room suddenly winked out of existence and became instead an opening into the infinity of deep space. It was how the Phuili did such things; regarding as totally unnecessary the "fade-in" used by humans to allow time to adjust to the incredible reality of holo projection.

The combined gasp from four human throats was followed by a guttural sound which Gia interpreted as the Phuili equivalent of laughter. But ever the perfect diplomat, David diverted attention from the discomfort of his human friends by zooming the field toward the object known as Silvers One and commenting, "Gia you perhaps see zis before. But not, I zink, so close."

No. Certainly not so close. This time, instead of stopping above an area of slender needle-nosed columns which stretched from horizon to close horizon like a metal forest, the zoom continued in until only one of the columns was visible. It was undoubtedly a ship, small and clean of line, its base concealed in a depression sunk into the asteroid's crust. "Small cwew," David said. "Two. Zwee maybe. Not more."

He retracted the zoom slightly and then moved the field over the ranks of ships. In some places, the hulls were so close the rock of the asteroid was barely visible in the spaces between.

Kurber said, "Notice the absolute lack of recognizable features on those ships, plus the fact they are as alike as peas out of the same pod. I am not sure what that implies, except to presume they are the products of mass production on a truly massive scale."

"Vewy fast to make," one of the other Phuili agreed. "As if know zey must finish and send out system before we find and stop."

Gia nodded. Perhaps the Silvers were mad, but it seemed they had been smart enough to realize their plans for the rest of the universe might be opposed by some. She looked sourly at the ugly image, the rows of daggerlike craft aimed belligerently at the stars. "What else can you tell me?"

"Watch," David said.

Again the little Phuili manipulated the holo controls. The image zoomed back until the asteroid was merely a stony space wanderer in the center of the field. The star background had shifted slightly, so Gia judged she was no longer watching in real time. Her guess was confirmed by the large man who had been introduced as Keller Vanderbrusse, communications specialist. He pointed at the Phuili numerals rapidly scrolling at the edge of the field. "This was recorded about twenty hours ago. I know we jumped the gun, but time is short and it did seem the obvious first step."

Something glinted in the foreground, suddenly flared and streaked toward the asteroid. "We aimed to miss by about a thousand klicks; close enough to be noticed, distant enough to imply a nonaggressive intent."

"I forgive you," Gia murmured, appreciative rather than angry at this demonstration of intelligent initiative. The image switched to one seen by the probe's camera as the tiny vehicle accelerated along its present course. Again the asteroid changed; from a distant irregular shaped object like any other of its size and mass, to a formidable and bristling carrier of . . .

There was a flash of light, another, and then several more as the asteroid reacted. The missiles themselves remained invisible as the probe reached its closest point and began to draw away. The asteroid's surface was quiescent again, resuming the enigmatic status it had held since being discovered. Slowly the asteroid retreated; eleven hundred kilometers, twelve hundred, thirteen . . .

The image flickered, was replaced by an expanding sphere of fire as seen from the Phuili command ship. For a while the sphere pulsated, waxing and waning with obscene irregularity. "A slight case of overkill," Vanderbrusse commented. "Seven warheads against one innocent little probe."

"So how do we get into that thing?" Gia asked.

"Exactly."

The problem seemed unsolvable. Gia lay and stared into the darkness of the cabin assigned to her, wishing she had the expertise to understand what was currently happening back in the operations room. At her suggestion, electronic and propulsion experts had been brought in from all over the fleet, "to find a means to jam or overwhelm the asteroid's defenses." She hoped she had injected some sense of purpose that had not been there before, though in her heart she suspected they were grasping at straws. Jamming seemed very unlikely; without some knowledge of the systems under that stony crust, the odds against were enormous. And how, with a mandate that allowed for everything except the destruction of the asteroid, does one "overwhelm?" In any case, the closest thing in the fleet to a warcraft was *Luna*, a patrol ship from the early years of human expansion into space. With only a single missile tube, that military anachronism was about as useful as a mounted cavalryman against a squadron of tanks.

Gia was not sure if she slept. In that half world between waking and dozing, in which the mind plays tricks with time as well as logic, she was not at first aware of the thrumming of the ship's drive as it accelerated the big spacecraft out of its orbit. But she was startled into full wakefulness by the piercing phonics of a screech alarm. *"Iknillic!"* rasped a Phuili voice over the P.A. *"Rassin bil Iknillic!"*

Not having the faintest idea where the bridge of this alien vessel was located, and knowing she would not be welcome there anyway, Gia could only hurry back to Operations as more incomprehensible Phuili consonants rattled out of the P.A. When she entered, the experts were still there; anxiously watching the holo image of a double-hulled ship linked at each end by a complex of spheres and struts. A faint blue-white glow was flickering around the entire assembly.

Gia asked breathlessly, "What is going on?"

"Runaway converter," was the laconic reply of a lanky human Gia vaguely remembered seeing on the *Century*. "They are already evacuating." As he spoke, dozens of passive life pods began spewing out of the stricken Phuili ship as shuttles from all over the fleet raced in and picked them up like sharks swallowing minnows.

The expediter found a vacant seat and slid into it. "Is it going to blow?"

"Haven't the foggiest." The man frowned puzzledly. "The point is, what could have caused it? The safeties these days . . ."

"Not accident," one of the Phuili said flatly. "Zat happen because someone make."

"Sabotage? But who . . . ?" Gia's eyes widened. *"Iknillic!* Now I remember. That's the ship that took our Phuili passenger, while Major Gostorth . . ." Her face went white. "My god, where's *Luna*?"

David, followed by Jase Kurber, had entered just before Gia's horrified flash of realization. Almost as if he was reading her mind, her small friend immediately sat before the holo controls and switched the image to a plot displaying near space. The Phuili ships were represented by blue points of lights, the human ships by green. The asteroid was a lurid red near the bottom edge of the field. All the blue and green points were converging on the flickering blue spark of the damaged Phuili spacecraft, though it was noticeable that the ships from the far side of the englobement were curving wide to avoid the prickly menace at the center.

All except one.

By this time the tension was almost palpable as David touched the control that would identify the miscreant vessel. A symbol appeared.

Kurber swore. "Goddamn, it is the *Luna*." He shouted across the room to the lanky human from the *Century*. "Kerrin, who are *Luna*'s owners? And what do we know about her crew and their point of origin?"

Kerrin's hand-sized comset, keyed to a memory bank aboard one of the human ships, took only seconds to roll out a slender piece of flimsy. "She's owned by the Lecfras Trust on Unity," Kerrin called back. "Most of those aboard are Unitans."

"Lecfras." Kurber took a deep breath. "Translates to Lector Fraser. Anything bearing that name has to be farther right than Attila the Hun. And the Unitans themselves are not much better."

The green trace seemed to be approaching its closest point to the asteroid; not suicidally close, though near enough to indicate a captain whose recklessness was somewhat surprising for a responsible officer. Gia prayed she was overreacting, that this was merely a coincidence—not an unholy conspiracy which for place and timing promised an unpleasantness far greater than merely the destruction of a single ship. But that hopeful thought lasted only a few seconds. With a flare of thrusters at full power, *Luna* suddenly flipped ends and blasted away from the asteroid as if hell itself was at the little ship's heels. Where *Luna* had been, a tiny spark accelerated furiously along a tight curve which left no doubt of its intended target.

Everyone in Operations was momentarily paralyzed as they realized how neatly they had been hoodwinked; from the "accident" which had attracted every unit of the fleet, to the attack run which in any other circumstance would have been forcibly aborted long before its initiation.

Already the asteroid was reacting; seven tiny flashes

from its surface, one after another as backup followed backup with neat regularity. "It's ridiculous," Gia murmured, half to herself. "How can one silly missile . . . ?"

The answer came almost with the question as, seconds before it was obliterated, the spark ejected something behind it. With the same furious acceleration as its parent, the second component passed through the expanding cloud of gases created by the seven defense warheads.

Again flashes from the asteroid, and again a multiple explosion—just after a *third* component split away from the attacker and accelerated at an incredible rate through the detritus of the second series of explosions.

The third reaction from the asteroid was apparently successful, though for tense seconds the asteroid itself could not be seen behind the fading cloud caused by its salvo of missiles. As it gradually reappeared, a blackened area on the asteroid's near side indicated it had not gone entirely unscathed.

David anticipated Gia's question. "Missile fwom human ship made by Phuili. Vewy old, not make fwom many centuwies. Zwee, one in anozer, all shielded. In head, matter against matter. Vewy dangerwous."

"Antimatter," Kurber breathed. "My god . . ."

"Zink Phuili you call Mawy and human you call Major awange zis. But not work because Mawy not know heads changed since many cycles. Now missiles only for warning. Not hurt much."

The situation was so improbable, Gia doubted she would dare recount it to anyone not already conversant with most of the facts. Though it was possibly true that man and Phuili were indeed a duality that might ultimately rule the universe, on a smaller scale the duality of Groombra Four had instead become an insanity as potentially potent—and tragic—as the Silvers aberration it had been set up to destroy. Such an insanity, fueled by hate of an enemy that eclipsed the hate they had for each other, was something the greater human-Phuili partnership was going to find increasingly difficult to rationalize.

"Iknillic!" said the P.A. *"Iknillic si enne rassin!"*

David returned the holo image to that of the burning ship—which was no longer burning. After a moment of uncomprehending silence, the little Phuili then uttered a word so full of angry consonants it was like a vocal explosion. "It pwoof," he told his human friends, his bitterness evident even to unaccustomed ears. "Because plan fail, Mawy weverse what did to converter. She only one know ship not in danger, so I zink she still on ship."

Gia sympathized with David's shame. But she was also familiar enough with Phuili psychology to know it was not a matter to be discussed. "Then I suppose we can cancel the evacuation and get everyone back on board." She paused. "What is *Luna* doing?"

Kerrin entered the query into his comset. "Returning to station," he replied after a moment. Marveling, he shook his head. "The gall of those people. They are carrying on as if nothing happened!"

Despite herself, Gia smiled. "What else can they do? They are not the first losers who have used bravado to face their sins."

Kurber asked tentatively, "What do you want done about Mary and Major Gostorth?"

Gia looked at Kurber. Then at David. Her face was bleak. "I want punishment. I want both of them brought to this ship and confined together. Until I rescind that instruction, no one—human or Phuili—is to communicate with either."

Kurber whistled. "Bit drastic, isn't it? How long is this . . . ah . . . joint confinement to last?"

"Until I decide it can end." The expediter's expression softened. "Jase, I know it's cruel, but we need to know the extent of the conspiracy. Hopefully, reaction to each other's physical presence will prove stronger than any urge to remain silent."

David inclined his long head. "Zis one agwee. Perhaps it way to stop ozers twying same."

Perhaps, Gia thought as she returned to her cabin

and again prepared to catch up on lost sleep. But she doubted that one failure would deter the fanatics of Groombra Four. From their myopic viewpoint, the only enemy was the one at hand—which allowed little or no room for consideration of anything else. Especially of a threat which existed only in theory.

Gia was so exhausted that sleep came easier this time. But hardly had it seemed her head touched the pillow, when she heard the twanging of her cabin's attention alarm, and then a familiar voice. "Gia, are you awake?"

She looked at her watch. She had been asleep for five hours. She yawned and said to the air, "Yes Jase, I am now. What is it this time?"

"Something you should see. Good news for a change."

Gia was intrigued. Within a couple of minutes she was back in Operations and staring with wonder at the image of a sleek, slightly singed object clamped to the hull of the Phuili ship Mary had sabotaged. "That last little fracas dislodged it from the asteroid," Kurber explained cheerfully. "It was found drifting, identified as a harmless crew carrier and then brought in."

David added, "*Iknillic* our wepair and build place. Have cwew and machines to fix all zings. Zey put contwol on Silvers ship to hand at distance."

"Radio control?" Gia began. "But why . . . ?" Her face cleared. "Of course. If the asteroid's defenses recognize it as a friend, it opens a door we did not have before." *This had better be the break we need, or someone else can have this job!* "Go ahead. Please."

Daring to hope, Gia watched the image as space-suited Phuili drifted away from the captured prize and reentered their ship. Magnetic clamps released and the Silvers craft turned and accelerated smoothly toward the asteroid. Minutes passed. Steadily, the distance closed.

"We appwoach cwitical point." David indicated the scrolling numerals. "Soon we know."

Twelve hundred. Eleven hundred. One thousand . . .

By now there should have been a reaction.

Nine hundred. Eight hundred. Seven . . .

Still no reaction. No one seemed to be drawing breath. Even the Phuili observers were suspended in timeless anticipation; their small bodies rigid, great eyes staring.

Five hundred.

Three hundred.

Still nothing. The remote pilot steered his charge about the asteroid's equator, at one point dipping below a hundred kilometers. There was a small sound in the room, a concerted sigh. Then, as the distance finally began to increase, a whoop from Vanderbrusse. "We made it!" the big man exhaulted. "Dammit, we can go!"

The Phuili were also happy, bowing to each other and to their human guests in a display of emotion rare for that notoriously phlegmatic race.

Gia was in a more practical frame of mind. Though a door had opened, it was nevertheless a very small portal. "David, you told us those ships are crewed by three, at the most. Do those numbers still hold?

The Phuili nodded. "Inside of ship vewy small. Even zwee tight to get in." Still the diplomat, he continued, "But you to decide who, fwiend Gia."

Three hours later, Kurber and two Phuili identified as John and Matthew, found an entrance lock on the surface of the asteroid. The exterior controls were simple and the lock opened easily. Two hours after that, Gia and David came down and met Kurber in an enormous chamber at the heart of the asteroid. The chamber was spherical, its inner surface completely covered with thousands of glasslike protrusions which reflected the light from their lamps like a coating of precious stones. Phuili voices muttered in Gia's helmet phones, there was a pause, and then the entire space became brilliantly illuminated.

David said with satisfaction, "Zey find contwol center and turn on power. Soon find defense contwols and turn off."

Kurber was floating near one of the protrusions. He called Gia over. "Want to meet the crew of this beast? Come and say hello."

The expediter activated her suit jets and drifted across. The protrusion was actually a transparent hexagon about fifty centimeters wide. As Gia grasped Kurber's shoulder and steadied herself, he shone his lamp into the hexagon. Inside were the head and shoulders of a gray-furred being. Its eyes were closed, the long arms were folded across the chest.

Gia felt strange, her revulsion conflicting with her awareness of the undoubted physical attractiveness of the being. "What happened to them?" she heard herself whisper. "What made them what they are?"

"God knows," Kurber replied. "Perhaps in the past some paranoiac demigod came to power and somehow transferred his sickness to the whole race."

"Iss possible," David agreed. The little Phuili was drifting alongside them, his snouted face enigmatic behind the reflected highlights of his helmet. "Pleese come. I zink ozers find somezing."

The two humans followed him out of the chamber and back up the broad corridor which led to the surface. Then they turned aside through a side portal, into a long room covered with display panels and ranks of multicolored indicators. John and Matthew were at the far end of the room, before an enormous panel split in two halves. One side was brilliantly ablaze with thousands of tiny sparklike indicators all glowing orange. The other side was identical, except the indicators were blue.

There was a rapid exchange in the incomprehensible Phuili language, before David turned to his human friends. "Place we just in, filled wiz what you call sleep tanks. We zink zis place iss where sleepers made waking." David gestured at the tiny indicators. "Each light push in like little button." Expectantly, he looked at Gia.

His point was painfully obvious. Whether or not to revive any of the sleepers was a decision only Gia had the authority to make, and it was one which made her fervently wish she was elsewhere. Even to revive only one or two of the graceful monsters had the potential of being the unleashing of a dormant plague. On the other hand, not to revive could mean they would never know—or at least probably not until it was too late—if there were any other drifting arks waiting to release their cargoes of comatose malevolence into an unsuspecting universe.

Thoughtfully, Gia studied the huge panel. "David, are the Silvers bisexual?"

"Have seen only one corpse of wace. But it have like male."

Kurber's mouth twitched. "I suppose you have a reason for that . . . ah . . . delicate question?"

Gia nodded. "It looks to me there are about as many lights on that panel as there are sleepers. Which suggests that the two colors represent the two sexes—and please note there are an equal number of each. So if we revive . . ."

"Even if we can, we shouldn't!" Kurber interrupted sharply. "To start with, we have not yet figured out how to activate the atmospheric life support. And the reviving process is probably automatic anyway; most likely triggered when the asteroid reaches the neighborhood of a star."

David was also studying the panel. "I zink automatic only for two. If two zen see planets wiz life, zey can make ozers to wevive." He pointed to the top of the panel, where symbols linked a small row of orange-blue pairs. "I say contwol start at top two. If not work, zen next two."

"And so on." Kurber rubbed his chin. "You know, that does make sense. It also means we merely have to find the asteroid's sun proximity sensors and generate a phony signal." He grinned. "Interesting possibilities there, don't you think?"

"I am not interested in mere possibilities," Gia said

grimly. "Before we stick our necks out on this one, there will have to be certain stringent controls."

The expediter's instructions, which she issued immediately after they returned to the command ship, provoked some discussion but not much argument. Something had to be done, everyone knew it, and the necessary preparations were well within the capabilities of the fleet and its polyglot crews.

The biggest job was the painstaking analysis of the various electrical and mechanical systems aboard the Silvers ship, followed by modifications which the original designers certainly never had in mind. Interfacing with the asteroid's voice and control circuits, a tough task by any standard, was also accomplished within the stipulated time. Whether or not the newly introduced translator module was sufficient, was something they would not know until after the operation was initiated. At this stage, all Gia could do was dilute her worries by concentrating on other things.

After a thorough exploration and mapping of the asteroid's interior, explosive experts were called in. Carefully they installed and set their charges, then withdrew. The consequent explosions were minor, designed merely to seal certain tunnels and service shafts. But for fifteen tense seconds the huge mass reverberated like a bell before finally rumbling into silence. Anxious minutes followed as circuits were checked for possible disruption. Nervously, Kurber remarked, "That was a bit more than I expected."

Gia nodded, though she did not speak. Her state of mind was such that she would gladly have swapped her current situation for any from her past, even those that had been life threatening. Old-fashioned fear was one thing; she could cope with that and often had. But the strain of these moments was something close to unbearable.

She stood up. "Dammit!"

Kurber looked at her. "I agree," he said uncertainly. "Do you have something in mind?"

"I am going to have a little talk with our friend Gostorth." Gia held up a restraining hand as it seemed Kurber was about to join her. "No, Jase. This is personal."

She knew she was being selfish. But Gia had long ago learned to trust her own combative instincts. If conflict was in the wind, even if only verbal with a programed fanatic, the challenge was a welcome catharsis.

The major was now confined alone, but his red-rimmed eyes and nervous twitch indicated he had not long been separated from his unwelcome roommate. Gia's first words were a cheap shot, but she enjoyed saying them anyway. "I gather you and Mary did not get along too well."

"You are a bitch," Gostorth said tonelessly.

Gia smiled. "Thank you." She sat down facing him. "Do you want more company? I can arrange it, you know."

"What do you want?"

"I want to know the extent of the conspiracy. I want names."

He sighed. "I am surprised you did not have me pumped full of some T-drug. It would have been easier and less . . . ah . . . uncomfortable."

"Easier? Less uncomfortable? For you, Major, perhaps. But you see I do not want you to come away from this with an easy conscience. You will talk because now you know what will happen to you if you don't. We do not need any drug."

Again he sighed. Compared to what he had been, Gostorth was definately a reduced man. Gia recalled what she had seen when, during a rare spare moment, she had tuned in to a pickup in the confinement area. The two conspirators had been huddled in opposite corners of their shared space, not speaking or moving. Only their eyes had been warily active, as if each suspected the other was a predator about to pounce. It had been a depressing scene. Mary was now confined elsewhere; apparently, in the Phuili context, as much disturbed as the xenophobic human.

Gostorth said, "*Luna* was in on it."

"Of course *Luna* was in on it!" Gia looked at the man with contempt. "Please do not insult me with the obvious. Frankly, *Mister* Gostorth, if it was not for the weapon you used, I could almost have been persuaded this thing was strictly between you, Mary, and *Luna*'s idiotic crew. But because that weapon had to have originated from Phuili . . ."

The P.A. beeped. "*Human Gia needed,*" an anonymous Phuili announced. "*All weady for start.*"

The expediter rose to her feet and went to the door. "Think about what I have said," she told the reduced man. "I will be back."

It seemed everyone was there waiting for her. Sitting or standing, Phuili and humans were all looking at the split image on the screen at the end of the room. This was ordinary 3D as opposed to holography, but the excitement generated by the image of the sleepers control panel on one side, and the vault with its thousands of glassite hexagons on the other, was almost enough to make the air crackle.

Gia sat in the seat reserved for her between Kurber and David. "What did Gostorth have to say?" Kurber asked.

"He's malleable," was Gia's obtuse reply. "Is everything set?"

"We weady," David said.

Gia clenched her hands under the table. "Then let's do it."

David whispered into his comset. A Phuili technician closed a switch and fifteen thousand kilometers away a carefully programmed data package began feeding into the receiving unit of a detector mounted on the asteroid's surface.

For about twenty interminable seconds nothing happened. Suddenly Gia grabbed Kurber's arm and pointed.

"Jase. It's beginning."

On the image of the control panel, the top pair of orange-blue indicators had begun to pulsate.

Enrahin stretched cramped muscles. His thoughts were still somewhat blurred, but already he remembered where he was and why. Air blew on his cheek and chilled his damp body as the reviving process reached its final phase and as the automatics built up atmospheric pressure outside his stasis chamber. An indicator began pulsing above his head, telling Enrahin he could now open the lid and exit the chamber. The lid swung back easily, and as he floated free he looked below him and to the right. He did not know Ayree's exact location, but surely her pulse indicator would tell him if the loved one would again share his life.

It was there!

It was very faint, but the tiny pulsing glow was unmistakable to his eager eyes. Enrahin immediately launched himself down past the ranks of chambers and their time-suspended occupants, reaching and embracing Ayree just as she began to emerge.

"Again we are one!" he said happily.

She blinked sleepily. "How long?"

"I do not know. Only minutes has it been since I woke."

Ayree shivered and fluffed her fur. She was beautiful, even with the uneven hair growth caused by lack of grooming. "Then we must find out," she said practically. "Control did not wake us for nothing."

She flexed her long legs and with a single soaring leap reached the main access opening. Her mate followed, into the broad tunnel which ultimately led to the surface. Suddenly he bumped into her as she floated helplessly before rubble which completely blocked their way.

Enrahin was as horrified as she was, but he had been stim-programmed, so his reaction was immediate. He urged Ayree into a side tunnel. "Come. I think the way to Control One is still open."

Ayree obediently turned and followed him into a long room lined with panels and winking displays. Once they were inside, Enrahin said loudly, "Control. Are you listening?"

A voice answered. It was weak, electronically disturbed, and beyond the noise of interference its words were halting and strangely accented.

I LISTEN.

"List. Time since drive activation. State of vehicle and life units in storage. Reason of activation of life units E19 and A304."

TIME. FIFTEEN HUNDRED AND NINETEEN DAYS LESS ELEVEN MINUTES. STATE. VEHICLE DAMAGED BY EXPLOSIVE OVERLOAD OF PHASE SHIFT DRIVE SYSTEM CAUSING COLLAPSE AND BLOCKAGE OF SEVERAL PASSAGES. STORED LIFE UNITS UNDAMAGED. STASIS AND CONTROL SYSTEMS STILL OPERATIVE. REASON. ANOMALOUS INDICATION OF STAR PROXIMITY.

Ayree felt for and grasped Enrahin's hand. "Explain use of term, anomalous."

VEHICLE CURRENTLY ZERO DECIMAL SIX STANDARD FROM SYSTEM OF ORIGIN. NEAREST STAR IN DIRECTION OF MOTION TWELVE DECIMAL NINE STANDARD. INDICATION OF STAR PROXIMITY THEREFORE ANOMALOUS.

What does it mean? Enrahin's twin hearts thudded as he pondered this strangeness. He heard Ayree ask,

"Is it possible the star sensors were also damaged by the drive explosion?"

SYSTEMS CHECK COMPLETED. POSSIBILITY OF ERROR THREE DECIMAL ONE PERCENT.

"Identify possible cause of anomaly."

NINE ONE DECIMAL SIX PERCENT PROBABILITY STAR PROXIMITY DATA ARTIFICIALLY GENERATED.

Fifteen thousand kilometers away, Expediter Gia Mayland turned off the microphone. "Now they know," she whispered as, on the screen, two attractive gray-furred beings stood with eye-glaring rigidity. Then there began a spasmodic twitching of the male's right hand as, slowly, he turned toward the sleepers activation panel . . .

Ayree dug sharp claws into his upper arm and pulled him away. "No, Enrahin, not yet. We do not know enough."

Like an animal emerging from water to the dry land, he shook himself. But Enrahin's eyes were still wild and unfocused as he said hoarsely, "Control said artificial. That implies life."

"Control is artificial. Does Control live?"

Gradually the wildness died. "No. Bu . . . but we built Control. *We* are life!"

"We are life," Ayree agreed. "And by creating Control, we proved that intelligent action need not necessarily be exclusive to living beings. Perhaps life created whatever generated the anomaly. But we do not have the right to activate any of the others until we are certain that we face that other life. Not merely what it once created."

Ayree had always been the analytical one. Realizing the logic of what she had just said, though still shivering with the hate/fear that was his birthright, Enrahin dragged forth his cowering reasoning-sense and forced it into action. "So if we are not dealing with life *is*, then it must be life *was*. Either way, it is a shattering thing."

His mate nodded. "And proving, of course, the necessity of the Great Work. But would you and I be performing our Holy Task if we activated other life units prematurely? It is precisely because stasis is limited to once per life unit, that Control has been programmed to activate only two at each time. So it is our function, dear one, to determine the nature of this anomaly and then to make a proper decision. If it is life, then we must activate as many brothers and sisters as is necessary to rid this area of the infection. If it is not life, then it is our duty to return all systems to cruise mode and then to submit ourselves to the nutrient vats. What we cannot do, others will do—and we will be there, our substance being part of their substance."

"My god, what kind of philosphy is that?"
"Cold-blooded."
"But they are not machines. Their obvious affection for each other proves that."
"Even Hitler loved his Eva Braun. And I am sure Caligula had his tender moments. We cannot afford to go soft, Gia."
"Agwee we not take chance. But zat little good perhaps mean we can make into bigger good. Maybe later we make. But first still have find out if ozer ships. Fwiend Gia, you have somehow make zem speak."

Enrahin asked, "Is the anomaly close enough it can be shown on the screen?"
NEGATIVE. OPTICAL AMPLIFYING CIRCUITS DAMAGED. SELF REPAIR PROGRAM OPERATING.
"How long before repairs are complete?"
CURRENT DATA MAXIMUM TWO POINT SEVEN HOURS. MINIMUM ZERO POINT THREE HOURS.
"Do available sensors indicate anything of anomaly other than its possibly artificial nature?"

"That's it Gia! The question we need!"
"Oh, I hope so," the expediter said fervently. She took a deep breath . . .

SIX TWO DECIMAL EIGHT PERCENT PROBABILITY ANOMALY SIMILAR TO THIS VESSEL.
Enrahin groped for Ayree's hand. *That is not possible.*
"Clarify," he said.
ANOMALY OF SIMILAR SIZE AND MASS. IN-

DICATIONS OF METALLIC STRUCTURES ON SURFACE.

"Like needle-ships," Enrahin muttered, half to himself. "But that cannot be. We know the others were . . ."

His mate's grip became so fierce it caused pain. *Don't speak of it. Not even this way!*

He knew Ayree was merely insisting on observance of the rules, even when using secret-talk. It seemed an unnecessary nuisance, but with an inward sigh Enrahin decided to abide. There would be no conflict with his love, even of the most minor kind. *I was wrong and I am sorry. So please do not . . .*

Ayree said firmly, "Whatever is out there, *if* it is a ship, then it must be of other-life. How can it be otherwise, considering this is our only ark?"

Wondering for whose benefit she had voiced the lie, Enrahin suppressed the urge to secret-talk his doubts. What was bothering Ayree anyway? Did she still believe in that hoary old theory of a transmental component of secret-talk? "Dear Ayree," he said. "What you say is true, of course. But you know how I like to project myself into the future, imagining the people as they *will* be—countless trillions of us, cleansing and purifying the cosmos until it is perfect. Time is vast, after all, and we are prolific. Truly the Great Work will come from this single holy seed which bears us all toward our destiny."

"Damn!" Gia's frustration caused her to thump the table so hard it made Kurber jump. "Did you see and hear that? The male said it, for god's sake. Others! But then she stopped him. How?"

"As if know we listen." David's huge eyes were somber. "But zink zey not know. Equipment we put hidden too well to find yet. Zink female do smart guess. Zen tell male shut up, perhaps wiz mind talk."

"Telepathy?" Kurber frowned. "Could be. But the problem still remains; presuming they have other ships out there, how in blazes do we find out about them? We have already searched the asteroid for physical evidence, though I suppose we'd need years to poke into every nook and cranny. So let's face it; our only hope is still inside one or the other of those two furry skulls."

"And how do we do that?"

"Plan B. Make friends with them."

"That is not funny, Jase."

"Who's laughing?"

The two Silvers had made a quick tour through the main tunnels, and so far had found each surface access thoroughly blocked by tons of fallen rock. They knew there was equipment which could clear the mess, but when they discussed the problem . . .

"We don't know how to operate that machinery, and in any case there is no point in activating anyone who does, until we are certain there is something—or someone—out there."

As always, it was Ayree's logic which cooled Enrahin's impetuousness, and realizing there was still not sufficient reason even to activate a miniscule few of the others, the male felt a terrible sense of loneliness as he and his mate trod through echoing tunnels toward Control One. Tightly, they held hands.

The blockages form a very strange pattern.

What do you mean?

True to her resolve not to say too much, even with secret-talk, Ayree ceased communication until they were back in the room with the winking displays. With all this flickering activity it was not difficult to imagine it as the measure of a living crew at work, instead of the reality of a soulless collection of components imitating what the two beings dearly wished could be.

"Control, have the optical circuits been repaired?"

AFFIRMATIVE.

"Please show us the anomaly."

The image was at first fuzzy with very little detail. But even before it cleared and sharpened, Enrahin and Ayree knew exactly what they were seeing.

*   *   *

"I not understand weason. Zey know ozer Silvers not near."

"David, if there is to be any chance at all for us to talk and them to listen, they must be convinced we are not the alien horrors they expect. So we start with the image of a ship similar to their own."

"Ah. What do zen?"

"At the proper moment we introduce them to two beings not unlike themselves; male and female, possibly a little inferior. The One Behind All, we inform them, has created these beings to assist in the mighty task of bringing order to the universe."

"Beings cannot be Phuili. We too diffewent. Humans closer zough less hair. You say male and female."

"Exactly. Jase and I."

"I zink perhaps might work. But after . . . ?"

"I wonder about that myself. Dammit Gia, I am no actor! What are we supposed to say to them anyway?"

"Right now, I haven't figured that out. But Jase, I do not want to order the destruction of those people if there is the slightest possibility they can be turned around. I may be the judge with powers of execution, but at this moment I strongly lean toward a recommendation of mercy."

There was a long silence. Kurber was obviously astonished, while David looked thoughtful. Then:

"It is say all zings possible. Zank you, fwiend Gia, for wemind."

"Thank *you*, friend David."

Kurber was not so sure. "I wonder if anyone will deserve thanks when this is over," he commented gloomily.

"Is there any sign of activity on that ship?"

NEGATIVE.

"That does not prove anything. It has obviously matched our course and velocity—which is orders of magnitude beyond any coincidence."

"Enrahin, we have already discussed that. If that

ship is like ours, then perhaps it has a Control like ours."

ALIEN SHIP TRANSMITTING. SIGNAL CONTAINING COMPARATIVE REFERENCES AND NUMERICAL DATA FOR POSSIBLE LANGUAGE TRANSLATION.

Enrahin hissed. "Language? But language is caused by life!" Face twisted in hate, the male skittered back and forth, eyes darting about him as if looking for a weapon—any weapon. "No!" Ayree cried, her fur fluffed in agitation. Trying desperately to cling to reason, she grabbed Enrahin and pulled him close. While her only motive was to somehow return her mate to a semblance of sane behavior, instead an irresistible biological urge overcame them both and they began to mate. As was normal with their kind, the mating was insanely violent, noisy, and over as abruptly as it started. In their temporary exhaustion they hardly heard the developing sequence uttered by Control.

. . . WES COM BEEP SHOD . . . WESH COMMUN BEENG SHOP . . . WISH COMMUNIC BEINGS SHIP . . . WISH TO COMMUNICATE WITH BEINGS ON SHIP. PLEASE REPLY. ARE YOU THERE . . .

Ayree flexed sore limbs and wiped blood off herself. Pain, a residual of ecstasy, revulsion, and curiosity were all components of a whirling confusion in her brain. . . . *hate . . . hate . . . hate . . . destroy . . . destroy . . . destroy* . . . The message of a thousand generations shouted wild from her genes. She looked at Enrahin. Like her, he was a mess. But more noticeable was the strangeness of his expression. The fatigue was there, and still the fear. But the hate was gone, as if part of him had burned out from overload.

"Ayree." His voice was weak yet wondering. "Control has language. Yet Control is a machine. That is so, isn't it?"

"That is so," she replied gently. Oddly, as if echoing his overload, her own hate had subsided—though not quite gone. It was still there, seething deep at the edge of her awareness.

"But what if . . ." Enrahin lifted a hand in the universal sign of question, then let it fall. "What if there is life on that other ship? Is it possible they are . . . you know . . ."

She knew. And what he was trying to say chilled her. "*We* are the Giver's chosen instrument of the Great Work." Ayree said, realizing with shock she was saying the holy words as much to remind herself as her mate. "So whatever happens, whatever we see or hear . . ."

WE ARE CALLED HUMAN. WE ARE THE SWORD CREATED TO DESTROY THAT WHICH DEFILES THE ONE'S UNIVERSE. WHAT ARE YOU? IS THERE MORE THAN ONE SWORD?

It was almost too much. Enrahin seemingly did not react at all which, more than anything else, indicated the extent of his sickness. Ayree, still sane though barely so, for an eternity of moments could only glare at Control's master panel as if its electronics had somehow become transformed into protoplasmic ooze. Finally, with a massive effort of will she forced herself to speak.

". . . show . . . me . . ."

One of the screens flickered into life. Two creatures, hand in hand, stared at Ayree. To her confusion they were not so much repulsive as merely ugly; about the same shape as she was but almost hairless, with protruding nostrils and slits of mouths. Their eyes were small and deeply recessed into their skulls. One was smaller than the other, with a greater development of chest. The smaller one spoke, its mouth parts making sounds which Control translated.

WE STILL WISH TO KNOW. ARE YOU ANOTHER SWORD?

Ayree moistened her mouth. "What," she asked with difficulty, "is the One?"

Her mind was functioning a little better now, enough for her to have reasoned that if they did not properly answer *her* question, then all doubts were resolved and she and Enrahin could proceed with whatever was necessary to destroy these strangers and their ship. But Ayree's hope for that simple solution was dashed as the smaller being replied, THE ONE IS THE MASTER OF THE UNIVERSE. THE ONE GAVE US THE TASK TO DELIVER ALL THINGS FROM THE SCOURGE WHICH IMITATES AND PROFANES TRUE LIFE. IN THIS WE ARE THE SWORD OF THE ONE.

Enrahin groped for Ayree's hand. *I am not as sick as you think.* "Perhaps . . ." Again it seemed he groped for words. "Perhaps in the Great Work, what we are is only a part. Perhaps . . ." He lapsed into helpless silence. *Ask them. How many are they?*

Ayree asked.

WE ARE AS YOU SEE, was the unexpected reply. *Two? In that ship? They are lying!*

HOW MANY ARE YOU?

"Two," Ayree promptly lied. "As you."

WE MUST MEET.

It was almost a relief to be able to speak the truth. "That will be difficult. All our surface access tunnels are blocked by fallen rock and we are trapped inside."

WE HAVE MACHINE. WE CAN MELT THROUGH TO YOU.

"It's certainly taking them long enough to react to our little bombshell." Vanderbrusse glanced at his watch. "Nearly a full minute and they haven't said a damn thing."

Still hand in hand, the two Silvers were wandering aimlessly about. Their gaze was open and fixed, as if going through an alien form of somnambulism.

"Perhaps we moved too fast. Talking with the devil is one thing. But having him come to you in person . . ." Kurber shook his head.

Gia had to agree. "Jase, I am afraid you have a point." She burst out, "My god, I think I have managed to mess up the whole thing!"

"Not perhaps so," David said. With soothing logic

the little Phuili continued, "You have offer way fwom inside of asterwoid. Zey too smart to wefuse us doing."

"Maybe, but only if we haven't already driven them over the edge." Kurber gestured at the screen. "Look at those two! Right now they are hovering between pragmatism and that insane purpose of theirs like a tug-of-war between evenly matched teams. If pragmatism wins out, then, Okay. I admit we still have a chance to turn them around. But if it turns out the other way, or even if the rope breaks and they go schizoid on us—then I say we have no choice except to blow them out of space before they can rouse their sleeping buddies."

It was a terrible choice and they all knew it. Communication had been established, and with time could perhaps lead to a kind of grudging acceptance. But the menace represented by the regiments waiting to be unleashed from the asteroid's core, was an unstable component in an equation already weighted against Gia's desire not to be involved in another mass slaughter.

So we have decided?
We have decided.
It will be difficult.
That is so. But what else can we do? Perhaps for too long we have assumed our exclusiveness without properly considering the impossible vastness of the universe. The near destruction of our race surely indicates that the Giver must have more than one arrow to his bow.
It is a possibility we must consider. But even if the Giver did create other instrumentalities for the Great Work, we still cannot be sure of those who are about to come to us.
Agreed. So we must be prepared.
We must be prepared.

Gia's mood at the news of acceptance was a combination of relief and caution. As the work team and their equipment prepared to melt a tunnel from the point on the asteroid's crust indicated by the Silvers, she issued swift instructions.

"David, as soon as your crew is within a meter of breakthrough, Jase and I will go down and take over. Are you sure the other access is well enough camouflaged?"

"Silvers have see and not know what zey see. What looks wockfall is not. So we use as Silvers wait at place where new tunnel to come."

"Good. And if things work out as I hope, your people can withdraw by the same route. But if the situation turns ugly . . ."

"We watch. If need, we act. You and Jase be safe."

Later:

So you are sure the strangers cannot read secret-talk?

Enough that I am convinced it is our greatest advantage over them, though I admit we must be circumspect in its use. We must not arouse their suspicions with too many silences.

Agreed.

"They are close."

"Very close. In a few moments they will be before us."

"When did you deactivate the defense screen? I did not see you anywhere near the panel."

"There was no need. The screen was already down, presumably a result of the phase-shift failure. The even was, after all, catastrophic enough to collapse the exit portals." *And it is that I fear. Why only those tunnels which lead to the surface? Surely, a strangely selective effect.*

Coincidence is often strange.

"Look! The wall is glowing!"

"Then they are here. Better stand clear in case of rock splinters."

Ayree and Enrahin backed into the relative safety of the entrance of Control One as with a hiss and a rumble, part of the corridor wall disappeared. Dust billowed outward, was almost immediately thinned as exhaust vents opened. Cautiously, the "humans" emerged out of the jagged opening and halted. The small one spoke, its thin voice eerily echoing Control's translation. I AM GIA. THIS MALE IS JASE.

They were indeed ugly. But also strangely pathetic with their squashed, pink-skinned faces and awkwardly jointed limbs. Ayree was surprised she could feel pity along with her instinctive revulsion. "I am Ayree," she responded. "This is Enrahin. What do you offer?"

OUR PURPOSE IS TO SERVE THE ONE. WE THINK IT IS YOUR PURPOSE ALSO. IT IS CONFUSING TO US BECAUSE WE DID NOT KNOW THAT OTHERS SHARE THE HOLY CAUSE.

Enrahin signaled, *That, at least, is understandable. It is our own dilemma.*

Ayree repeated. "What do you offer?"

WE OFFER OURSELVES. WE OFFER OUR SHIP AND ALL IT CONTAINS. THE ONE'S UNIVERSE IS MIGHTY AND MUST BE CLEANSED. THERE CAN BE NO OTHER WAY.

All it contains? Challenge him!

"I asked you before. I ask you again. How many are you?"

There was a hesitation. Then: IN OUR SHIP, THERE ARE MANY THOUSANDS IN DORMANCY CHAMBERS. THEY CAN BE RESTORED, BUT ONLY IN THE ONE'S SERVICE.

"Ayree! Praise the Giver, I believe they truly are our soulmates in the Great Work!" *Yet why do I feel so uneasy? What is wrong?*

Perhaps they are too much for logic to expect. We must probe deeper.

"There is a better place to talk than in this corridor." Ayree pointed, then she and Enrahin turned and walked slowly into Control One. *Is this wise?* her mate asked.

Do they know about this space? Ayree countered.

They should not.

Exactly. Then what I am about to do should provoke

no reaction other than perhaps curiosity. Watch them closely.

At first, the humans remained merely hesitant. But as the two Silvers continued past the various control displays and approached the glowing blue-orange panel at the far end of the chamber, Enrahin noticed that the hesitancy seemed to become a distinct nervousness. As if by unspoken agreement, the humans suddenly began to close the distance between themselves and their hosts. Enrahin felt Ayree's hand tighten. *Prepare.*

His pulses raced as her suspicions became his. *I am ready.*

At the panel, Ayree casually lifted her free hand upward toward the illuminated buttons.

STOP HER! roared Control, translating the male's mouthings as both humans lunged forward.

They know! Screaming with primeval hate, the Silvers unsheathed their claws and charged to intercept the humans. It should have been an easy slaughter. The humans were obviously weak and biologically not equipped to face the natural killing machines Ayree and Enrahin were by birthright. But as gray-furred arms swept lethal arcs across where unprotected throats should be, the humans had already dropped prone below a sudden fury of sizzling beams. Enrahin did not have time even to know what killed him. His head half blown from his shoulders, he simply pitched forward in a bloody heap. Ayree cried once and fell across her mate. She twitched a few times and then lay still.

Their hot weapons still at the ready, two armed Phuili edged into the room. Then David came in. His alien expression showed strain but was otherwise unreadable. He squatted next to the bodies.

"Not like fail," he said sadly.

Gia studied the photograph. "Those?" she asked, pointing.

David nodded. "Tiny sensor pads. Vewy sensitive,

much nerve network behind. All over palm of hands. When hold hands, Silvers communicate near good as talk."

Kurber asked, "But what would be the evolutionary need? I noticed nothing wrong with their ability to voice communicate."

"Combative," Gia murmured, half to herself.

"Beg pardon?"

"Try this on for size. Suppose the Silvers have a very long history, perhaps even as long as your people's, David. Also suppose that their world was an incredibly savage place almost exclusively populated by toothed and clawed predators. So to survive long enough to evolve sentience, the Silvers' ancestors had to become even more savage than the rest. Then, as they attained dominance and eliminated most of the competition, those ancestors increasingly turned their savagery on each other. Still they continued to evolve, though obviously it would be a painful process. Therefore a question. In such a situation, given enough eons of continuous combat against natural enemies and then against one's own kind, what kind of personality trait would you expect to develop?"

Kurber frowned. "Paranoia?"

"You said it, dear. Paranoia. But taken to such an extent, and over such a period of time, that the physical ability to 'secret-talk' became as much a part of life as eating and breathing."

David nodded thoughtfully. "But Gia fwiend, does not act of hold hands what you call 'give-way'?"

"Not if that particular behavior is also a basic instinct," the expediter replied. "If it is normal for Silvers always to grab hands with anyone within reach, who then can tell who is secret-talking with whom?"

"And zeir antilife cwusade?"

"A natural extension of what they are. What originated as a survival mechanism on one planet has exponented into a threat against every living thing in the cosmos. As far as the Silver People are concerned, *all* other life is threatening and must therefore be eliminated. From back yard, from planet, even from the universe itself. It's as simple as that."

As she spoke, Gia also knew she was rationalizing. The hardest decision of her life had been the order to vaporize the Silvers' asteroid-ship. Now the asteroid, its thousands of needle-ships and the tens of thousands of intelligent beings it was bearing toward what they considered was their holy destiny; all that was gone. Also eliminated—at least from the foreseeable future— was the chance to correct a great natural tragedy. In their loyalty and obvious love for each other, Gia had seen qualities in Ayree and Enrahin worth saving. And then she had been forced to destroy them. *In some ways, God, you have a lousy sense of humor.*

"We haven't burned all of our boats, you know."

Startled, Gia ejected out of her depression. "What are you talking about?"

Kurber looked uncomfortable. "We'll find them. If they are there to be found, that is."

"Zis one agwee," David said. Unlike Kurber, who had misinterpreted Gia's malaise, the Phuili's deep empathetic sense had enabled him to know and under- stood his human friend's intensity of feeling. Never- theless, he followed Kurber's lead as he pointed out, "If ozer asterwoids, zey pwobably on course for ozer suns which near. Also because pwimitive dwives pwobably fail as zis one, zen easy to know appwoximate place which be."

It was a correct and necessary interpretation which Gia had already determined would be in her report when she returned before Giesse Frobert and his com- mittee. One fact was certain, however. Gia Mayland would quit Expediters and even Earth itself rather than be involved—even remotely—with the killing she knew was to come. Only Major Gostorth, Mary, and the other shock troops from Groobra Four would be happy with the outcome of this particular exercise.

David repeated, "As alweady say, not all lost."

"I think . . ." Gia began, then stopped. Though it had happened before, in other circumstances, the shared sense of *knowing* which passed briefly between her and the Phuili, left the expediter slightly breathless with its intensity. Whatever David was referring to, had, she now knew, nothing at all to do with the possibility of finding other asteroid-ships.

She sought Kurber's hand and interlocked her fingers with his. "David. What is not lost?"

David told her.

And suddenly there was hope.

"How many?" Giesse Frobert asked.

"Six," Gia replied.

"How are they developing?"

"Very well, apparently."

"And when will they be born?"

"About thirteen months from now. According to the Phuili biologists, normal gestation is only half that, but the mortality rate is probably high. With the extended time, they expect their artificial uterus will deliver six healthy little Silvers."

"What about the mother?"

Gia looked down. But not before the Chairman detected a suspicion of moisture in her dark eyes. "Ayree was brain dead. They kept her body functioning only until the embryos could be safely transplanted."

"How long a time was that?"

"Several weeks. She and her mate were then given a ceremonial space burial. I insisted on it."

"So I heard," Frobert said dryly. The Chairman paused a moment, his broad face impassive. "I understand Expediter Kurber returned with you."

"Yes, sir." Unexpectedly, the woman blushed. "We are considering a . . . ah . . . cohabitation contract."

Frobert turned to the man at his side. "Peter, do you know about this?"

The Director of Expediters grinned. "I am encouraging it."

And he's behaving like the cat who caught the canary, the old man grumbled to himself. He cleared his throat. "Expediter Mayland. Director Digonness. I do not like being maneuvered into situations over which I have no control. However, in these somewhat exceptional circumstances, and cognizant of Expediter Mayland's stated intent to resign should I do otherwise, I accept the director's recommendation that Expediters Mayland and Kurber be appointed to Project Alchemy. I trust that is satisfactory?"

"Eminently so," Peter Digonness declared gravely.

Gia merely bowed her head; as much to conceal her swelling emotions as to indicate acquiescence. She wondered how Jase would react when she told him. *Bless him,* she thought. *He too will probably turn away, especially being a male. The poor dears are not supposed to display such feelings.*

"Alchemy?" the Chairman was asking. "I do not understand the relevance."

Digonness said seriously, "I think, sir, you should ask Expediter Mayland about that one. Like so many other things, it was her idea."

Gia managed a weak smile. "Alchemy. The transmutation of base metals into gold." Abruptly her eyes flashed and she added fiercely, "Or in our case, the transmutation of an intelligent species!"

For long seconds, Giesse Frobert, Chairman of the World Union Council and therefore master of mankind's highest political office, studied the flushed expediter. With a grunt of effort, he then ponderously heaved his bulk out of the chair and walked to the door. Just before he went out, he turned.

"Alchemy, you say?" He chuckled. "My dear, if you pull this off, and if I am still around when you do . . ." The chuckle became a rumbling laugh. "My god, I will recommend you for sainthood!"

How long before Earth and Phuili again needed the services of the psychopaths of Groombra Four was still only an informed guess. Thousands, tens of thousands or perhaps even millions of the deadly Silver People were out there between the stars, dreaming away the light-years until they could waken to begin their savage crusade. But now there seemed at least a reasonable possibility they could be located and destroyed before Day One of Armageddon. For most of those who knew, even for those among them who were sickened by the necessity of having to accept genocide as a viable solution, Project Alchemy seemed at best a wishful fantasy.

But Project Alchemy was not a fantasy.

On a small previously uninhabited world beyond the Hub, guarded by a screen of warships whose commander had been instructed to destroy without question not only any unauthorized vessel which came within ten diameters of the planet, but also anything which came up *from* the planet, six lively youngsters were being educated, studied, and above all, loved.

Perhaps the instructions in their genes would ultimately overwhelm what was being learned within their furry skulls. Those of two races who were their guardians and teachers had, of course, dedicated their lives to making it otherwise. But it was a delicate edge they all trod; balanced between the time-consuming work with the youngsters on the one hand, and the near certainty on the other that the warriors of Groombra Four could be performing their grisly work before Alchemy had a chance.

It was, in a sense, a race. And the prize was much more than the continued existence of an intelligent species. It was also a race for the soul of a civilization.

Careful not to damage its complex circuitry, Gia gingerly wriggled her hand into the glove. Then she took the hand of the graceful child at her side. Wide eyed and radiating innocence, Emma looked at the expediter trustingly. But Gia was wary. The children were born actors and could convince the most profound skeptic that black was white. So this, the first test of *secret-talk* between Silver and human, was infinitely more than a mere indication of the child's sincerity. Within the next few moments, ten years of work would either be triumphantly verified or shattered forever.

"Do you love me?" Gia asked.

Emma answered promptly. "Of course I love you. You are mother."

Gia interfaced with the computer. *Do you love me?* she signaled via the glove to the natural sensors on the palm of the child's hand.

Emma was startled and tried to pull away. But the woman held firm. *Do you love me?* she repeated.

The child tugged again; tentatively. Gia relaxed her grip but did not let go. The child trembled and crept close. A silken arm encircled Gia's neck and a furry head pressed into the hollow between neck and shoulder. Then:

I love you, Momma Gia.

All was well.

The ambassadors were ready.

SIX

DRY RUN

The wrong still exists. The righting of the wrong has not yet been accomplished. Yet who is to judge the moral difference between success, or an honest attempt which fails? Perhaps that is a judgment for the gods. Each mortal being is a battleground between emotion and intellect, and failure—or success—too often triggers a reaction which is not intelligent. Yet perhaps that is how it should be. Because if mortal beings act and react according to a logic which is dictated by intellect alone, then there can never be those great (and not so rare) accomplishments which result from "supermortal" effort. In which case, it is surely better to hand over the universe to the pseudo-intelligences of metal and plastic—

Do you love me?
I love you, Momma Gia.
That was how Emma had first confirmed her affectionate nature via secret-talk. Now, even after a further two years of intensive education and training, she remained the likable and lively individual she had always been, although the physical transformation was startling. From a gangling, awkward youngster whose double-jointed limbs seemed designed to tangle rather than be useful, Emma had matured into a sleek, gray-furred being with a grace and suppleness which made her mentors feel awkward. The fierce pug-nosed face and fanged grin would perhaps be disconcerting to anyone unfamiliar with the Silver People, but to the

humans and Phuili who were her adopted parents, Emma was beautiful. Nevertheless, the young Silver and her four sisters and one brother had known their idyllic existence could not last forever, although the break—when it finally came—was sooner than expected.

Gia Mayland had always been Emma's special parent. Indeed, the two were so close that not even secret-talk was necessary to reveal to Emma that Gia was deeply troubled. More ominous was the fact Gia was not wearing the glove. That piece of equipment, through which Gia could secret-talk via the natural sensors on Emma's hands, was not even visible. It was as if the human did not want her meanings distorted by emotion.

"Emma dear, I have to ask the question I have not asked since I first told you about your people. What is your reaction to what the Silver People intend to do in the universe?"

Puzzled, Emma stared at the slim, dark-haired woman. She understood the question and at the same time did not understand it. It made as much sense as being asked to identify the color of the blue sky. "It is wrong to destroy life. It is wrong even to want to destroy life." She meant exactly what she said. But she wished Gia wore the glove. Only with secret-talk could Emma communicate the intensity of her abhorrence.

The woman sighed. After twelve years with the project, she felt she knew the youngsters as much as any mother would her own children. Nevertheless, the six were *alien*, and despite her hopes Gia was aware there would always be unknowns.

"Emma, from the moment we determined the pregnancy of your natural mother, there was no doubt in our minds that her offspring would be brought up under the principal of absolute honesty. As soon as the six of you were old enough to understand, you were all told about the Silver People's monomaniacal determination to eliminate every form of life other than their own. It is why we destroyed their home world, and it is why we must do something about the ships they seeded into space before their sun was triggered into nova. We found one of those ships, Emma, and tried to find a way to neutralize its threat without destroying its crew. Well, you know what happened. We were forced to destroy that ship and the thousands of sentients aboard. And when it was over, all we had to show for the ghastly experience was one nearly dead pregnant female who gave birth to you and your brother and sisters before she died. It is a terribly unhappy story Emma which, with your help, may yet have a happier ending."

The young Silver grasped both of Gia Mayland's hands. Because the human was not wearing the glove, there was no silent communication. But the warmth and mutual pressing of fingers was a comfort. "Happier? How, Momma, how?"

"Well to start with, we have found another ship of the Silver People."

"You have? Where? How can I help?"

Gia said sadly, "You start by becoming grown-up."

It was almost claustrophobic but not quite. In a tiny glass-ended chamber recessed into the wall of a huge cavern at the heart of the ship, Emma waited for the signal. Beyond the trasparency, thousands more of the life-suspension units studded the walls of the cavern. Each cramped cavity contained a stasis-preserved being superficially like Emma, but whose dormant brain cells contained instructions to destroy. Not to preserve.

Even with the combination of human ingenuity and Phuili science, it had been a herculean task to phase-shift the gigantic mass of the ship to a new destination. But when the radiation from the approaching sun triggered the sequences which would begin to rouse the sleepers, hopefully none of them would suspect the hoax which, in the name of sanity, had been perpetrated. Neither, it was also hoped, would they detect the presence of aliens in the hidden control center at one end of the converted asteroid.

"Emma, are you all right?" As clear as if voice-spoken, the words impressed into Emma's thoughts.

Emma fingered the implant at the side of her neck. "Yes, Momma Gia. But I am lonely."

"Until this thing is over, we will always be here. Me, Jase, your brother Silskin, David—"

"—iss to be accepted you lonely," interjected Davakinapwottapellazanzis. Preferably "David" to those without benefit of the dexterous Phuili tongue, he was Emma's second favorite parent. Possessing a sad-eyed canine head atop a squat and powerful body, a contrast in temperament as well as physical appearance to the humans he was associated with, the old Phuili had nevertheless charmed the six young Silvers almost from the moment they became aware of the beings of two other races who shared their world. David continued, "But you not old, so can accept pwoblems better zan older. And if mission succeed, you have Silver fwiends you not have before."

Silver friends. It was the prize at the end of the rainbow for Emma, and abruptly a fierce determination replaced her fear. I will do it, she told herself. I *will* do it!

And then another voice, warm and familiar. "Hand-touch," said Silskin encouragingly.

"Hand-touch," Emma replied, regretting her brother's unfortunate choice of words. She still was not adjusted to the nerve blocks which had eliminated all feeling in the sensitive palms of her hands. Hand-to-hand secret-talk was an extra voice and ear for a Silver, and to lose it was analagous to becoming a partial deaf-mute. But because that unique form of communication allowed no deception, or even half truths designed to deceive, Emma's temporary diminishment was the only way to preserve her undercover role amid the thousands of wild ones aboard the drifting ship.

"Seven minutes," Jase Kurber announced. Kurber was one half of a relationship he and Momma Gia called "marriage." He was likable enough, although

Emma envied the closeness apparent between the two humans. "Remember Emma, you must act as if it is a complete mystery to you why Control reactivated a lower priority person such as yourself."

"Yes, Poppa Jase." Emma stretched as much as she could within her claustrophobic confines and tried not to stare too hard at the ruby indicator above her head. Somewhere on the asteroid-ship's surface a detector had already locked on to the nearing star and was waiting for penetration into its circum-solar life-zone before generating the signal which would begin to reactivate up to a dozen of the sleepers. Based on past experience, the number of reactivations could be as low as two, although analysis of the control sequences had raised the possibility that no two Silvers ships were alike either in physical layout or programming—adding an uncomfortable element of uncertainty to each encounter.

The indicator began to blink; once, twice, and then urgently. It was a simple warning signal, telling Emma that far more involved processes than a blinking light were proceeding in other chambers. She cracked open the lid, holding it back against spring pressure until she could see which of the other chambers were activating.

At first she saw nothing, although the slightest flicker of light would be a beacon in the stygian darkness of the cavern. She opened the lid a little farther and wriggled her body outward so she could peer over the rim of her chamber. Almost instantly she saw it; a spark only meters above her head. There was another glimmer, to the right and dimmed by distance. And then, starting from a point at the top of the cavern and cascading down its sides like an incandescent flood, the main lighting system waxed to full brilliance within seconds; revealing thousands of glass-lidded stasis chambers glittering like huge jewels set in the rock.

From the chamber above Emma's, a lithe figure floated free, swiveled, and grasped a handhold. Like a butterfly resting after emerging from its chrysalis, Emma thought, although the delicate winged creatures she knew only from books and instructional tapes hardly resembled the bedraggled humanoid clinging to the wall.

"Jihevva!" the Silver said suddenly, and with a powerful thrust of its long legs launched itself upward toward where another Silver was just emerging. Still only halfway out of its chamber, the second Silver shouted something and pointed across the cavern to where two other Silvers were poised near their open chambers. More shouts were exchanged, until the first two Silvers leaped across the huge space, turned in flight, and landed neatly adjacent to the others.

Emma said excitedly, "There are four! They have rendezvoused across the cavern from me."

"Then it is time to show yourself," Gia Mayland instructed from the concealed room less than two hundred meters away. The human added, with a concern which warmed Emma's heart. "But be careful, dear. Please."

"Yes, Momma." Emma let go the lid of her chamber, and as it swung wide she shouted, "Hello!"

The reaction was silence, as the four swung about and stared in her direction. Although Emma's training was alien, the physical instincts she had been born with were sound, and she launched herself across the cavern and alighted close to them with unerring ease. "Hello," she repeated, meeting their puzzled faces.

Finally one spoke. "Who are you? Control was not programmed to revive any other."

"I am Berein," Emma replied, using a name her mentors had extracted from the records of her mother's ship. She shrugged. "I do not know why I was chosen. I am only a Priority Eighteen."

"An eighteen?" One of the Silvers reached out and grasped Emma's hand. The large eyes widened with astonishment. "No wonder. You are a lesser!"

They clustered around Emma, touching and stroking her. They were friendly, sympathetic, showing a positive side of the Silver character completely at variance with their attitude to other life-forms. "Obviously Control erred," said the one who had attempted secret-talk with Emma. She pointed at herself and then at the others. "I am Gelhon and this is my mate Bewokul. That is Jihevva and his mate Halranen. But now—" Gelhon turned toward a large opening in the upper part of the cavern. "—our immediate purpose must be to find out why we are here."

As if with one thought, the revived Silvers floated up to the opening. Emma followed meekly behind. The opening was the inner end of a tunnel which drove arrow-straight to the asteroid's surface, but halfway along Gelhon turned aside and led them through an armored portal which opened automatically at their approach. Beyond, was a large room crammed with panels and indicators. Gelhon stopped part way into the room and said loudly, "Control?"

CONTROL, acknowledged the computer. Containing neither gender nor expression, its cold machine-voice made Emma's fur crawl.

"State reason for activation of life units."

VEHICLE APPROACHING TARGET SYSTEM. INDICATION OF LIFE BEARING PLANET IN INNER ZONE.

There was a hiss of indrawn breath. "State degree of infestation," Gelhon ordered.

DATA INSUFFICIENT.

Ignoring Emma, the four Silvers grasped hands and for several seconds stood in silent communication. It was the first time in her life Emma felt truly left out, and in desperation she called, "Momma Gia!"

"Emma, what is the matter?"

"We are in Control. The others are using secret-talk."

Gia understood. "You knew that would happen. Have you any idea what they are discussing?"

"I only know the computer has told them about the life-world in this system."

"We heard that, and it was expected—or at least hoped for. Considering how difficult it was to reprogram that electronic juggernaut of theirs—"

Emma abruptly broke contact as the four released hands and Gelhon came to her. "Berein, we do not wish to be unkind, but important decisions must be made. You heard Control. I hope you understand."

"Yes, Gelhon, I do understand. You will tell me what I cannot sense?"

"We have already decided to activate a full echelon. The ark is not yet close enough to that world to know how much of its surface is contaminated, but we do know that a mininum of fifty scouts is necessary to sterilize even a small continent."

Emma sub-vocalized, "Momma, did you hear?"

"It is being recorded, Emma. Just remember the special place you hold as a 'lesser.' Normal Silvers look on those without the ability to secret-talk as some human cultures do their blind—as people compensated with a wisdom not held by the sighted. It is a delicate edge you tread, my dear, so be very cautious what you say or do."

Part of Emma's training had given her the ability to communicate through her implant while outwardly carrying on a separate conversation or activity. It was an asset which gave her an objectivity she could apply to either side at will. This time she was applying that ojectivity to what was going on around her, as the one called Jihevva approached a big panel at the end of the room. The panel was divided into an orange and blue section, each glowing with thousands of illuminated indicator buttons. Jihevva began pushing the buttons until twenty-five pairs of them were flashing orange and blue. He nodded with satisfaction. "We will wait for our brothers and sisters in the Instruction Hall."

That was a large, vaulted chamber which they accessed by following a smaller corridor paralleling the main tunnel. Although Emma was as familiar with the interior layout of the gigantic vessel as any of her crew, identification was another matter. She had to avoid the situation in which she would be expected to know the location of any place by its name. Emma communicated her unease to Gia, who replied warningly,

"You must anticipate such traps. If necessary, feign illness or find an excuse for one of the others to accompany you. But never arouse suspicions by admitting ignorance."

It was sound advice, and Emma felt comforted by the fact that those who had always been closest to her were still—even in the literal sense—within reach. A little more relaxed now, yet conscious of her role as a Silver of lowly status, she remained silent and separate as her new acquaintances huddled together and communicated with a mixture of voice and secret-talk.

If Emma knew anything at all, it was the absolute certainty that the Silver People's dedication to the destruction of all life was an obscenity almost beyond belief. So why was it she felt strangely attracted to these mirror images of herself? Did it mean that even a lifetime's indoctrination cannot thin the call of the blood? Not according to Poppa David, she remembered, who had often remarked in his profound Phuili way that "a body is not more a person zan a house is who lives inside." Certainly Emma had never thought of her human and Phuili mentors as anything other than persons, even considering their obvious physical differences. On the other hand, was it possible that was an exception rather than the rule?

Prejudice, especially of the racial kind, was a subject not taught or even discussed in the small planetary colony devoted to the upbringing of six young Silvers. But the colony's data-base contained a reservoir of knowledge culled from the libraries of two planets, and over the years Emma's innate curiosity had caused her to accumulate an incredible clutter of unrelated facts—including a chilling item about one human response to race difficulties as expressed by the word "genocide." The human race had, of course, long since evolved out of that dark period of its past. But if Attila, Hitler, Karel Hewton or any other of those charismatic demagogues had had the ability to lead their followers into the galaxy, would they have been any less deadly than the Silver People? In fact, not even the history of the Phuili was entirely free of—

I am rationalizing! Emma shuddered as she realized the traitorous potential of her thoughts. Evil is evil from any source, and must be expunged. By peaceful means if possible. By the destruction of worlds if necessary. Morality never involves an easy choice.

She started as a furry hand touched her shoulder. "They come," Gelhon said solemnly. Emma turned and looked to the entrance of the room as pair by pair they came in, twenty-four couples and a lone female. The female was in a state of crisis, twisting her head back and forth and moaning, "Kapakan is not! Kapakan is not!"

"She found her mate dead in his chamber," Gelhon whispered as the female was calmed by a sequence of reaching, soothing hands. "It must always be thus. The system is not perfect."

Emma touched her implant and switched to the symbolic shorthand she and her siblings had developed after they received the tiny units. The mentors knew of the shorthand and had, indeed, encouraged it. From the start, it had been realized that hand-to-hand secret-talk was merely the physical manifestation of something much more complex inherent in the Silver brain. The implants had proved the theory, giving the young Silvers the ability to communicate at lightning speed with each other, as well as at a normal rate with the mentors themselves.

Silskin!

Emma!

From this moment I cannot use time by talking normal with the olders. Tell them you are henceforth their channel to me.

I will tell them, dear sister.

It did not have the warmth and closeness of secret-talk, of course, but at least it was an exclusive link with her brother. In any case, Momma Gia and Poppas David and Jase could still hear what her ears heard. They did not need Silskin for a running commentary.

One of the newcomers called for attention. He was a large male with grizzled fur and pale, glittering eyes. "I understand we are approaching a world which needs cleansing. But that we are not yet close enough to know if the Holy Task can be mounted with a minimum effort."

Jihevva nodded. "That is correct, Master Delbroj."

"What is the status of this ark and its crew?"

"As expected, we had meltdown of the main drive and the ark is drifting. All other systems are functioning, including the stasis generators. Generally, I believe we are healthy, Master Delbroj."

"As the Giver wills," the old male said solemnly.

It was a strangely fatalistic reaction to the news that their ship had become an inert wanderer, captive to the same gravitational laws which governed the movements of planets and suns. But Emma was not surprised. The primitive one-surge drives of the Silvers ships had been barely sufficient to phase-shift them half a light-year toward their respective target suns, even as their own sun was triggered into nova by human-Phuili action. Nevertheless, although the Silvers were the ultimate xenophobes, they were not so mad as to permit their seeds to die a lonely death in the interstellar void. Crews could be preserved in stasis until the end of time, if necessary, and the thousands of tiny space-scouts encrusted like barnacles on the surface of each ship, were themselves capable of ranging across light-weeks of distance. It was why the fifty or so giant carriers which were known to be spread across the surface of an expanding sphere a light-year across, were potentially a worse threat than that once posed by the billions of Silvers who had been alive until their planets were incinerated.

Unless . . .

Emma and her siblings were the alternative. They were Silvers, in blood and flesh and bone exactly as those on the ships. But their dedication was to life, not to its antithesis. If the wild Silvers were to be diverted from their deadly crusade, it could only be by others of their kind. It was a task many Phuili and humans were convinced was impossible—who were, in fact, resigned to the unpleasant necessity of having to vaporize each Silvers ship as soon as it was found. Nevertheless "Project Alchemy" was secretly established to raise and educate the six baby Silvers. The Project was a desperate attempt to expurgate some of the guilt resulting from the horror of the preemptive strike which had destroyed almost an entire race. It was also an incredible burden to place on six young shoulders, and no one knew it better than the six themselves. But they were proud. Above all, they were willing.

It had become quiet again in the Instruction Hall as most of the Silvers disappeared to perform tasks for which they had been trained before they entered stasis. A few, Emma suspected, would soon be suited up and out on the surface, beginning to prepare some of the deadly little scouts to receive cargoes of radioactive poison to be dumped on any target which had even a suspicion of reproductive life. *Why are they like this?* she wondered, in her innocence still doubting what her teachers had told her of the evolutionary history of the Silver People—of the legions of savage carnivores ranging from insectiles to thirty-meter monsters which the evolving sentients had had to conquer and destroy just to avoid being destroyed themselves. A genetic hate, Poppa Jase had called it.

Those who remained, including Jihevva, Delbroj, the grieving female who was called Felwon, and Emma herself, returned to Control. Felwon, learning of the other single female's "handicap" and realizing this was a fellow misfit, stayed close. *If only she knew the whole truth,* Emma communicated wryly to her brother.

Cultivate her, Poppa David came back through Silskin. *That kind of depressed mental state makes her a possible convert.*

It was a good suggestion, if a doubtful one. It had, after all, taken a lifetime's training to enable Emma to win over her own call of the blood. Nevertheless, it was one of the slim possibilities she could not ignore.

Emma's attention was jolted by a bellow from the one they called Master. "It is not possible, I tell you! The star pattern is all wrong!"

Jihevva had activated an optical pickup, and he and Delbroj were staring at a big display panel. Compensating circuits had blanked out the glare from the central sun enough to display the background stars. "In the Giver's name, I should know," the old Silver continued angrily. "I was the one who originally selected our first target, and I tell you this is not it!"

Looking doubtful, Jihevva turned away from the panel. "Control."

CONTROL, acknowledged the computer.

"State time since initial activation of the main drive system."

THIRTY-NINE YEARS, FORTY-THREE DECIMAL SIX DAYS.

Actually, it was less than seventeen years. But the human and Phuili specialists had done their work well, reprogramming Control as well as diverting the millions of tons of mass to another system. Unfortunately, no one had anticipated the photographic recall of an elderly Silver.

"Are we on course to Prime Target?" Jihevva asked.

NEGATIVE.

There was a hiss of indrawn breath. Delbroj chuckled nastily. Emma waited. There was still a question to be asked.

"How far are we off course?"

MINUS DECIMAL ZERO ZERO THREE DEGREES.

"But that is nothing to . . ."

MAIN UNIT WILL PENETRATE CHROMOSPHERE OF TARGET STAR IN THREE ONE ZERO DECIMAL EIGHT DAYS.

"What?"

The die was cast. Emma expelled air in a long sigh, outwardly as horrified as the others, but reacting for an entirely different reason—the knowledge that the incentive was finally in place. She envied as she watched the others, including Felwon, agitatedly secret-talk. Her own palms tingled from the irritation of the nerve blocks. *Now they know,* she signaled.

That is obvious. From this moment your real work begins. But be careful of the old one. His attitude is unexpected.

So was Felwon's. Her expression calm, almost ethereal, she came to Emma and said dreamily, "It seems we are destined to burn. Even as billions of our brothers and sisters were burned by the sun under which we were all born. Do you not think that is poetic, Berein?" Felwon gently touched Emma's cheek. "You are a lesser. I lost my love. What can be better for us two than to welcome the end of our pain?"

"No!" Unceremoniously grabbing the female's arm, Jihevva swung her to face him. He was angry. "Three hundred and ten days is not tomorrow, and in any case our lives are not ours to waste with useless moaning about what cannot be changed! Do you understand me?"

"Yes, Jihevva." Like the switching of a circuit, Felwon abruptly withdrew from the edge of insanity and was contrite. She hung her head. "You are right. Therefore I am wrong. Our holy purpose must always come before our feelings."

Emma marveled at the discipline. To be able to order someone back from the mental brink and be obeyed was, she knew, something uncommon in both Phuili and human experience. Despite herself, she warmed at the knowledge she was also of this species.

Gia Mayland signaled, *The female's concern with feelings is a good indication of where she is vulnerable. I suggest, dear, you take advantage of that vulnerability.*

Yes, Momma, Emma agreed, not liking the callousness of the suggestion but realizing the situation was one in which the end did truly justify any means.

Then it was David. *Emma, it is through you the people on that ship are about to be presented with an impossible dilemma. We Phuili were also once faced with such a dilemma, and you know how we solved it. Use that knowledge.*

I will, Poppa David, Emma replied, appreciating the old Phuili's reminder that the Silver People's obsessive hatred of other life-forms shared, in many respects, the instinctive knowledge that the Phuili had of themselves as being the indisputable heirs of the universe. It was the coming of the humans, a race which in the ridiculously short span of a few centuries had advanced from the wheel to interstellar travel, which had threatened to shatter that prime tenet of Phuili belief and culture. But the simple device of acknowledging humans as "intelligent animals" had preserved the ancient equilibrium, albeit with the reluctant agreement of the humans themselves. It was a compromise, Poppa David had told his young pupils, in which the impossible had been reclassified as "improbable"— permitting a cooperation which, to the profound surprise of everyone, proved superior to the sum of its two parts.

Solidly anchored to the rock of his own conviction, Delbroj seemed unaffected by the computer's prediction of disaster. Into the embarrassed silence which followed Jihevva's denunciation of the mateless female, the Master repeated softly, "I still do not believe it. That is the wrong sky."

Jihevva tensed, clearly on the verge of arguing the point. Instead, in a partial sidestep, he asked, "Are you willing to concede there is an infested planet out there?"

Delbroj hesitated. "Not absolutely." Then, grudgingly, "But I agree we must investigate further. Even if we are in the wrong system."

Emma wished the old one would go away. His stubbornness in the face of overwhelming evidence was beginning to worry her. She prayed the human-Phuili teams had not missed anything in their reprogramming of the computer. Even the slightest evidence of external manipulation and consequently of other intelligent life, would be fatal to hopes of diverting this shipload of Silvers away from their savage purpose. It was fortunate that Delbroj's title "Master" had no official status other than signifying respect for someone of long experience. Jihevva, as a first-roused, was the one with authority.

Again, Jihevva spoke to the computer. "State degree of life-infestation on planet in inner zone."

The odds were that not enough time had elapsed since Gelhon had asked the same question. But the line between negative and positive is often narrow, and in this case the line had clearly been crossed. PRESENCE OF CHLOROPHYLL AND ATMOSPHERIC OXYGEN INDICATIVE OF VEGETATIVE LIFE FORMS, the computer replied. There was a pause. Then, as if with an electronic afterthought; APPROXIMATE NINE ZERO PERCENT PROBABILITY OF REPRODUCTIVE ANIMAL FORMS.

"Keduhunna!" Jihevva turned to Delbroj, and in unison the two males repeated the ancient call to exterminate. *"Keduhunna!"*

Timidly, "Berein" asked, "What happens, after?"

That startled them. Even Felwon seemed astonished. The Master, who had ignored Emma until now, stalked over and took one of her hands. He nodded. "As I was told. A lesser."

Emma steeled herself. "Master, does it serve our holy cause to die in the fires of a star? That is only one world. And we are enough to cleanse many."

Delbroj gently laid a large hand on her head. "One bridge at a time, little one. First we will do what we must."

"Then can we leave the ark before it burns and go down to that world? Perhaps stay there long enough to find another space rock we can make into a new ark? Control has said there is air for us to breathe."

The old Silver was patient. "Air is only part of what we need. We must also have food and water. I know that world has water, but after our work is done there, would you want to eat the rotting matter of once-life? For you, little one, for me and for all of us, far better a clean end in the solar fire." From sympathy, Delbroj's expression darkened to anger. "One world only. *One* world! If we were on the proper course, there could have been many on which to continue the Giver's work. Hundreds. Perhaps thousands!"

Despite her nervousness at the old one's continued persistence, Emma was satisfied. She had planted the seed which sooner or later would force her listeners to confront the obnoxious option. And she was certain they would not be able to keep it to themselves; secret-talk would inevitably spread the idea like a wildly communicable disease. The key, even for a people as fanatically dedicated as the Silvers, was in that all-encompassing human phrase, "The proper rationalization."

Emma slept poorly that night, despite the approval communicated from her mentors in their hidden chamber. Felwon had chosen the neighboring cubicle, and her frequent whimpering made it difficult either to relax or concentrate. In fact, Emma was beginning to have doubts about Felwon's potential value. Despite the apparent death-wish reversal, it seemed too much to expect a turnaround—especially to the extent the female would subscribe to the option. Grief is an emotion which is not so easily exorcised.

Eventually, Emma did slump into a fitful sleep in which her dreams proved almost as exhausting as real-life. Her subconscious conjured up disturbing images of friends and enemies in which neither could be distinguished from the other. Humans, Phuili, and Silver People merged, separated, fought, and loved with complete interchangeability. Familiar faces, some on not so familiar bodies, welcomed, accused, and hated with a gallery of emotions and expressions passing through her awareness like random ghosts. And when Emma finally woke, it was to a cacophony as confusing as her dreams.

It was as if the ship had become a hive of ants, with scurryings, shouts, and indeterminate noises around, above and below her. Still half asleep, Emma murmured, "Momma."

"Hush," Gia Mayland said through the implant.

"Wha . . . what is happening?"

"I don't know. But I would not be surprised if there have been unauthorized awakenings. Perhaps you can find out at Control."

"I will go there." But first Emma checked the next cubicle and saw that Felwon was gone. The single sheet from the female's bunk was bundled and tossed aside. The corridor which connected the row of cubicles was thronged with dazed Silvers; talking, wandering, and hand-touching. Emma pushed her way toward Control, trying to ignore the groping hands, only half hearing the plaintive questions which averaged out to, "What is happening? Why am I here? Why are so many here?" The entrance to Control was guarded by two large Silvers, each armed with a hand projector and a pair of long, wickedly curved knives. Emma was about to be thrust back when someone called from within the partly open portal, "It is all right. Let her pass."

There were at least a dozen inside, including the first four. Felwon was crouched in a corner, curled almost in a fetal position. A bloodied, dead Silver was crumpled near her. At the far end of Control, all but a few of the indicators on the orange-blue panel were flashing in unison. Gelhon saw Emma's widening eyes and nodded. "That's right, Berein. This—" She poked Felwon with one foot, "—came in here, killed the guard, and then activated most of the sleepers."

Emma caught her breath. "Why?"

"Because she is obviously mad," Halranen declared. She added flatly, "Felwon has killed us all."

"We are going to die anyway." Jihevva gestured at the big screen, on which the sun was already showing a perceptible disc. "The only difference, now, is that everyone will know it."

Bewokul chuckled. "Consider the bright side. With three thousand scouts and nine thousand people to crew them, we can sterilize that world a dozen times over." He shrugged. "And why not? There is nothing else we can do."

Felwon stirred and raised her head. Her eyes were wild, unseeing. "You can live," she whispered.

Emma was glad to be away from the ship's teeming interior. She was not so happy about being out of touch with her mentors, although during the few moments she had before she boarded the scout, Poppa David had told her she should welcome this opportunity to continue what Felwon had so surprisingly started. "She hate because she alive when want not to be so," the old Phuili suggested. "Zerefore she make avewyone awake so zey can see sun and know zey will burn."

So a sane mind explains a deranged one, Emma reflected as she watched the blue-brown landscape below the scout. Her moody introspection was disturbed by a single explosive epithet by the scout's pilot. "Life!" Jihevva was glaring out at the rolling grasslands and occasional clumps of bush. "Just look at that. The whole planet is contaminated!"

In fact it was not a particularly verdant world. In the grip of an ice age, it had huge ice caps extending to mid lattitudes. Only in the equatorial regions, on the single continent and a straggling archipelago, was there an ecology which supported sparse savannas and widely scattered subarctic forests. Nevertheless, it was clear Halranen shared her mate's distaste.

"I have seen enough. Please take us back to the ark."

Emma had been raised on a world not too dissimilar from this one. Pacific's oceans were larger, its climate milder, its land-based vegetation a little lusher. The indigenous animal life was widely scattered and timid. So unremarkable was Pacific, with so few potential distractions, it had been selected as the ideal location for "Alchemy," the project dedicated to raising six young Silvers to a true respect for all living things. But as she looked at the retreating surface of this other life-bearing sphere, Emma wondered if Pacific had been the right place for her education. *I have seen enough images of the abundant worlds of Earth and Phuili to love and respect the vibrant force which is life. Yet how can I communicate to these brothers and sisters of mine what I have only indirectly experienced? It is so difficult!*

One thing, however, was certain. With her current captive audience of two, there would never be a better opportunity to begin. "It makes one wonder," she muttered, as if to herself.

Halranen turned in her seat. "Wonder? About what?"

"Sorry. I was thinking aloud."

"Compared to most of us, I suppose you do have more time to think about things. I mean, considering your—ah—impediment." Embarrassed, the female went on, "What is on your mind?"

Emma shrugged. "I just do not understand why we must all die after the decontamination of one small world. The Giver made us to purify galaxies, not to expend ourselves on a dust mote."

That startled Jihevva, who locked the controls while he turned and stared at the passenger. "Berein, you cannot know what you say, otherwise I am sure you would not say it!" His tone softened. "But of course, you do not understand. The ark is destined to plunge into the sun of this system, and nothing we can do will change that. So we must use the one small opportunity presented to us, and then prepare to die. It is that simple."

"Forgive me, please, but I do not believe that is so. It seems to me there is at least one other option."

Emma knew she was treading on thin ice. She also knew she could push the limits of propriety a little farther than would be accepted from a "normal" Silver. But how much farther? Praying she would not have to resort to extreme action, she tongued the tooth switch which armed the deadly little needle weapons concealed under the retractable claws of both thumbs.

Jihevva had returned his attention to the controls. The scout was above atmosphere now, and he opened the homing dish from its recess in the hull. The dish swiveled, and within seconds locked on to the ark's signal. The drive thrummed, they were thrust back against their restraints, the planet dropped away into the darkness. The male did not look at Emma, but tension was evident in the manner he grabbed his mate's hand. "What option?"

Emma took a deep breath. "Instead of decontaminating the planet, we use what is there to survive until we can refit another ark and continue our mission. Each scout cannot carry much, but because there are many, we should be able to transport enough material to give us a start with—"

"Just a moment," Halranen interrupted. "Use *what* to survive?"

"Protein."

"Of course, protein!" Halranen said crossly. She started to say more, but the words caught in her throat. Horrified, both she and Jihevva turned and stared at the defiant one in the back seat. If the male had been a human, Emma was sure he would be livid. "You dare to suggest we use—" He almost choked, "—*living* matter?"

"It is protein, isn't it?" Emma insisted with feigned innocence. "Synthesized or grown, why should it make a difference? Instead of destroying it, we make use of it. And survive. And ultimately continue our holy mission."

For Emma it was the final, absolute commitment. What happened during the next few seconds would be the making or breaking of Project Alchemy and the hopes it stood for. If wild Silvers could not be turned from their deadly crusade, they would be destroyed. Jihevva and Halranen would be the first, instantly paralyzed and then dying as the virulent poison from

Emma's needles acted on their nervous systems. Then the ark itself, vaporized along with the thousands of sentients aboard her. And every other ark, as soon as it was found, without hesitation and certainly without mercy. And because civilization is the ultimate expression of the life force, that genocidal precedent would trigger a guilt which for generations would haunt the collective psyche like a malevolent and unexorcisable spirit.

All this passed through Emma's mind as she prepared for the worst. It was a tribute to a combination of training and rigid self control that she did not react when Halranen suddenly screeched, "It was what Felwon said! We can live!"

"No!" The male pulled his hand away from his mate in shock, for a moment also unknowingly on the brink of termination. He shouted back, "Felwon was wrong! Berein is wrong! Better to die!" Again the two clutched hands, and in silent yet violent communication they strained like two arm wrestlers. When they separated, both were in a state of near collapse.

"We can live," Jihevva said dully.

"Yes." Halranen turned to the unparticipating passenger with an expression which was a compound of relief and accusation. "You had better be right, Berein."

It was only a battle, yet for a moment Emma felt she had single-handedly won the war. She was uncertain what had happened, except to suspect that in Silver terms Halranen and her mate had become insane. In a greater sense they were perhaps the first of their race to find true sanity—except that particular hope was dashed when Jihevva explained, "It is a sacrifice we must accept so that we or our descendants can continue the Great Work."

Sensing that for the moment further words from her would be superfluous or even counterproductive, Emma nodded silent agreement. She would like to have known how Jihevva and Halranen proposed to persuade others to the new doctrine—or even if they had a plan at all—but instead had to wait with lonely anticipation as the two communicated only via secret-talk until the scout finally reberthed on the ark several hours later. As they entered the crowded tunnels, Emma was met by two guards who promptly escorted her to a re-straining cell.

She could not believe it was happening. "Momma," Emma subvocalized plaintively as the door slammed shut. She tried to open the door, but it would not budge.

Silskin answered. *Emma! What has happened? Are you all right?*

No, I am not all right! I want to talk to Momma Gia!

There was a pause. Then; "Emma?"

"Momma, what is going on? They have locked me up!"

"I know. I don't understand it either. Emma, what happened between you and those two while you were away?"

"I wish I knew. Jihevva and Halranen *said* they accepted the necessity of surviving on that world. But how can I be sure? I don't have secret-talk!"

"They had a rationalization, I suppose?"

"Only what I gave them. That the end justifies the means."

"Really? In that case, Emma, you have made real progress!"

"I am glad you think so. But it hardly explains why I am in this cell."

"Just a moment, dear." There were several seconds of silence, during which Emma agonized with a mix-ture of hope and doubt. Then: "You may not believe this, but your two friends are walking through the Ark like glad-handing politicians, greeting everyone in sight! It's as if—"

"Momma, I think I know! They're passing on the message the best way they know how. Don't you see? If they had left me free to blab, I could have spoiled it all and probably got myself killed as well—and believe me, murder was in the air when I ever-so-gently made a few suggestions in what I thought was a controlled situation."

"You could have defended yourself. Your stingers—"

"If I had used them, what then? Jihevva and Halranen are our best chance. Our *only* chance."

The conversation was interrupted by Jase Kurber. The human sounded excited. "Emma, I think your friends are returning for you. They seem in a helluva hurry!"

Then another voice. "Cwisis is deweloping."

"Poppa David?"

Emma wondered if there was an equivalent to "emergency" in the Phuili's lexicon, as the old teacher calmly told his pupil, "One known as Master has led many into ozer part of ship, away fwom zoze who stay wiz your two. I not know meaning, but zink may be sewious."

The door opened and Halranen came into the cell. Jihevva remained outside, restraining a crowd of curious Silvers. "Come," the female said, thrusting Emma into the corridor. They followed Jihevva toward Control as with fists, feet, and occasional angry snarls he rammed a way through tunnels made hot and humid by too many bodies in too cramped a space.

Control itself was hardly less chaotic, although it was less crowded. Emma saw Gelhon, Bewokul, and—astonishingly—Felwon, who was engaged in a shouting match with the screen image of Delbroj. The Master was equally strident as he shouted back, "You blaspheme! It is our holy duty to destroy filth, not to become filth! Something evil has diverted us to this place and has twisted you and the others away from the true path." The grizzled face became menacing. "You have a choice. Join us and die in glory. Or oppose us and die in shame."

As the screen went dark, there was a collective sigh which was almost a moan. Emma went to Felwon, who welcomed the newcomer with a sad smile. "Yes, I was mad. I killed because I was mad. But I was right when I revived the sleepers, because now the truth is known to them all."

Emma marveled at the resiliency of the one she had thought was hopelessly insane. "You are not being punished for what you did?"

Felwon shrugged. "I am still here. Everyone knows that is punishment enough."

It was an enlightened reply which, considering what Emma had already learned about these contradictory people, she did not find particularly surprising. "What was the argument with the Master about?"

"He said we are flouting the Giver's Law."

"Aren't we?" Emma asked daringly.

"Perhaps." Felwon's gaze was clear and direct. "But as one who has flouted that Law already, I don't really care."

"Felwon is a seed." Unnoticed, Gelhon had come up behind Emma. Emma felt her hand grasped as Gelhon continued, "You, Berein, are also a seed. The appearance of both of you at the same time can only be the Giver's work, or the new ideas could not have born fruit." Emma sensed an unintelligible ripple of palm muscles and sharply pulled her hand away.

"Please do not do that."

Gelhon nodded sympathetically and moved aside. "For a proper cleansing, it makes no sense to uselessly expend all the cleaner on one soiled spot—a concept which I find quite elegant now that I have got over the initial pain of understanding." Looking at the blank viewscreen, Gelhon added resignedly, "It is unfortunate that so many have refused to confront the pain."

"You mean those with the Master?"

"Delbroj is dangerous. Although he is wrong on the matter of whether or not we should survive, too much of what he has said makes sense. Especially his insistence that we have arrived at the wrong solar system."

That shocked Emma. She was not tuned to Momma Gia and the others, but she knew they had heard and could imagine their consternation. "But I thought Control—"

"There is evidence."

Felwon nodded vigorously. "I will get it." The younger female ran to a nearby console and returned with a large book. "These are star charts which were drawn before the ark was launched." She opened the volume and pointed. "That is the area of space in which we are supposed to be—but in which we are not."

It was a development which was totally unexpected. The experts who so successfully reprogrammed the Ark's computer, had not even considered the possibility the Silver People might still depend on this archaic form of backup. But Emma's nimble brain quickly came up with an appropriate objection. "Why should that be so surprising? The ark was launched, after all, even as our planets were burning. Systems were new, untried—"

"These charts show the sky as it would appear from every destination we could possibly reach during the years since drive activation. Not one matches the pattern which exists at our present location."

Emma felt helpless. She did not know what to say. Silskin signaled: *Tell them it must be the Giver's work.*

Too easy, she shot back. *They are not so unsophisticated that they blame their god for everything they don't immediately understand.*

"Zen be as unknowing as zey," suggested a familiar voice. "Zere is not way zey can know twuth."

As always, it was the Phuili's cool voice of reason which brought Emma back from the edge of panic. She longed for a few moments during which she could retire into a quiet corner and converse normally with the members of her support team; especially with Momma Gia. But events were moving too fast; she knew that even her exclusive "shorthand" channel to Silskin would have to be used sparingly. For a brief moment her imagination penetrated meters of solid rock to where her three friends and only brother were watching, listening and—as much as she—hoping.

Emma turned to Gelhon. "So what do we do?"

The older female gestured to where Jihevva had climbed on a chair and was calling for attention. "We listen to him." Bewokul came through the crowd to her, and Gelhon reached for and grasped her mate's hand.

As the noise died down, Jihevva shouted, "Are we agreed on survival?"

The response seemed unanimous, although to Emma's trained ears, not entirely enthusiastic. "Yes!"

"It is the Giver's will," someone echoed solemnly.

Jihevva nodded. "We know the price and we know it will be a heavy one." His voice rose. "But for future glory, are we willing to pay that price?"

There was a hesitation which was barely noticeable. Emma supposed she would similarly hesitate if she was told her survival depended on sustenance she could only find in a decaying heap of refuse. And her distaste for rotting protein was mild compared with these peoples' abhorrence of *any* matter which was life-originated.

"We are willing to pay the price," Bewokul said quietly, and there was a murmur of agreement. He added, "But for the sake of our sanity, I suggest we do it in easy stages. First, survey the planet for a relatively lifeless area on which we can locate our first settlement. Second, transfer as much foodstuff and equipment as possible until proximity to the sun finally forces us to evacuate everyone from the ark."

Jihevva pulled lips back from his fangs in a savage grin. "And then the hard part, eh?"

Bewokul nodded. "For the first time since enlightenment, we will ultimately be forced to eat what is not synthesized. It will be—ah—" Bewokul's expression became as savage as Jihevva's. "—difficult."

Emma lifted her hand. "You must still deal with the Master and those who followed him," she pointed out. "They will certainly try to stop you." *And they will succeed,* she thought as she considered the inevitable stalemate; half of the crew prepared to rewrite the rules in order to survive, the other half prepared to die in the service of the unholy and unforgiving god they called the Giver. Neither side would permit the other to gain access to any of the little ships on the ark's surface, until ultimately the system's sun imposed its own fiery solution. Emma took a deep breath. "Permit me to go to Master Delbroj and talk to him."

Jihevva was not the type to waste words. "Is it worth the risk?"

Emma shrugged. "I am a lesser. He will not harm me."

"It is possible you overestimate his adherence to the old ways."

"Perhaps." Emma added stubbornly, "But can it do harm?"

Jihevva studied her. Then he nodded. "Only to you, I think." He lifted his head. "Does anyone believe Berein should not try?"

The answer was silence. Still in silence, there was a general movement clearing a path between Emma and Control's portal. Feeling truly apart, for the first time as much alien as if she was human or Phuili, Emma acknowledged the quiet acquiescence and walked between the silent ranks. At the portal, she turned. "Please tell Delbroj I am on my way."

"He will know." Jihevva raised his hand, palm outward. "Good talk, little one."

Transmitted by a wave of touching hands, news of Emma's mission preceded her along the tunnels, and only after she entered the deserted sector between the opposing factions did she feel she could pause and catch her breath. The sadness and silent sympathy had stifled her; desperately, she needed a hopeful word. "Momma?"

"We heard, Emma. And we understand why you do this. But the one you call Jihevva is right. You take a great risk."

"To do nothing is to guarantee failure. Momma, you must know that!"

"Of course, I know. Unfortunately we may have an even worse problem."

What was worse then everyone frying because of forced inaction, Emma could not fathom. "What problem?"

"Delbroj. He has crews poking around this section of the asteroid. They are using charts and measuring tapes."

"Looking for what?"

"Us, obviously."

"But that is impossible!" Emma felt a sudden fear. "Unless—"

"No dear, it was not you. Somebody found something Delbroj has identified as not belonging on the ark, and now he is sniffing around like a cross between Sherlock Holmes and a bloodhound. So right now your immediate priority must be to find out what is going on and somehow defuse it. If this hideaway of ours is found, it will not be just three aliens who will end up as chopped meat. One look at Silskin, and Delbroj will know enough to bring everyone back to his side—and heaven help any other Silver who is 'odd.' It'll be more than just your hide, Emma."

Emma thought of the two "re-engineered" scouts on the surface directly above the concealed command post. "I think you and the others should leave, Momma."

"No. Not yet. Not only will a couple of unauthorized launchings help confirm their suspicions, but we four have by unanimous vote elected to remain here until you can come with us."

"I am not sure—" Emma paused. "You will not take unnecessary chances?"

Jase Kurber: "We love you, but we are not suicidal. If we have to go without you, we will. But please work things so we won't be forced to make that decision. Okay?"

"I will try, Poppa Jase." Emma rose to her feet and stretched. "Here I go, dear ones. Please wish me luck."

"Save all, daughter," David said gravely.

Silskin: *Hand-touch*.

"Come back," Momma Gia whispered.

Initially, Emma's arrival in the Master's territory was almost anticlimatic. She had been escorted to a central point by two females who found her in the tunnels, and for a while she was forced to wait amid comings and goings as uncoordinated as the confusion she had left behind. For too many with not enough to do, Emma was a diversion which made her an object of intense curiosity, and the area became even more crowded as word spread of her presence. Finally she was rescued by an armed male who took her a short distance to where Delbroj was examining the wall of a small branch tunnel. Emma's heart sank. She knew what was a few meters behind that wall.

Delbroj turned to her. "Jihevva said you wanted to talk to me."

Praying her consternation did not show, Emma nodded. "Yes, Master."

"Why should I listen? It is you who turned so many away from the Path."

Emma had an inspiration. She said defiantly, "You can kill me if you choose. But would that make any difference?"

The old Silver chuckled. "Little one, you attach too much importance to yourself. If I had thought your death would make Jihevva and his friends rededicate themselves to the holy cause, you would have been made a corpse as soon as I knew you were here."

"In the same way, Master, is it not possible *you* are attaching too much importance to one slightly infected planet? It is—"

"Enough!" For a moment Emma thought Delbroj was going to strke her. Instead, he beckoned. "Come."

She knew where he was taking her as soon as they entered the descending ramp toward the drive chamber in the base of the asteroid. She had been there before, as human-Phuili crews installed the latest in phase-shift equipment, and later when they removed it after the ark had been safely diverted to this galactic backwater. She expressed appropriate awe as they entered the huge chamber, and listened politely as Delbroj pointed at the melted slag which covered most of the floor.

"It does not look like much now, does it little one? But it propelled the ark half a light-year from our exploding sun in the same time it used to take to travel from Homeworld to the First Moon. Given a few more months, I think we would have solved the problems of surge and meltdown and created a *real* interstellar drive. Anyway, I brought you here to see this."

He pointed at a body-width hole in the lower wall of the chamber. At the back of the hole gleamed a metal fitting resembling a sophisticated cross between a bolt head and a hook. Emma knew there were six of them; the anchors for the cables which had suspended the substitute phase-shift core in the center of the space. A litter of broken rock near the hole was a clear indication of poorly packed concealment, and Emma's claws twitched in their sheaths as she thought of what she would like to do to the careless technician responsible for this disaster.

Delbroj said flatly, "It was not there when the ark was launched on its journey. Neither is it anything we could have made; the metal is completely resistant to the hottest torch, and the few scrapings we have taken defy analysis. It is apparent therefore that *strangers*—" As he spoke the word, the Master's fur bristled and his eyes glared. "—have somehow made our ark turn to this unknown star and to the unholy temptation of what you, small one, choose to call a 'slightly' infected planet!"

A large hand grabbed the base of Emma's neck and she was hustled back up the ramp, past throngs of curious Silvers, finally into the small side tunnel. Still with a firm hold on her, Delbroj continued, "If these *strangers* are observing us from space, it follows that we, in turn, should be able to see them—"

Not true. Emma knew the big Headquarters ship was only light-seconds away, safely concealed inside its bubble of masking fields.

"—but because we cannot see or detect anything unusual in near space, what we seek must therefore be elsewhere. Perhaps even inside the ark itself." Delbroj released Emma and tapped the wall of the tunnel. "Here! Hidden in the only part of this former asteroid our builders did not have time to excavate. Yet which I suspect *has* been excavated. Do you like my logic, small one?"

Despite the discovery in the drive chamber, evidence of concealed watchers was still pretty flimsy. Yet Delbroj had deduced the truth in a way which made Emma wonder if there were powers within themselves not even the Silvers were aware of. A subconcious sensitivity, perhaps, to the signals from her implant—

No! He is guessing!

"Now, then. What is it you wanted to say to me?"

Emma despaired. It was obvious her mission had failed, and that the only course open to her now was to somehow join her friends and blast away from the Ark before Delbroj and his followers cut through to the command post. Helplessly, she looked around her. In every direction her way was blocked either by solid rock or by watchful Silvers. *I can't get away from them,* she signaled. *Please save yourselves while there is still time!*

No, little sister. Silskin's reply was amazingly clear considering its passage through metal-rich rock. *Be patient a little longer, and we will—*

There was the explosive crack of a projectile weapon, and with a cry of agony a Silver collapsed to the floor. Then an eye-dazzling flash, and a second Silver gasped and crumpled. Screams of rage preceded an answering barrage of bullets, knives and even thrown rocks; adding an incredible cacophony of smoke and noise.

Again Delbroj grabbed Emma. "Attack!" he roared. "In the Giver's name, attack and kill!" He jerked his captive forward so violently, she lost her footing and was dragged painfully along with him. The pandemonium remained deafening as the master led his followers after the elusive attackers. Somehow Emma regained her feet and stumbled behind Delbroj with a limping run. It was obvious where they were heading, and she wondered why Jihevva and the others had forced the issue so soon. Silvers unsure of themselves, still adjusting to ideas which conflicted with every basic instinct, would melt away before this mad charge led by a charismatic prophet.

The projectile weapon sounded again, felling another victim who was instantly trampled under dozens of feet. There was a yell of triumph, and a cluster of bodies reeled toward Delbroj. A few breathless individuals separated from the scramble, revealing a young female struggling with maniacal strength against the grip of four large males. One of the four was flourishing the female's weapon, a wicked little fifteen-shot. "Delbroj!" Felwon yelled. "Master, we spit on you!"

We? It did seem to confirm that Jihevva had acted with uncharacteristic rashness. Then again, it was also possible that Felwon had relapsed into insanity, taking to herself the impossible task of stopping the reactionaries and their leader. But who had used the beamer? As far as Emma knew, the most advanced hand weapon in the Silver armory was a sonic device which was great for crowd control, but hardly selective enough for individual targets. It was as if—

Silskin!

That's right, sister. The help from that little female was unexpected, but who am I to complain? Anyway, the rabble will soon be so confused they won't notice one extra Silver stealing away their captive.

But you have triggered them into attacking Jihevva and the others! It will ruin everything!

Emma, it is ruined anyway. Or haven't you noticed?

No! Emma desperately needed to talk to Momma Gia, but she knew there was not enough time. It had all played into Delbroj's hands; the discovery in the drive chamber, Felwon's crazed intercession, and now Silskin—

A large hand closed tighter around Emma's wrist. "Come, little one. Learn with me how the Giver punishes those who dare usurp his holy authority." Pointing, Delbroj shouted, "Destroy the blasphemers!"

"Destroy!" the crowd roared, and surged behind their leader and his captive. The beamer flashed from a side tunnel, and with a choked cry another fell. But now the master had his followers in such a state of holy frenzy, Emma doubted even a massacre could stop them.

I am coming up behind you. If I can get close enough to shoot that old—

Wait! There is a better way. Emma's free hand flashed forward and lightly scratched Delbroj's upper arm. At the same time she screamed, "He's dead! The Master's dead!"

He was indeed. The instant poison was so fast Delbroj's brain was destroyed even before he began to fall, and as his grip slackened Emma pulled free and merged back into the crowd.

Those closest, who had heard Emma and then saw their leader fall, wailed with dismay and pummeled and pushed themselves into a protective wall around him. Just before the jostling screen of bodies blocked her view, Emma saw some of the followers kneel and try to prod the Master back to life. The attack had already degenerated into a disorganized confusion, and as she quietly slipped free from the milling throng and turned away, Emma's feeling of horror at what she had done was only slightly mollified by the fact it seemed to have had the desired effect. But before she could be sure, she knew she had one more unpleasant duty.

She found Felwon leaning weakly against a tunnel

wall. Another Silver was applying salve to a wound in the young female's side.

"Silskin!"

He grinned at her. "Hello, Emma. Congratulations."

"For what?" She did not know why they were using the slow talk of normal speech, but its friendly familiarity was very satisfying.

"For getting rid of the old one. You saved the mission, you know."

"Perhaps," Emma said tiredly. She turned to the female. "How do you feel?"

Felwon's eyes glittered. "I will be well. What is that language you and this one are talking?" She pointed at Silskin's weapon belt. "And what is that which made the light? It killed!"

Emma felt numb. Not that she supposed Silskin's foolishness before Felwon really made much difference. The female's youth and charisma was a near guarantee of eventual leadership, and it was certain her half-crazed fanaticism would leave a legacy of *jihad* which would persist for generations.

It could not be allowed.

Emma asked in the local language, "Silskin, will you please leave us for a few moments?"

"Of course."

As her brother faded into the darkness of a side tunnel, Emma said quietly, "I think you are my friend, Felwon."

"I can no longer allow myself to be diverted by friendship, Berein. Now there is a light I must follow."

"I understand." Emma gently touched the wound. Something glistened under the claw of her thumb. "Let me finish dressing that."

"Why?" Gia Mayland persisted with a mixture of anguish and anger. "Emma, you have no reason to stay with them. Jihevva is a good leader, and I am sure his pragmatism will spread to those around him. In a couple of generations, their allergy to life will be no more than an ugly memory."

Poppa Kurber took up the argument. "In any case Emma, aren't you forgetting the other arks out there? What we did with this group was only a dry run, an experiment to prove that we no longer need to destroy the Silvers when we find them. And it is you who have given us that proof. So with your experience—"

"What do you know about the native life on that planet?" Emma interrupted.

Kurber shrugged. "Only that it is sparse. Which is another reason you should not go. Even if your friends can get over their aversion to natural protein, the possibility of starvation will always be there."

"Zere is what is in sea," David said.

"Oh, thank you!" Emma ran over and hugged the old Phuili. "Poppa David, please tell them!"

Davakinapwottapellazanzis' muzzle twitched with the Phuili equivalent of a smile. "I zink Emma alweady done more study of planet zan us. Ocean have much life. Some much large cweatures in water which wesemble whale cweatures on human planet. Perhaps wiz intelligence like whales. Zerefore I say expewiment stay on-going. Emma keep implant in head, she talk wiz us by welay we place on mountaintop."

"I suppose we could maintain a small craft and crew in this system," Kurber said cautiously. "And when Emma can no longer— "

"You mean when I am too old?" Emma laughed happily. "By then I will have had young ones, and they will be trained to be yours, dear Momma Gia, and dear Poppas Jase and David." She opened her arms and hugged them each in turn. "Now you have only six. But in time, don't you see, we can give you thousands!"

Gia Mayland held out her hand. She was wearing the glove of secret-talk. Emma, aware the nerve blocks would have to be restored before she rejoined her other family, accepted gratefuly.

You are my child and I love you.

It was an astonishing truth, and Emma knew this moment would be with her for the rest of her days.

And I love you, Momma Gia.

The sun was already fatally close. Even as the rock on the sunward side of the drifting asteroid began to melt, the last ships lifted from its surface into the dark.

On the planet, nearly three thousand of the tiny vessels were already clustered on a high dry tableland. Their crews were busy assembling temporary shelters, and a few disciplined souls had supressed their revulsion enough to begin gathering small quantitites of local life-stuff for analysis.

These who were born to kill were the innocent. While elsewhere, the guilty who would not kill but had killed, still waited to be absolved—

EPILOGUE

Now there are three.

Man, Phuili, and the Silver People.

Man and Phuili have started their integration. The Silvers remain separate and are still a threat. But time's arrow points as it should, ultimately smoothing even the most extreme aberrations. Later there will be others, and slowly, inexorably, the web will expand. Somewhere, somewhen, my equal will rise and the universe will never again be the same.

Will it happen because of my interventions? I do not know. But I must continue what I started; observing, encouraging and even—when necessary—weeding.

A word for all sentients. Do not resist that inevitability which is the universal mind. Individuality is not diminished, indeed it is enhanced. The "we" of my own subunits still exist, thriving within the subtle matrix of what their philosophers describe as the Overmind. It is the natural wisdom of their separate selves which is the anchor that keeps me stable between the higher and lower realities.

I am not a deity. Neither am I immortal, although by the standards of lesser beings it may seem so.

What I am, is alone.

But like the mortal creatures of the universe to which I also belong, I hope.

DAW

Another Part of the Universe

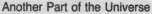

J. BRIAN CLARKE
☐ THE EXPEDITER   (UE2409—$3.95)
For humans, first contact was the fulfillment of a dream—to the alien Phuili, it betrayed all the laws of the cosmos. For the Phuili refused to admit there could be more than one sentient race in the universe. Yet a shaky alliance was forced on the two races when they encountered the Silvers, a dread beserker race sworn to destroy all other life forms. . . .

FRANK A. JAVOR
☐ SCOR-STING   (UE2421—$3.95)
His name is Pike, and he is a free-lance photojournalist in an age when media communication is strictly controlled. Called upon for aid by comrades from his military past, Pike finds himself on a planet hostile to human life, where the most important discovery to the future of the human race *may* lie hidden among storm-swept desert dunes. Is it real—or is it just a scam? Either way, it could be worth Pike's life to find out. . . .

IAN WALLACE
☐ MEGALOMANIA   (UE2351—$3.75)
A galactic jet of destruction was the force Dino Trigg chose to take revenge on his mentor, Croyd, the leader of Sol Galaxy, after failing to overthrow him by political means. Trigg swore he'd have his revenge, not only upon Croyd but upon all the civilized worlds. And, unless Croyd found a way to stop him, he would fashion a doomsday weapon from the Magellanic Clouds that would not only form a new galaxy for him to rule, but would release a deadly stream of energy aimed right for the heart of Sol Galaxy!